MAIN LIBRARY

@ 1986

WITHDRAWN

#3 in Madoc Rhys Series

**DO NOT REMOVE
CARDS FROM POCKET**

A DISMAL THING TO DO

By Alisa Craig

A DISMAL THING TO DO

ALISA CRAIG

PUBLISHED FOR THE CRIME CLUB BY
DOUBLEDAY & COMPANY, INC.
GARDEN CITY, NEW YORK
1986

The author has taken liberties with the organization and operation of the RCMP and no doubt with those of some branch or other of the Canadian military. She would wish the reader to believe this was done in order to avoid any identification with actual persons or circumstances, but it was mostly plain ignorance. All characters and events in the book are her own invention, and any resemblance to anybody, anything, anywhere would be coincidental.

Library of Congress Cataloging-in-Publication Data
MacLeod, Charlotte.
    A dismal thing to do.
    I. Title.
PS3563.A31865D5   1986   813'.54   85-16194
ISBN 0-385-23263-2

FOR GEORGE, IVAN, THARON, MARY, AND JANE
and All Their Kith and Kin

2273270

"After such kindness, that would be
A dismal thing to do!"
"The night is fine," the Walrus said.
"Do you admire the view?"

"The Walrus and the Carpenter"
from *Through the Looking-Glass*
by Lewis Carroll

A DISMAL THING TO DO

CHAPTER 1

Janet Wadman Rhys was not much given to cussing, as a rule. She was doing some now, partly at the neighbor who'd given her the directions, but mostly at herself for having been fool enough to follow them. This was one hell of a time to be out on a strange road with the snow piled six or eight feet high on either side and just about room enough for a weasel to squeak past her.

Thus far, she'd been lucky enough not to meet an oncoming vehicle. Her luck, however, was about to run out. Here she was, almost to the top of a fairly steep hill and a truck coming at her over the crest. Now what was a person to do? That truck wasn't wasting any time, either; spiked tires, most likely. Janet wished to heaven she had them, too. Driving this little car over hard-packed snow that had been glazed by the thaw and freeze of early March was like riding a puck over a hockey rink.

There was a turnoff plowed out in front of the one lone house perched atop the hill. If she could only make that before the truck bore down on her—but she wouldn't. The truck was there already, not slackening speed at all. It would roar down this icy channel and she'd be—great God Almighty!

Janet couldn't imagine what caused it. She couldn't believe it had happened. The truck didn't brake, didn't skid. It simply flopped over and lay there with its wheels spinning. Its left-hand side—the driver's left—was down into the snowbank. The rest of it was clear across the road, looking to be high as a meeting house steeple, showing underparts chunked up with greasy, filthy ice.

"How am I ever going to get him out?"

That was all Janet could think of. Somebody was inside that cab. Somebody had to get the door open and help him out. Or her, or them. Janet hadn't had time to notice before the crash. She couldn't see anybody now, but she could see clearly enough there'd be no escape for anybody through that down-side door. She had a shovel in her trunk. She could tunnel through to the door, maybe, but what if the whole rig came crashing down on top of her? She'd have to work from the high side.

Maybe the driver wasn't much hurt, only dazed from the shock. The truck had gone over so softly, so easily. No matter; a person couldn't sit here waiting to find out if they were alive or dead. She must climb up there and get that cab open and—and what? And how?

Janet Rhys was a small woman, young and slender, wearing a lovely new coat of handspun Welsh wool in a gentle tapestry of blues and grays, with touches of gold and a bronzy brown that matched her hair. The coat had been a present from Sir Emlyn and Lady Rhys, who still couldn't understand how their tone-deaf younger son had managed to snare himself a charming, sensible, well-brought-up wife like Janet. They'd settled for shameless pampering and increasingly unsubtle hints about a first grandchild.

Janet hated the thought of ruining their handsome gift on those scarily exposed internal workings, but that wouldn't have stopped her. What in fact was going to stop her, Janet realized once she'd got out of her own car and gone to look the situation over, was that the cab door was so high up and she was so low down.

At the angle the truck was tilted, she could see no way to climb up. She thought of driving her own car closer and standing on the roof, but there was no room to maneuver. She thought of going to the house for help, but with that flopped-over body blocking the way, she couldn't even see whether there'd been a path dug, much less get at one. It wasn't going to help the trapped driver if she tried to cut across the field, foundered in snow far over her head, and smothered herself to death. Anyway, if there was a path, and people in the house, why hadn't they come out by now?

Twenty meters or so behind her was a tumbledown barn, built smack up against the road. Maybe there'd be a ladder inside, or at least a board she could use for a ramp. She yelled as loudly as she could, "I'm going to look for something to climb over," in case the driver was conscious and worried. Then she returned to her car and backed down.

There was a pretty high drift between her and the barn, but Janet thought it must surely be packed hard enough to climb over. She picked up her pocketbook, then tossed it back under the seat. She'd want both hands free for the ladder if, God willing, she found one. She did take along the emergency blanket Madoc wouldn't let her travel without, though. This was a space-age oblong of some silvery synthetic material that weighed nothing to speak of but was tough enough to serve as a carrier or a sled.

The drift was frozen solid, and boards were off the barn. Janet had no trouble getting inside. It was a rickety old place and the hay in the loft stank of mold, but there was a ladder of sorts leading up. She was shaking the sides, trying to free it from the puddle of ice that was sticking it to the floor, when the truck blew up.

Janet didn't know it was the truck, not then. She only knew she was flat on her face with spoiled hay in her mouth and half the barn on top of her. She assumed she'd been knocked senseless; she had no idea for how long. She didn't think she was seriously hurt. Her thick wool hat, heavy winter clothing, and the mounds of hay must have saved her skull and bones. By dint of some painful squirming, she managed to get out from under.

Probably she was in shock. She spent a fair while straightening her hat, picking straws out of her coat, kicking away splintered boards to clear a path to the drift. Then she realized she was smelling oily smoke and burning metal, and thought to look up the road. The hilltop was one mass of flame.

"Oh God," she murmured, not swearing this time. She might as well forget about the ladder. Nothing was going to help that driver now. And what about the people in the house? Why hadn't they come out to help? Or had they, and met the blast head-on?

She must get back to her car. She must somehow turn around and go for help. Janet picked up her survival blanket, perhaps because it was the only thing left whole and familiar in this direful place, and climbed back out to the road.

Her car was not there.

Janet decided after a while that she hadn't been knocked silly. She knew perfectly well she'd left the car right beside the barn. She could see her own footprints on the road where she'd stepped out and walked around to clamber up over the packed snow. Her first thought was that the car must have been blown up along with the truck, but there was no debris of the right sort. Her car had been a shiny bright blue, with blue plastic seats. Nothing she could see was bright enough or blue enough to have belonged to it, not that Janet was any expert, but neither was she blind or stupid.

What had happened was clear enough. The driver had managed to get out of the cab, probably through the window on the high side, and jump down, which would have been a darn sight easier than climbing up. He'd hopped into her car while she was inside the barn, coasted backward down that slippery hill, and been able to drive away because she'd been fool enough to leave the keys in the ignition. He'd panicked, she supposed. He must have known the truck was going to explode. But damn and blast him, he might have had the decency to blow the horn rather than leave her stranded.

He'd meant to leave her stranded. That was why he'd coasted, so she wouldn't hear her engine starting. He'd been a hijacker, most likely. Now what was she to do?

There really was only one thing she could do under the circumstances, which was to stand there watching the fire, hoping somebody would see the flames and smoke and come along. She hadn't passed a house in ages, and it wouldn't make much sense to go prowling around unknown roads by herself on foot with the sun going down. Maybe there was something up ahead she could get to when the road became passable.

As to expecting the person who took her car to have an attack of conscience and come back to get her, she might as well forget it. He'd find her registration and plenty of gas money in that handbag she'd so kindly tossed back before she went into the barn. He'd even find a box of gingersnaps to munch on if he got hungry. She'd meant to drop them off with old Briard Dupree, one of her sister-in-law's many uncles, having been under the mistaken assumption that Muriel's directions would take her close to where he lived. She hadn't the remotest idea where she was now, but it surely wasn't anywhere near Uncle Briard's.

Oh well, somebody was bound to come along soon. So Janet kept telling herself, but nobody did. Why not? A blaze like this must be visible from a considerable distance. At least she wasn't cold. The heat was intense enough to warm the air even down here where she was standing, away from the smoke. It was also melting the snow, sending a running stream down to soak her boot soles. She climbed up on some of the shattered barn boards to get out of the wet, and kept on standing.

All that water had to affect the fire at last. The flames were dying down, the twists of metal turning from red to black. Pretty soon she'd be able to pick her way around the mess and find the path to the house. There had to be a path. It was going to be pitch dark in a little while. Janet took yet another look at her watch, a charming whimsy Madoc had given her for Valentine's Day so she could count the shining hours they spent together. She'd meant to be home early so she could fix him a special supper tonight.

Why in the name of all that was good and holy didn't anybody come? She still could see no sign of life over at the house. Maybe they were off doing their shopping, or gone to Florida till the spring thaw. Well, she had to get a move on regardless. The fire was really down now, just a mess of junk, cinders, and slop. The cold was getting into her bones. Janet flung the insulated blanket around her like a shawl and began to circle the wreckage. It was impossible to keep out of the puddles and these new boots of hers, she found, were less waterproof than they'd been cracked up to be.

At least there was a path, though not much of one. It looked to her as if somebody with big feet had tramped it out during the first storm of the year, then depended on added footpower to keep it barely passable. Janet floundered along over the bumps and holes as best she could, with a sinking feeling that she'd find nothing at the end but an empty house and a locked door.

The house did appear to be deserted, but the door was unlatched. Janet knocked and called out a few hellos, got no answer, and decided this was no time to stand on ceremony. They'd be back from wherever they'd gone; whoever they were. It hardly seemed likely they'd have left the place wide open if they were going to be gone for any great length of time.

Not that there looked to be anything here worth stealing. The small vestibule in which Janet found herself held nothing but a scrap of old carpet and a lot of dirty footprints. To her right was the front room, or the remains of one, with a broken-down chesterfield and a couple of armchairs that had wads of gray stuffing hanging out of them. There was a rusted airtight stove with a galvanized coal hod beside it that held only a few sticks of kindling. No furnace, she supposed. No electric lights that she could make out. No running water, like as not. And no telephone, darn it.

At least she might be able to keep from freezing to death. Whoever had left that kindling wouldn't begrudge a traveler in distress. Janet only hoped to the Lord they'd left matches, too.

They had, not wooden matches but a couple of little cardboard folders with advertising on them from some bar and grill in a foreign country. Bangor, Maine. Funny, Janet wasn't used to thinking of the States as a foreign country. Maybe it was because she felt like a foreigner herself, here in a strange house on an unknown road with not a soul around to tell her where she was, much less get her away.

She wadded up a piece of newspaper—just an advertising circular, unfortunately, with no address on it that might help her orient herself —and put it in the stove with some of the kindling. Nobody had bothered to rake out the ashes for ages, she noticed. Whoever lived here certainly didn't go in for housework. Or else nobody really lived here at all.

Madoc had told her about what he called "squats," derelict houses that people with no place else to go simply moved into, making out as best they could with none of the facilities people nowadays had got accustomed to. Maybe this was a squat. All right, she'd be a squatter. Janet touched one of the cardboard matches to the newspaper, waited till she saw the kindling start to catch, and shut the stove. She'd have to go easy on the firewood unless there was a cache somewhere. Too bad she hadn't brought some of those barn boards. If, God forbid, she got stuck here for the night, she supposed she might go back there and drag in a load, using her trusty plastic blanket for a skid.

Think positive, she adjured herself. Somebody absolutely had to come along pretty soon. The road had been plowed, so it must lead from somewhere to somewhere. Any car that tried to get through would be held up by that mass of wreckage in the road. She could rush out and yell to its driver for help. In the meantime, she'd better hunt around for something else to burn. She might even find a kettle and the odd tea bag. She could melt snow for hot water on the stove if she had to.

And, please God, let there be a bathroom, or at least a privy she could get at without wallowing through any more snow. Janet didn't relish leaving the meager warmth of the stove to poke around this dark old place by herself, but she had no choice, so she went.

The next room had nothing in it at all except more dirty footprints, but there was a kitchen of sorts beyond it, and a woodshed behind that. There she did find some stove wood. She'd also, judging from the reek, found out where the squatters did their personal squatting.

This was perhaps the most distasteful act Janet had ever performed, but by now she was in no condition to cavil at local custom. At least she had a few tissues in her coat pocket. She used one as daintily as possible under the circumstances and took it back with the logs to burn in the stove. A detective inspector's wife knew better than to leave any clue that she'd actually peed on somebody else's woodshed floor. Then she opened the front door to wash her hands in snow and take a long look up and down the road. Then she sighed and went back to see about that tea bag.

There wasn't one, but she did find a bottle of brandy about two-thirds empty and a few smeary tumblers on the counter. She ignored the glasses, took a dusty teacup down from a shelf, wiped it out on her petticoat, poured herself a modest slug after having sniffed with care to make sure the stuff in the bottle really was brandy, went and got another dollop of snow to tone it down a little, and carried the cup back to the front room.

She also took along an oil lamp she'd found while she was looking for the tea bag. The chimney was smoked up and the wick in need of trimming, but there was still oil in the bottom, so she lit the lamp and set it in the window, for whatever good that might do.

The stove was sending out some warmth now, not enough to encourage taking off one's hat and coat, but enough to suggest setting one's wet boots underneath and hoping for the best. Janet dragged the less ratty of the armchairs as close as she dared, wrapped herself in the emergency blanket, and took a sip of the brandy. It landed in her empty stomach with an agreeable wallop.

Now that darkness had made it impossible to see the shambles around her, the yellowish glow from the lamp and the bit of red showing through the stove's open damper made the room seem almost cozy. Janet was tired, she realized, more tired than she ought to be. Now that she had nothing to do but sit and count her aches and pains, she discovered quite a few. Lots of bruises, no doubt, from getting the barn dumped on her. Madoc would have a fit.

Whatever had been in the truck to create such a blast? Could an exploding gas tank knock down a building a fair distance away? That had been no great tractor trailer, just a truck. A top-heavy truck. Janet could see it well enough even now, lying there across the road with its roof in the snowbank. Like a horse box, she thought. High in proportion to its length. Bigger, of course. A giraffe box? Silly! A moving van. A van for moving giraffes. This must be terrible brandy.

And why had the explosion been so long in coming? Janet was sure she'd seen no sign of fire while she was standing there wondering how to get up to the cab. She'd had time to back her car down to the barn, time to get inside. The person in the cab had had time to get out, time to run down and make a safe getaway in her car.

Why should there have been an explosion at all? The truck hadn't crashed, it hadn't lost a wheel or snapped an axle, it had simply tipped over and nestled into the snow. Janet couldn't even remember its making any noise to amount to anything.

But there must have been something. Damage to the body on the side she'd never got to see? Inflammable cargo? Acid dripping out of broken carboys into—what? Crates of kitchen matches? If the driver had hijacked the truck, he might not have known how to drive it properly, and that was why it tipped over. Maybe he'd then set the fire himself before he ran off, trying to cover up what he'd done. Anybody who'd steal a lone woman's lovely new car and leave her stranded in the middle of nowhere when she'd only been trying to save his life would do anything. Janet finished her brandy and went to sleep.

CHAPTER 2

She woke at half-past seven on the dot. Her watch said so. That meant she'd been stuck on this hill for four solid hours, and still nobody had come. Unless there'd been cars going by while she slept. But how could they? That mass of wreckage must still be blocking the road. They'd have honked or got out and tried to move it, or seen her lamp and come here to ask what had happened. Besides, she hadn't been asleep so very long, probably not more than an hour by the time she'd been held up by the wreck, blown down with the barn, waited around all that time for the fire to go out so she could get in here and do the various things she'd done before she nodded off.

She had to go and do one of them again pretty quick. She must have caught a chill in her kidneys standing around out there with wet feet. She'd better fetch in more firewood while she was about it. Sighing, Janet stuck her feet back into her boots, warm and fairly dry inside by now, thank the Lord, picked up her security blanket for company, and dragged herself back to the woodshed.

What the heck had she been dreaming, anyway? Something about dinosaurs prowling around outside, making strange noises. That must have been the wind. Up here, with nothing to break its force, it was roaring loud enough to wake the dead. If she were to get stuck in this old shack all night, she'd have to hump some to keep herself from freezing.

But first things first. Janet was attending to her most urgent need when all of a sudden she heard voices beyond the door she'd instinctively closed. And here she was, the wife of a detective inspector in the RCMP, with her panty hose down around her knees.

That embarrassing circumstance no doubt saved her life. Now they were in the kitchen, two men, talking plenty loud enough to hear.

And the first thing she heard was "Did he have sense enough to kill the woman before he took her car?"

"He claims he did, says he knocked her down and kicked her head in, then tossed the body in the barn under some boards so it would look as if she was killed when the roof caved in."

"The hell he did. That kid would say anything. I'll bet the crazy bugger didn't even wait to make sure she was dead. She might still be down there, yelling her head off."

"Not by this time she isn't. Anyway, who'd have heard her? Come on, quit swilling that rotgut. We've still got work to do."

"Like what, for instance?"

"Lug the furniture out in the road and set it afire."

"I thought he said to torch the whole house."

"Yes, but we've got to account for the burnt patch in the road. With the wreckage gone, people are going to wonder what caused it. We take away the detour signs when we leave, remember. The blaze is bound to attract attention then, and it's got to look reasonable."

"What's so reasonable about burning the furniture in the road?"

"Nothing, that's the point. We're just teenage vandals having some fun."

"Oh, I get it. Not bad. What gets me is why the kid bothered to light the stove and the lamp. He claims he took off right after the truck went over."

"Huh, I know that lazy bastard. He'd never dream of hiking out on foot. He came in here, made himself comfortable, and waited for a lift. Along comes this woman, sees the lamp he's put in the window for bait, and comes trotting up here looking for somebody to move the nasty old truck so she can get by. So he whomps her one, dumps the body, and takes off in the car. I'm surprised he didn't just leave her here."

"Damn shame he didn't. We might have had some fun with her. Here, quit hoggin' that brandy. I've got a mouth on me too, you know."

There was a pause, then the sound of glass smashing against the wall. Teenage vandalism. Janet didn't know what else to do, so she simply froze where she stood until the dishes quit crashing and the men left the kitchen. She didn't leave the woodshed then, either, though she did make sure her garments were in order. From the grunts and curses she could still hear, she assumed they must be juggling that gone-to-pieces chesterfield out the door. There was silence for a bit, then some more tramping and swearing and sounds of splintering wood, then a great crash that must have been the parlor stove going over, then a small explosion that was no doubt the oil lamp tossed on to whatever they'd piled up for kindling. Then the fire began to catch and the flames to outroar the wind.

They wouldn't wait around now. No doubt they'd already set fire to the stuff in the road. They'd toss a bottle of burning gasoline into what was left of the barn, then they'd make tracks. As for herself, it looked like a case of fry or freeze.

The woodshed had an outside door, frozen shut, with drifts piled against it probably higher than the door. Janet wasted no time there. She did the only thing she could do: wrapped the emergency blanket around her, ran back into the kitchen with smoke tearing at her lungs and flames already licking in through the doorway; tried the one window, found it stuck, pulled the tough plastic over her head, and jumped through, glass and all.

CHAPTER 3

Detective Inspector Madoc Rhys had gone off duty. This was a matter for mild jubilation, since he'd been on a good deal longer than he'd intended to be. Time had been when hours meant nothing to him, but now he was a married man with a wife to come home to. He savored the thought of his Jenny waiting for him in the house his mother had badgered them into buying, or imagined she had. Lady Rhys could badger as effectively long distance as she could in person, but nobody badgered Janet, not really. She just let them think they had, if it made them happy.

They'd bought the house simply because they'd needed a place to live. The miserable bachelor pad he'd occasionally roosted in before his unexpected marriage at Christmastime hadn't been worth trying to make livable for the two of them. They'd read all the articles, listened to scads of advice, then gone out one Sunday afternoon and seen a place vacant with a cupola on top and etched glass panels around the front door, and that was it.

Like most New Brunswick women, Janet had a passion for antiques, or reasonable facsimiles thereof. She'd insisted they do the house in period, partly because it was obviously the only thing to do and partly because it meant they could use a lot of old furniture various relatives had tucked away in their lofts and attics. If she wasn't at home right now, it was because she was out chasing down a Morris chair or a black walnut whatnot. She'd get the seller to deliver it free of charge, too, not by coercion or seduction, heaven forfend, but because she was Janet.

Jennet, she called herself. That was the way they said it around Pitcherville. Madoc's brother Dafydd, the famous operatic tenor, had teased her about that. "A jennet's a lady mule," he'd insisted. She'd just given him the full force of those dark gray eyes, shown her dimple ever so slightly, and replied, "That's right." Madoc treasured the memory.

Madoc ran the old Renault into the carriage shed, raising his eyebrows when he noticed the empty other half. Then he went in through the side door, kicked off his boots, hung up his storm coat, and went to put the kettle on for tea. He was surprised Janet wasn't here to do it for him, not that he minded waiting on himself but because he'd told her he'd be home early tonight for once and she'd been glad to hear they'd have a little extra time together.

She'd put some beef to marinate in a basin beside the sink, he noticed. Red wine, bay leaves, and various other odds and ends; one of Annabelle's mother's recipes, no doubt. Janet had known he'd be hungry for something special after living on what snacks he could grab for the past two days and nights.

He opened the refrigerator door and stood staring in, the way men do when their wives aren't around to say, "Shut it." She'd got salad greens crisping, mushrooms ready sliced to put into whatever would come out of the basin. She'd promised him a pie; where was it? All Madoc could see was a blob of what might well be piecrust dough wrapped in waxed paper.

"Resting its gluten," Janet had explained rather hilariously after she'd watched a cooking program on television. The Wadman women had always let their dough set a while before they rolled it out, but they'd never quite known why. Madoc didn't know why now. It was a quarter past five, early for him but still later than he'd meant to be. Damn it, why wasn't she here rolling out that piecrust?

If she were, he might have coaxed her into doing something other than rolling piecrust, but that was beside the point. Madoc began to fret. This was not like Janet. Had she popped down to the grocery store for something she'd forgotten, and run into a problem with the car? Why should she? The car was new, but they'd had it long enough to get the bugs worked out. Anyway, she could have had the kid from the garage drive her home while it was getting fixed. She could have phoned their neighbor Muriel and asked her to pin a note on the door. She could have called headquarters and asked him to pick her up himself. Not that he meant to be a possessive husband, but where the bloody hell was she?

Madoc was drinking his tea, thinking up any number of perfectly harmless and innocent reasons why Janet might have had to pop out on the spur of the moment, when the phone rang. Ah, there she was now, stuck with a flat tire she wanted him to come and fix. He sprinted for the phone. "Hello, darling!"

"That you, Inspector?" replied a basso profundo voice.

Madoc gritted his teeth. Didn't they know he was officially, positively, irrevocably off duty? "What's the matter, Sergeant?" he snarled.

"Sorry to bother you, Inspector, but we've had a report."

"About what? Well, come on, spit it out." If they thought he was going anywhere tonight—

"Er—would Mrs. Rhys be with you now?"

What the hell? "No, she's not."

"You haven't heard from her?"

"No, I've just been—look, what is this?"

"Now, Inspector, don't get excited. The thing of it is, her car's been reported found."

"Found? What do you mean? Found where?"

"Gone off the road down near Harvey Station."

"Harvey Station? What would she be—Sergeant, what about my wife? Where is she?"

"They don't know. There doesn't seem to be any sign of her, except her pocketbook. It was under the seat, with all her stuff in it. Money and everything. Some kids on a Skidoo found it."

"What about the car keys?"

"Still in the ignition."

"Oh Jesus!"

Madoc didn't realize he'd whispered. The sergeant started talking faster.

"The car wasn't smashed up, Inspector. It may have been deliberately ditched. There were no footprints, no bloodstains, no—"

No body, that was what the man was trying not to say. Of course there weren't any signs in the snow. Those kids would have mucked them up with their damned snowmobile, trying to be heroes. Blast their souls to hell. No, that was not fair. They'd only done what anybody would who didn't know better.

"How deep is the snow there?"

That was a stupid question. Deep. There hadn't been a real thaw since December. On the other hand, there hadn't been a fresh snowfall recently. The snow wouldn't be soft and fluffy, the kind an unconscious person could sink into and smother. The crust would be thick.

Thick enough, God willing. If the sergeant answered, Madoc didn't hear. He was already on the case.

"Send around a car. Now."

He wouldn't trust himself to drive the Renault. Anyway, he wanted lights flashing, sirens whooping. He wanted time to sit and get his head together. He wanted both arms free for Janet.

What the bloody, flaming hell could she possibly have been doing at Harvey Station? Nothing. Therefore, maybe it hadn't been Janet who ditched the car. She was a careful, sensible driver. She wouldn't go off that far without letting him know. She wouldn't leave the car without taking her handbag.

But suppose she'd had her handbag snatched. The thief would then have her keys and registration. Suppose he'd located the car, driven off hell-a-whooping toward Harvey, skidded off the road, panicked, and run, forgetting about the money in the bag.

That wouldn't explain why Janet hadn't called. If it was a simple case of snatch and run, she'd have got a message to him somehow by now. Unless it hadn't been only that. Unless she'd been knocked out and dumped in another ditch, someplace where she wouldn't be found.

Driving himself crazy wasn't going to help. Madoc put on the coat and boots he'd been so glad to take off, and started out the door to meet the car they were sending. Then he stopped. What if Janet was all right? What if she tried to phone home and nobody was here to answer? Why hadn't he asked for a spare man?

Because he knew damned well everybody who could be spared was already either out there or on the way, sticking long poles down into the churned-up snow around the little blue car, hoping to God they wouldn't hit anything solid.

Muriel, the neighbor, she'd come. He picked up the phone again. Muriel was over in a flash, a coat clutched around her, house shoes on her feet, nothing on her hands.

"But I talked to her just at noontime," she was protesting. "Janet was fine then."

"What did you talk about?" Madoc demanded. "Did she say she was going anywhere?"

"Not that I recall. She said she was sewing on some curtains for that spare bedroom she's fixing up for when your mother comes. Oh, and I told her about the washstand."

"What washstand?"

"Well, you know Janet's been wanting one. The old-fashioned kind, with a hole cut out for the basin and a shelf underneath to set the pitcher. It's to hold that nice decorated ironstone set your friend over in Pitcherville gave her. You know, that belonged to the old lady Janet was so fond of."

Madoc knew. Marion Emery, Bert and Annabelle's neighbor, had brought it over from the Mansion. She'd thought Janet would like a memento of the late Mrs. Treadway. She'd also, as Annabelle pointed out, saved herself the price of a wedding present. Madoc could see Janet now, laughing over the gift and dashing away a tear or two at the same time. Yes, she'd mentioned a stand, but she hadn't been about to pay what they were asking for one in the antique shops.

But Muriel had seen one in a flea market out on a back road somewhere. At least it hadn't been a real flea market, just somebody's barn with a few bits and pieces, most of which a person wouldn't give houseroom to. But there'd been this perfectly decent washstand they were only asking thirty dollars for, and she'd thought Janet would want to know.

"Did you tell Janet where the place was?" Madoc asked with his heart thudding against his back teeth.

"Oh yes. She asked me about four times, till she was sure I'd got it straight. You know how I am about directions."

Madoc did know how Muriel was about directions. He made her go over them a few times, too, scribbling frantically on Janet's grocery list as he listened. They looked easy enough once he'd got her pinned down, but Muriel's directions always did. Janet and he had found that out on a couple of other abortive missions.

The one clue that popped out of his jottings was that if Janet had in fact gone to look for the washstand on the strength of what they purported to indicate for a route, she might have wound up in one of several places, all of them fairly close to Fredericton and none of them on the road to Harvey. So now what did he do? He had to check out Janet's car for himself, but instinct told him to head the opposite way. He compromised by switching on the siren and telling the driver to go like hell.

Yes, that was her car, all right. Madoc opened the door, stuck in his head, and sniffed like a hound on the trail. At first the interior didn't smell anything but cold. Gradually, though, he picked up a trace of—what? Oil and smoke. He put his nose to the nylon carpeting and sniffed harder. Oily smoke, no doubt about it, and a smudge of grease in front of the gas pedal. He reached into the glove compartment for the flashlight he'd put there himself, and beamed it at the stain.

"Who's been in here?"

"N-nobody."

That was one of the kids from the snowmobile, chilled to the marrow, no doubt, but not about to quit while there was any excitement going. "We couldn't see anybody through the window, so we opened the door."

"Both doors were properly shut?" Madoc snapped.

"Yeah, that's right." The kid's teeth were chattering. "Just shut. Like as if you just got out and shut the door and walked away. Only there weren't any footprints. None at all. We looked."

"How? Did you drive around in the Skidoo?"

"No, we had snowshoes. But we didn't need 'em, really. The crust bears you up."

"So it does."

Madoc realized he hadn't even thought about putting on snowshoes himself. He was not a big man, but he outweighed Janet by at least thirty pounds. She could have walked away from here without even cracking the surface. Only she hadn't, because she wouldn't have left her pocketbook.

Unless she'd been dazed. She hadn't been dazed. She hadn't been here. Somebody had got the car away from her, as Madoc had thought from the first. Somebody with big feet and heavy boots, who stank of burning.

"Any fires around here today?" he asked the kid.

"Fires? You mean like a house burning down?"

"Or a dump, or a car that caught fire. Give a sniff."

The boy followed Madoc's example, cupping his nose between his mittens to thaw it out. "Hey, yeah! That's like we smelled when we opened the door. ⌐irst we thought it was the wires under the hood, and jumped back for fear she was going to blow. Remember, Pete?"

Pete remembered. There'd been this funny stink, sort of like burning rubber. He'd wanted to lift the hood, but Duane said they'd better not, so they hadn't. Anyway, it hadn't been all that much of a stink.

"More as if somebody wearing smoky clothes had been in the car?" Madoc suggested.

"Yeah, like that," said Pete. "But then we found this lady's purse."

"Where?"

"Underneath the driver's seat. We didn't notice it right away."

"Did you open it?"

"Well, sure," said Duane. "I mean, what the heck, why not? We had to find out who owned the car, didn't we? We never took anything, honest."

"All right, I'm not blaming you."

Madoc picked up the slender pouch of dark blue leather. Janet wasn't one to clutter herself up with a bunch of stuff she didn't need. Her checkbook, a wallet with fifty dollars in the billfold and two dimes in the change purse. Driver's license, registration, charge cards from a couple of department stores, a snapshot of himself that might have earned him a kidding from the sergeant if the situation had been less dire. A clean blue plastic comb, a blue pen to go with the checkbook, a lipstick in a light coral shade that went well with Janet's bronzy brown hair, and a clean handkerchief with forget-me-nots embroidered in the corner and a scent of lavender wafting from it. That was what the car should have smelled of, if anything. Madoc's sister Gwen had presented Janet with a great flagon of Welsh lavender cologne to take away the whiff of sheepdip while they were over visiting Great-uncle Caradoc, and she'd been dabbing it on herself and her possessions, though not to excess because Janet didn't go in for excesses.

They hadn't raised any fingerprints from the wheel, but there was again that odor of greasy smoke, along with something more pungent that none of them could identify. Janet's handbag, on the other hand, smelled only of good leather and just barely of lavender. So it would appear that the lout who'd had his greasy gloves on the wheel hadn't handled the bag at all. Maybe he'd never even noticed it.

"I'd say she got out of the car for one reason or another, and some thief jumped in and drove off with it," he told his driver.

"Sure, Inspector," the constable replied kindly.

"Damn it, she must have!"

Madoc kept on pawing around until he found it jammed down behind the gadget the seat belt fitted into: a slip torn off Janet's grocery pad like the one he had in his pocket, with more or less the same directions scribbled on it. So she had gone to look for the wash-stand and he'd wasted all this time fiddling around in the wrong direction.

"Come on," he barked, and raced back to the police car.

This time Madoc drove while the constable sat beside him and recited poetry to himself, for the constable was a man of literary tastes. "Back he spurred like a madman, shrieking a curse to the sky." Funny how this mild-mannered wisp of a Welshman, who seldom raised his voice above a murmur and tended to disappear into the background unless one kept a pretty sharp eye on him, could turn into Sir Francis Drake all of a sudden. "If ever she needs me, living or dead, I'll rise that day." Only Mrs. Rhys, not England. That was Alfred Noyes, too, only a different poem. The constable was all mixed up.

He wasn't the only one, the constable decided some while later, after they'd sped back past Fredericton and over toward Oromocto. Those directions Inspector Rhys was trying to follow were getting him lost, from the look of things. Instead of being furious, though, he was acting grimly pleased.

"That's what happened, you can bet your boots on it."

This was the first thing Madoc had said since they left the Harvey Road. The constable was naturally nonplussed by the remark. Being also outranked and somewhat unmanned, he agreed.

Abruptly, Madoc slewed the car around in a hair-raising swoosh. The constable started to say, "What—" then he shut up. He could smell the smoke, too, and see the glow in the sky to the northeast. This might be the wrong fire, but any fire was better than none.

Even as he was straightening out of his deliberate skid, Madoc pointed at the sawhorse and the detour sign tossed into the snowbank at the corner of the side road that led to the glow.

"Firemen must have done that," he grunted. As he wound his way up the long lane that had turnings enough but nothing around them, though, he neither saw nor heard any sign that engines had arrived. Maybe the fire hadn't even been reported. How could he radio in an alarm when he still hadn't the foggiest idea where they were? Muriel had really outdone herself this time.

"Open the window," he told the constable. "Keep your ears peeled."

But it was Madoc himself who heard his name called, and caught the silvery glint of a plastic emergency blanket being waved wildly from the middle of a snowfield between two separate fires.

CHAPTER 4

He either ran or flew over the icy crust. Madoc couldn't have said which, and it didn't matter. Janet was in his arms, smelling like a finnan haddie and shivering like a toad eating lightning, but all there in one piece, self-possessed enough to warn him, "Watch out how you hug me. I expect I've got slivers of glass in my coat."

"What from?"

"The kitchen window. It stuck when I tried to open it, and I didn't have time to fuss."

Madoc started to laugh. He laughed a good deal longer and harder than the situation called for, and it finally occurred to him that he was having a fit of hysterics. That sobered him down enough to ask, "Were you really shouting my name just now?"

"Of course. I knew it was you."

"How?"

"I just did. You didn't think to bring along a cup of hot tea, by any chance?"

"I hope so."

The constable was coming toward them, carrying the snowshoes Madoc had again forgotten about. "Have we got a thermos?" Madoc yelled.

"Ayuh."

What the hell was the man's name? Michael? Gabriel? Raphael? Something that went with Archangel, anyway, or ought to be. Janet was telling the constable so as he handed her a red plastic mug full of scalding coffee. It would be loaded with sugar and she preferred hers plain, but no matter. When they got back to the car, the archangel even produced a box of sweet meal biscuits.

"Always keep a little something in the car," he remarked. "You never know."

"You don't, do you?" Janet agreed politely as she accepted a biscuit. "Madoc, how did you think to look for me out here?"

"Muriel's directions. Actually, how it started was that your car was found ditched and empty except for your keys and pocketbook down on the Harvey Road."

"Oh Madoc, I'm so sorry. It was my own stupid fault. If I hadn't left the keys in—" Janet stopped eating her biscuit. "If I hadn't left the keys, I'd be—"

"You'd what, darling? Here, what's the matter? Put your head down between your knees."

"No, I'm all right."

They had her in the back seat with her feet up, a woolly gray blanket wrapped around her and the emergency blanket on top of that. Madoc was supporting her head and shoulders against his chest, nicking his finger on a shard of glass that was, sure enough, caught in the soft wool of her coat, and not giving a damn. The constable was back in the driver's seat, fiddling with the two-way radio, letting them know back at headquarters that the lost had been found, that there was a fire out here but he didn't know where here was and it didn't much matter now anyway because Mrs. Rhys said the place was derelict and there'd been nobody else inside.

She didn't say anything else till the driver had turned his car around in the melted-out circle that had been left from the burning truck and they were passing the smoldering remains of the barn. Then she remarked rather offhandedly, "I'm in there."

"What?" Madoc was jolted. "Jenny, are you—"

"I mean they thought I was. That's why they burned it. The man who stole my car claimed he kicked—I tried to dry my boots but the stove wasn't—and then they pushed it over."

"We'll have you home soon." Madoc had never before in his life felt so totally useless.

"Delayed reaction," said the archangel in charge of biscuits. "She'll be okay once you get her home. You warm enough, Mrs. Rhys? Want me to turn up the heater?"

"I think she's asleep."

Madoc thought perhaps he was, too. The driver began a long and confusing conversation with the dispatcher about how to get out of wherever they were. Eventually they achieved a meeting of the minds, then there was no more talk until the car drew up in front of the right house. That set off a bustle of explanations and cups of tea and hot soup and sandwiches—Muriel knew how to find her way around a kitchen well enough—and at last Janet was in bed with her boots off and her nightgown on and her short hair still damp from a hot bath. Her gown was respectably hidden by a fancy blue bedjacket Grandma Dupree had crocheted, no doubt with visions of Janet's cutting a dash in a maternity ward. She put on the prim and proper expression Madoc liked to tease her about and said, "Now I expect you'd like me to make a statement."

"Ayuh," said Arthur. That was the constable's name, Madoc had remembered at last. Good man, Arthur. Maybe they'd name their first son Arthur. He still felt a little woozy himself, but Janet appeared to be in full possession of her faculties, thank God.

"Muriel, I never did find that place with the washstand."

It was a beginning, anyway. Janet picked up steam once she got going. Madoc was trying to take notes and keep his arm around her at the same time, perhaps so she wouldn't take a notion to go back for the washstand. He was joggling her sore ribs, so she had to protest.

"For goodness' sake, Madoc, either let go of me or leave the note taking to Arthur."

Janet settled the matter for him by taking the pencil out of his hand and hanging on to the other arm so he couldn't take it away. "Anyhow, I got mixed up somewhere along the line and there I was, out on this long, empty road, when I met a truck coming toward me over the top of the hill. I was wondering how on earth we were going to squeeze past each other when all of a sudden the truck tipped over."

"How do you mean it tipped over, Jenny?" Madoc was still a detective, come what might. "Did it skid and jackknife?"

"No, it wasn't that kind of truck, more like what your father would call a pantechnicon. A big box on wheels. It didn't do anything that I could see, just flopped over on its side in the snow and lay there with its wheels spinning."

"I'll be darned!" exclaimed Muriel, who naturally wasn't about to be excluded from the denouement when she'd been, so to speak, the author of the drama. "Whatever did you do?"

"Stopped the car and sat there like a lump. The truck was all across the road. There was no way to get around it and no place to turn back. Then it came to me I'd better try to do something about getting the driver out."

"Could you see him, Jenny?" Madoc asked.

"No, I couldn't. The truck was over on its left side, with the cab half-buried in a drift. He'd have been on the down side. I thought he might have bumped his head and got knocked unconscious or something. Anyway, I got out to have a look, but the truck was so high and I'm so short I couldn't figure out how to climb up and get the door open. Am I making myself clear?"

"Clear enough. Go on."

"There was this old barn next to the road a little way back, so I decided to look in there for a ladder or some boards or something I could get up on. I yelled up to the driver so he wouldn't think I was leaving him stranded, then I backed the car down to the barn and went in over the snowbank."

"Leaving your keys and pocketbook," Madoc amplified, "but taking that plastic blanket."

"That's right. Actually I started to take my purse, but tossed it back because I figured it would just be in my way. I wanted my hands free to carry the ladder or whatever, and I thought maybe the blanket would come in handy one way or another. I was assuming the man was trapped, you see. It made sense at the time."

"Of course it did, Jenny. So you got into the barn."

"Yes, and I did find a ladder. An apology for one, anyway. Only it was iced into the floor, and while I was trying to pull it free, the barn blew in on me."

"Jenny, what—"

"I'm sorry. I should have said the truck blew up and the explosion knocked the barn down. About half the roof landed smack on top of me."

"Jenny!"

"Now Madoc, don't get all hot and bothered. I landed on a heap of moldy straw. That and my heavy clothes saved me from the worst of it. A few bruises here and there, that's all."

"A few bruises?" Muriel burst out. "You should see her—"

"You don't have to draw them a blueprint," said Janet with an old-fashioned glance at Arthur. "Anyway, there I was, trying to wiggle out from under and wondering if I was going to bring the rest of the barn down on me and there he was, out in the road pinching my car, if you please. If that wasn't enough to curdle the milk of human kindness, I'd like to know what is. You don't have to write that down, Arthur."

"About this explosion, Mrs. Rhys," said Arthur. "You're sure it was the truck? I mean, mightn't the man who took your car have blown up the barn and then gone back with a crane or something to get the truck away? The thing of it is—"

"I know," Janet interrupted. "You're going to tell me you didn't find any wreckage in the road. All you found were the remains of an old red chesterfield and a couple of armchairs."

"Well, as a matter of fact, yes. What we think was, it must have been a moving van and some of the furniture inside it caught fire so they shoved it out, but the truck itself—"

"Arthur, I stood there for darn near two solid hours watching that truck burn down enough so I could get safely past it to the path into the house. Fool-like, I never thought of trying whether the crust would bear my weight. I was too scared about what might happen to me if it didn't."

Madoc's arm tightened around her till she squeaked. "I'm sorry, Jenny. Darling, what happened to the burned truck?"

"They came and took it away. With a wrecker, I think."

"Who did?"

"The men who set fire to the house and barn. I never did get to see them, but I heard them talking. I'd built a fire in the parlor stove to keep from freezing, and fallen asleep. When I woke up, I decided I'd better go back to the woodshed for some more firewood, and luckily I was still out there when they came into the kitchen. They had a bottle of brandy they were drinking. I'd taken a little nip of it myself earlier on. What happened was this."

Janet told them every bit she could remember, except what she'd really been doing in the woodshed and what they'd said about having fun with her. She was not about to let anything of that sort sneak into Arthur's notes. The wife of a detective inspector ought to be *sans peur et sans reproche*, and what Janet hadn't learned about *reproche* growing up in Pitcherville wasn't worth writing home about. Maybe things were different in Fredericton, but she didn't intend to find out the hard way.

They let her talk almost without interruption until Arthur had got it all down in his notebook. Then everybody had another cup of tea and a piece of the cake Muriel's husband Jock had brought over as an excuse to get in on the excitement, naturally enough. Then Arthur said he'd better clear out and let Mrs. Rhys get some sleep. Muriel and Jock took the hint, though they'd obviously have preferred to stay and hash over the details.

Madoc started taking off his clothes, putting his shirt, socks, and underwear in the hamper, leaving his shoes where he could jump into them, not taking the stuff out of his trousers pockets because a man in his position never knew when he'd have to get dressed again in a hurry. Janet had spruced him up a good deal, but he still bagged about the breeches. All the Rhys men bagged, Janet had learned on her honeymoon visit to the ancestral sheep farm. Sir Caradoc bagged the most, of course, because he'd worn his trousers longest. Madoc's brother Dafydd bagged the least because if half the rumors were true, and she could well believe they were, he never kept his on for long at any given time.

"I suppose you'd like to go straight off to sleep," Madoc said in his gentle, wistful way as he reached for his bathrobe.

Janet was still propped up against the pillows, wearing her fluffy bed jacket. "Go take your shower and let me think about it," she answered. By the time he got back, she'd taken off the jacket and hidden his pajamas.

CHAPTER 5

"Sleepy now, love?"

Madoc had been very gentle with his wife. Janet's bruises were every bit as spectacular as Muriel had intimated. As far as his extensive researches could show, however, nothing was broken. He still thought she ought to have X rays in the morning. Janet didn't.

"I'm all right. Truly, Madoc. It's just so good to be home."

She tried to burrow closer to him, but that was hardly possible, so she stayed where she was. "No, I'm not sleepy. I suppose I'm still keyed up. You know, those hijackers or whatever they were must have been awfully well organized in some ways. Putting out detour signs to keep other cars off the road till they could clear away the wreckage took some doing, wouldn't you say? Those were great big hunks of metal. I don't see how they could have managed it all by themselves."

"I expect they'd brought acetylene torches to cut the wreckage into manageable pieces. One of them was probably driving a dump truck to cart the junk away in, and the other a tow truck to hoist it aboard. It's a wonder you didn't see them."

"If I had, I'd probably have charged out and got carted away with the rest of the wreckage." Janet could say it matter-of-factly now that the risk was over. "It must have been that awful brandy I drank that put me to sleep and saved my life. I do remember having a weird dream about dinosaurs prowling around outside. I suppose that was the noise they were making."

After an interlude for comforting, Janet went on. "You know, Madoc, the scariest part of it all was watching that truck tip over. I'd swear it didn't skid or anything; it simply flopped. Like a toy rabbit I had when I was little that was supposed to sit up, but its bum wasn't padded right. I'd get Bun all settled and then over he'd go. You know, I think the truck must have been top-heavy to begin with, like that old bull box Perce Bergeron's got sitting by his barn back home in Pitcherville. His father built it to haul his stud bull around to service the cows on the different farms. He heightened the box in case they happened to be in the mood for privacy. Some cows are awfully prudish, you know."

Janet managed to smile despite her battered face. "And I think they'd aggravated the situation by loading it too high inside. You know how that bamboo coatrack of Maman Dupree's falls over if you pile too many coats on the same side? I'll bet the load shifted coming up the rise and when the truck got to the top of the hill where a big gust of wind hit it, that was enough to finish the job. Does that make sense to you?"

"All the sense in the world, Jenny. I've been thinking pretty much the same thing myself. No doubt it's also occurred to you why they went to such lengths to get rid of all the wreckage."

"Because they had something in the truck they didn't dare let anybody find out about. What do you suppose it was?"

"Your guess is as good as mine, love. Any ideas?"

"Well, of course livestock came into my mind on account of Perce Bergeron, or maybe that was the brandy. I remember something about giraffes. But that couldn't be it, Madoc. Anything alive would have made plenty of noise when the truck went over, and smelled like cooking meat when it burned. And it didn't burn like that."

"How did it burn?"

"Hot. Really hot, I mean. Hotter than—hotter than I'd ever have imagined a truck could burn, not that I'd ever seen one afire till then. But I think I must have been lying there in the barn for a while before I came to and got out, and I could still feel the heat like a blast furnace. I had to back off down the road a way, and couldn't begin to get closer for at least one solid hour. By then, the snow had melted all around and the water was running down the hill in a steady stream. I had to climb up on some of the debris from the barn to get out of the wet. And it kept going for another hour. Wouldn't you say that was no ordinary fire?"

"Over two hours? Jenny, are you sure?"

"As sure as I can be. I didn't have much to do except look at the fire or look at my watch, so I kept switching from one to the other. I suppose I'd have done better to start walking back down the road, but it was so cold, and I wasn't sure how badly I'd been hurt. I knew I hadn't passed another house, and there was that one right handy if only I could get to it, so I just kept hoping."

"It's a damned good thing you didn't start. If they'd spotted you walking along the road—" Madoc forgot for a moment to be gentle. "You did the best thing you could possibly have done, Jenny."

"The best thing I could have done would have been to have sense enough not to trust Muriel's directions." Janet sighed. "Now I don't suppose I'll ever get that washstand."

"My dearest darling, I'll take you out there tomorrow, myself."

"Out where?"

"Out wherever it is."

"Fibber. You want to go back to where the fire was and snoop out what was in that truck."

"I already know."

"What?"

"A fuzzy rabbit with a lopsided bum. Good night, Jenny *bach.*"

CHAPTER 6

Janet didn't get her ride the next morning. She tried getting up to fix breakfast, but Madoc took one look at the way she was walking and carried her back to bed.

"And mind you stay there. I'll make the tea. Could you fancy a poached egg on toast?"

Janet could have, but she opted for boiled instead. One thing about a boiled egg, as her sister-in-law had remarked on a similar occasion, you don't have to take the stove apart and scour it after a man got through cooking one. So Madoc put the eggs on to boil, set the little plastic timer, and got a phone call in the midst, so they turned out hard as brickbats after all.

"Who was that on the phone?" Janet asked as she forced her spoon into the yolk.

"He who must be obeyed. I'm to be down at headquarters in an hour."

"But you were supposed to be getting time off."

"I know, love, but some big bug's flying in from Valhalla or Olympus, I forget which, and they want me there to genuflect."

"You're lying, aren't you? It's about that business with the truck, and it's all my fault. What have I got you into this time?"

"Jenny, I'm not lying. I'm telling you what was told to me, though not in those precise words. It may turn out to be about the truck, and you may indeed have got me into something, in which case you must consider yourself under bed arrest until further notice. Nita Nurney will be over to keep you company till I get back."

"Nita? Madoc, I don't need a policewoman here."

"That, my love, is a matter of opinion. Bear in mind that this ape who stole your car has your registration number, can thus find out who you are and where you live, knows perfectly well he didn't kill you, and may decide to finish the job before the others find out he was lying when he said he did. The odds are that he forgot to write the number down and wouldn't come near you anyway because there'd be little point in killing you now and he hasn't the guts or he'd have followed you into the barn instead of concentrating on saving his own filthy neck. You will no doubt pass an uneventful though possibly somewhat boring day listening to Nita tell you how she won the bobsled race from Ghent to Aix. However, I don't know how long I'll be kept and I'm not going to leave you here alone, not for one solitary minute. I expect your full cooperation and no back talk."

Janet sat up straight and gave him a kiss on the nose. "Your mother warned me you'd turn into a brute and a bully, like your father."

Sir Emlyn had once in his life been heard to raise his voice in anger. The incident had occurred in the midst of a rehearsal for Handel's *Xerxes*, and the rebuke had been directed less at the basso who'd sneezed than at the tenor who'd said, "Gesundheit."

"Yes, dear. Be a good girl and I'll buy you another fuzzy rabbit. More toast?"

"I'll split the last piece with you. When's Nita coming?"

"Before I leave, of that you may be assured. It's probably silly, Jenny. The odds are that chap was in too big a swivet to notice whether the car had a license plate or not. Put it down to my brutish bullying."

"All right, you bullying brute. Not those awful old trousers again! Put on your new gray suit and a white shirt, and that lovely silk tie your mother sent you from Liberty's. Come over here and let me fix your hair."

The bullying brute got himself togged out as directed and beguiled the time kissing Janet goodbye until Officer Nurney arrived and he was free to keep his engagement with the big bug from Valhalla.

His big bug turned out to be two big bugs: one of them a deputy commissioner from NCI and the other a large and deeply upset man who was wearing civilian garb but would, Madoc thought, look more at home in the uniform of an army major, colonel, or possibly adjutant general. He opted for colonel, although the man was, it appeared, to be addressed simply and inscrutably as Mr. X. Mr. X was upset because he had lost something.

"And what did you lose, Mr. X?" Madoc asked with all the humble deference at his command, which was a good deal.

"I am not at liberty to say," Mr. X replied stiffly.

"Well, sir, could you drop a hint or two? Would this object, for instance, be large, heavy, and possibly bigger at the top than at the base, requiring to be transported in a high-bodied vehicle something in the nature of a moving van? Would the object be something the thief or thieves would be more apt to destroy than to risk being caught with? Would it be made of metal packed with some substance that might first explode and then burn with unusual intensity for a considerable length of time?"

Mr. X was by now decidedly bulgy about the eyeballs. He turned to the deputy commissioner in high dudgeon.

"How the hell did this man get hold of classified information without being briefed?"

"Inspector Rhys is inclined to be like that, Mr. X. That was why he was selected for this assignment. I suggest that you either confirm or refute his hypothesis, Mr. X."

"Hrmph. I'm not—er—saying it wouldn't fall into that general category, Inspector. What did you mean, burn for a considerable length of time?"

"Roughly two and a half hours, according to my wife's watch."

"What has your wife's watch to do with my object?"

"Well, Mr. X, I suspect your object may be the object she narrowly missed being killed by yesterday afternoon."

"Impossible! Was she trespassing on—er—trespassing?"

"No sir, she was trying to buy an antique washstand."

"What?" Mr. X chewed that one over for a while, then he muttered, "Good God!"

The deputy commissioner, who had progressed from deeply concerned to quietly amused, suggested mildly, "Suppose you tell us precisely what happened, Inspector Rhys."

"Certainly, sir, though I should explain that my wife's deposition, taken last evening, is already on record here. She herself is at home nursing her injuries and being guarded by Constable Nurney of this division."

"Guarded? Have you reason, then, to believe she may be in danger?"

"I'm not sure, sir. It depends really on whether the man who was supposed to have murdered her before he stole her car happened to make a note of its registration number, and whether the two who came to clear up the debris from the truck stopped to hunt for her body before they set fire to the collapsed barn in which it was supposed to be buried. If we've managed to keep the incident out of the news so far, she may be safe enough. If we haven't, then she's definitely a sitting duck and I'd like permission to go to her at once."

"Stay where you are, Rhys. This is more important."

"Not to me, sir."

Mindful of his mortgage and confident of Janet's common sense as well as Constable Nurney's efficiency, and having listened to the news on his car radio and heard no mention of the incident, Madoc nevertheless decided to stay. He gave a full report of what had occurred, based on Janet's testimony and his own observations.

"All in all, Mr. X," he finished, "it would seem to me that my surmise about your object's being involved could be a reasonable explanation for an otherwise baffling incident. These men were ruthless, well briefed, and quite efficiently organized. The van was of an unusual type and drastic measures were taken to disguise the fact that it had ever been in the area. This would indicate the object must have been something easily identifiable even in a ruined state and extremely dangerous to get caught with but well enough worth stealing to have warranted the risk and bother in the first place. Would you say your object fell into such a category?"

"Definitely. Mind you, that's off the record and highly classified. I'll even go so far as to say—in strictest confidence, mind you—that the van would have had to be internally braced in a somewhat complex manner in order to support the object at the only angle in which it could safely be transported."

"And that this bracing, even if the van had been later found empty, would have been enough to tip you off that the vehicle had in fact been used to transport the object?"

"Let's rather say the possibility would have had to be gravely considered."

"If you prefer, Mr. X. May we not also gravely consider the possibility that if the bracing hadn't been done properly, the object might in fact have overbalanced and caused the truck to fall over as Mrs. Rhys saw it do?"

Mr. X puffed out his cheeks, squared his shoulders, looked Madoc square in the eyes, and said, "We may."

"And that the penalties for being caught stealing this object would be extremely severe?"

"Damn it, hanging would be too good for the blaggards!"

"No doubt, Mr. X," said Madoc politely. "Could you tell me, please, who might possibly want this object? Would it be of any practical use, for instance, to somebody like myself?"

"Maybe, if you were planning to start a revolution."

"Are you, Rhys?" asked the deputy commissioner.

"Only if it should become necessary in line of duty, sir. Getting back to this object, Mr. X, is it something you have a good many more of?"

"What the hell kind of question is that?"

"I'm trying to determine whether there'd be any point in kidnapping the object."

"Kidnapping?" Mr. X turned to the deputy commissioner. "Is the man mad?"

"Oh no. What Rhys means is, would it be a worthwhile venture to seize the object, hide it away somewhere, and demand a ransom for its safe return? Happens all the time, you know, with works of art and so forth. If your object was one of many, it would hardly pay to steal it in the expectation of making a profit on the venture, aside from possible espionage, of course. On the other hand, if the object was some sort of experimental model that would be extremely costly and a great nuisance to duplicate, then the prospect of collecting a ransom could be considerably brighter."

"By George, I never thought of that."

"You are perhaps not accustomed to the devious workings of the criminal mind," said Madoc softly. "Then may we take it that the object might possibly provide that sort of temptation?"

"The—the outfit I represent would never pay ransom!"

"Would-be extortionists don't always consider that possibility, sir."

"Well, all right, then," Mr. X replied grudgingly. "No, we don't have a lot of them. In fact, now we don't have any."

"Is this loss going to incommode you seriously, Mr. X?"

"Hell no. I was dead against the damn thing in the first place."

"Really, sir?" Madoc could believe it, whatever it was. If the cavalry saber was good enough for Lord Cardigan, it was no doubt good enough for Mr. X. "Could you tell us roughly under what conditions this object was being kept? Was it under constant guard in a secured building, for instance?"

"As a matter of fact, the object was in transit. From Point A to Point B. I'm afraid I can't be more specific than that."

"Quite understandably, Mr. X. Point A and Point B will do nicely for our present purpose. May we assume that some part of the route from Point A to Point B lay over public highways, and that these highways were within the Province of New Brunswick?"

"You may, provided you don't ask me to specify which highways."

"Thank you, Mr. X. And may we assume the object was being transported in a conveyance closely resembling the one my wife saw yesterday?"

"Since I have only a second-hand description of that conveyance, you can hardly expect a definitive answer to that question. However, I will say theoretically it might not be unreasonable to hypothesize some resemblance between the conveyances."

"Might it not even be reasonable to hypothesize it was the same conveyance?"

"That's putting me out on a limb. How am I supposed to assume anything until I get some concrete facts to go on?"

"The point is well taken, Mr. X," said Madoc humbly.

The deputy commissioner went into a coughing fit. "Sorry, frog in my throat. Can we offer you a cup of tea, Mr. X?"

Mr. X considered the question in its various ramifications, then went out on a limb and boldly asserted that, yes, he could do with a cup of char. When it came, he opted without hesitation for milk but no sugar. Having thus established the fact that there was a firm hand on the helm, he loosened up and became almost recklessly loquacious.

"Fact of the matter is, it was decided by certain persons who shall be nameless that the object should be transported in an unmarked van driven by personnel who were either civilians—that is to say, not in the—er—company uniform or—oh hell, they were got up to look like a couple of truck drivers. Which of course they were," he added hastily. "The idea was to disguise the object as a load of what may be loosely referred to as merchandise. Saved having to line up a goddamn convoy and advertise the fact that we'd got hold of something we—er —had got hold of. Or were about to get rid of, as the case may be."

"Diabolically clever," Madoc murmured.

Mr. X gave him a somewhat puzzled glance and went on. "To make a long story short, the drivers were got at."

The deputy commissioner raised his eyebrows. "Money talks, eh?"

"Not money, damn it. Good heavens, man, you don't think trusted members of the—of our company could be bribed? This was worse. Far worse."

"Could you elucidate?"

"Er, hm. Needless to say, the personnel in the truck were instructed not to stop for any reason other than safe driving requirements. They were given lunches to carry, including a thermos of coffee. The food and drink were prepared in a maximum security area, or what we thought was one. Well, damn it, in an officers' mess, if you want the unvarnished truth. I mean, damn it, is nothing sacred any more?"

Mr. X struggled manfully with his natural outrage, then redonned his mask of inscrutability. "Nevertheless, in some manner totally incomprehensible to me at this juncture, either the food or the drink was tampered with. After having had their snack en route as directed, both the driver and his—er—assistant became so violently ill that they found it absolutely imperative to halt the vehicle and open both doors of the cab."

"Oh dear," said the deputy commissioner.

"Precisely. As they were leaning out to—er—eject the tainted matter, they were pulled from the cab by masked assailants, thrown into the back of a closed van that had apparently been trailing their vehicle waiting for this—er—occurrence to occur, and kept in confinement for several hours. The object of this maneuver was clearly to keep them from sounding the alarm until the truck could be driven to whatever destination the hijackers had in mind."

"Point C?" suggested Madoc.

"No doubt. The van was eventually found driverless on a side road not far from where the hijacking had occurred. The two kidnapped personnel were locked inside, still suffering from severe stomach cramps but otherwise unharmed."

"Would these personnel be available for questioning?" asked Madoc.

"They've already been questioned *ad nauseam.*"

The deputy commissioner coughed again. "With all respect, Mr. X, wouldn't it have been *post nauseam* in this case?"

"Hah! Got you there. It would not. They both started puking again after the interrogation."

"Poor devils. I stand corrected. Have your people been able to determine what substance was used to induce this gastric upset?"

"I am not at liberty to state."

"Could you at least tell us," Madoc asked shyly, "whether it was a substance that the average person could come by without a lot of fuss? Something like ipecac, for instance?"

Mr. X's eyelids flickered. "I believe the substance might be said to fall within that category, loosely speaking."

Ipecac, then. That must have been pretty ferocious coffee, Madoc thought, but perhaps the men had assumed that was how it was drunk at the officers' mess.

"As to the preparation of this lunch they carried," he went on, "wouldn't it be rather an unusual circumstance for kitchen personnel at an officers' mess to be asked to prepare a picnic for a couple of truck drivers?"

"Naturally, said kitchen personnel would not have been informed as to whom the lunch was for. They were merely instructed to get it ready. An orderly then collected the hamper and carried it to Point A, where he turned it over to the—er—top-ranking man in charge. That man in turn instructed a lesser-ranking person to put it into the cab. This was done just as the drivers were about to set off for Point B, which means the hamper was under guard the whole time."

Undoubtedly. And nobody would have known a thing about the hamper except the sergeant, the private, the orderly, the cook, his minions, and all their respective buddies at Point A, not to mention whoever was expecting them at Point B.

"This hamper and thermoses," said Madoc, "were they distinctive in any way, or were they what might be designated as standard issue?"

"They would fit more appositely into the latter category."

"Ah, then others of their ilk might be procurable at short notice."

"They might," Mr. X conceded after due deliberation.

"Then," said the deputy commissioner. "I expect you haven't ruled out the possibility of a substitution somewhere along the line."

Madoc hoped they also hadn't ruled out the possibility that the drivers had taken along their own ipecac. He decided not to bring that up just now. Mr. X was already having a hard enough time keeping his qualifying remarks under control.

Perhaps Mr. X was tired of the struggle. "All this talk isn't getting us anywhere, damn it. Let's see that deposition of Mrs. Rhys's."

"By all means," said the deputy commissioner. "Rhys, would you—?"

Rhys would, and did. They spent a while passing Xeroxed pages back and forth. Mr. X did a fair amount of grunting. Then he nodded briskly and stood up. "Right. Let's go see whether Mrs. Rhys can give us a description of those men."

"She didn't see them, sir," Madoc protested.

"Well, damn it, she must have seen something. Some—er—something or other. Got transport, Rhys?"

"No sir, I walked over."

"No matter. Got a driver outside. Unless he's been hijacked," Mr. X added with a slightly worried smile.

He hadn't. Unless Madoc was much mistaken, the driver had been taking a nap. However, he snapped briskly enough to attention and held the doors for the delegation. Madoc got in last and sat up front so he could tell the driver where to go, which wasn't far. They could all have walked, for that matter, but he'd known better than to make any such suggestion, even though he could have done without this hulking great vehicle blocking up his driveway.

As to the visit itself, he was happy at any excuse to get back to Janet and confident of her ability to have the household under control, bedridden or not. This proved to be the case. Before he'd got the key turned in the lock, Muriel was at the door to welcome the delegation, whisking off her apron and hiding a dustcloth behind her back.

"I just thought I'd drop over and tidy around a bit," she explained to Madoc. "That nurse doesn't seem to want to lift a hand, just stays up there in the bedroom with Janet. She wouldn't even let me inside. Took the tea tray right out of my hands, told me Mrs. Rhys was resting and couldn't be disturbed. Janet's not all that bad, is she, Madoc?"

Madoc could have said, "No, and neither is her housekeeping." The place was spotless and inviting, with its new William Morris wallpapers, stripped woodwork and shining floors, against which their salvage from the barns and attics cut a pleasing figure. Mr. X would be thinking Detective Inspector Rhys must be on the take. He voiced none of these thoughts, but merely said gravely, "We'll know better after the examination, Muriel."

"Wouldn't happen to be another cup of tea around?" barked Mr. X.

"Oh yes, Doctor. I'll boil up the kettle right away. Shall I bring it to you myself, or will you send the nurse down? She might like a little change of air," Muriel added cattily.

"We'll send the nurse," said the deputy commissioner. "You've got all your equipment, Doctor?"

"Er—oh yes. In my—in here." Mr. X waggled the large attaché case which he had in his hand and possibly padlocked to his wrist. Madoc never did find out whether the case was part of his disguise or crammed with secret plans and vital documents, because Mr. X never opened it in his presence.

He was, however, relieved that his superior and Mr. X appeared not only content but even pleased to have Muriel regard them as visiting physicians, more relieved that Dr. X's request for tea had sped Muriel kitchenward out of earshot, and most relieved of all that Nita Nurney was sticking to Janet like glue.

No doubt Nita had been alert to their arrival. When the delegation got to the head of the stairs, the bedroom door was ajar, and Nurse Nurney was standing on the threshold, all deference. Janet was propped up on a multitude of pillows, her bedjacket demurely tied at the throat, her hair neatly confined by a bonny blue ribbon, and her hands folded on the perfectly smooth counterpane in such a way that Mr. X could see her lovely antique diamond ring and realize Madoc was a man of status in his own right. Lady Rhys would have done the same for Sir Emlyn.

"Thank you, Nurse Nurney," said the man of status. "I see your patient is ready to be examined by these two noted specialists. As you will not be needed during the examination, I suggest you go down and engage Mrs. Muriel in conversation. Perhaps on the subject of some light but nourishing snack she might have ready for us in half an hour or so, since she so obviously burns to be helpful."

"Tell her to take whatever she likes from the fridge," said Janet. "Just don't let her cream it. Perhaps I'd better—" she caught Madoc's eye and went back to being fragile.

"Jenny dear," said Madoc when Nurse Nurney had bustled away in correct medical style and closed the door firmly behind her, "I believe you have met Deputy Commissioner Lawlord. And this is Mr. X, who would like to ask you some questions."

"Of course," said Janet. "I expect it's about what happened yesterday, so you know why I'm in bed and I don't have to apologize. What was it I left out of my statement?"

"For one thing," said Mr. X, "you gave no description of any of the three men involved."

"That's because I never laid eyes on any of them. I thought I'd made that clear in my report. The truck flipped over before I could get a glimpse of the driver, and I couldn't see into the cab after that because of the way it was lying. That was why I went hunting for the ladder."

"And as for the two men who came to the house later," said the deputy commissioner, "you say you happened to be in the woodshed when they entered the kitchen, and that the connecting door was shut tight."

"I don't recall having said tight," Janet replied. "It was shut. There was no crack big enough for me to see through. Considering how anxious they sounded about my being properly murdered and my body safely disposed of, I had no special inclination to sneak over and take a peek. I just froze stiff and prayed they wouldn't take a notion to open the door themselves, which they didn't."

"But you were able to hear them well enough," said Mr. X. "Does that mean you'd be able to recognize their voices if you heard them again?"

"I should think likely."

"Why are you so sure? Did they have foreign accents?"

"No, not at all. I'd say they both came from the Maritimes."

"Were they speaking English or French?"

"English."

"And you'd say English is the native tongue of both men?"

"Such was my impression, for what it's worth. It's hard to be sure nowadays, with so many kids growing up completely bilingual."

"Kids? Were these young fellows?"

"Sorry, I didn't mean to mislead you. No, they didn't sound all that young. I'd guess they were full-grown men, maybe in their thirties or forties. They referred to the one who drove the truck and stole my car as a kid, and they were joking about teenage vandals in a sarcastic way while they were breaking dishes and lugging the furniture out to be burned. I don't think real teenagers would have done that, and I don't see them as having been really old, or they wouldn't have been able to do so much heavy work in so short a time."

"But you can't remember anything unusual about them? They didn't talk like educated men?"

"Well, I rather doubt they'd have been professors from the university. They talked just like ordinary people."

"Yet you're positive you could recognize their voices if you heard them again."

"I expect I could. The voices mightn't have been anything out of the ordinary, but the circumstances under which I heard them certainly were."

Mr. X wanted to belabor the issue, but Madoc wasn't standing for that. "Jenny, is your head still aching? Are you sure you're up to any more talking?"

"I expect I could stand it if I had anything more to tell, but I'm afraid I'm pumped dry. Why don't you take Mr. X and Commissioner Lawlord down and give them their lunch? If one of you happens to think of something worth waking me up for, I'm afraid that's what you'll have to do. This stuff I've been taking for the pain is making me terribly drowsy."

She held out her hand, drooping limply from the wrist as she'd seen Lady Rhys do in moments of extreme fed-upness. Mr. X came all over gallant.

"Wouldn't think of disturbing you again," he assured her, patting the hand lightly as he held it. "You get your rest, Mrs. Rhys. You've earned it. Most grateful for your help."

"Indeed we are," said the deputy commissioner. "Rhys, you'd better stay here till we send Officer Nurney back upstairs. Not that anything's likely to happen, but still—"

"Exactly, sir," said Madoc. "You'll find your way."

Left alone with Janet, Madoc was all for improving the moment, but she put her hand over his lips and pushed him gently away. "Madoc, I have to tell you something. One of those men came from Bigears."

"From where?"

"Bigears. It's kind of a widening in the road out back of Pitcherville. They tried calling it Little Pitcher, but since little pitchers have big ears—"

"Yes, darling. How do you know?"

"They've got a funny way of pronouncing some of their final letters out there, very emphatically with a little sigh at the end."

She demonstrated on the "end." It wasn't quite like "endde," but somewhat in that general direction. "Every one of them does it over there, and I've never heard it quite the same anywhere else. It's just a tiny thing most people would never notice, but you can't miss it once you do."

"Darling, that's marvelous. Too bad it didn't happen to strike you while Mr. X was grilling you. You'd have made his day."

"Oh, it struck me, all right."

Madoc stared at his wife. Then he shook his head. "Jenny love, have you been being clever?"

"I hope so. He doesn't realize what he's doing, you know. They never do, and they get mad if you point it out to them. I expect his mother was a McLumber and his father was a Grouse, or vice versa. There are just those two families, and they keep marrying into each other. The ones that stay, anyway. Most of them get out as fast as they can. Here's Nita coming. Go get your lunch. Oh, and make sure you explain that I've just been having a nervous attack from being reminded, and want to go and stay with my folks."

"Being careful not to mention who they are or where they live, right? Wouldn't the Grouses and the McLumbers know the Wadmans?"

"Mr. X is a little too young to have been at school with my father, and too old for Bert's crowd, but I can't imagine he's never heard of us. Now scat. Hello, Nita. Did you eat?"

Madoc scatted, to take his place at the dining room table, which Muriel had set with the best silver and some placemats Annabelle had embroidered. She was impressed by doctors, and thought it nice of this pair to have flown in from Halifax or Saint John or Montreal or maybe even Boston.

She'd know they didn't come from Fredericton, since there was precious little about Fredericton Muriel didn't know. Anything pertaining to the military, would be a different story, and just as well. Mr. X, or Major Grouse or Colonel McLumber as the case might be, was not precisely a master of disguise. If he were, he'd watch his final consonants. Now that he knew what to listen for, Madoc had no trouble picking up the little extra emphasis, the quick expulsion of breath.

"Doctor, I'm sure you noticed how tense my wife was despite her efforts to appear calm and collected. I think I should tell you that we

had a small nervous crisis just now. No, Muriel, it's quite all right.
Nurse Nurney is giving her a sedative. But the gist of it is, Janet
thinks it would be best if she got away to her people for a few days.
They're a close-knit family, and she says she'd feel safer among them.
I must say I agree. Complete rest, quiet chats with her relatives—"

That was laying it on a bit. Fancy anybody having a quiet chat with
Annabelle, the one-woman soap opera. But Annabelle was fond of her
young sister-in-law, and Janet would indeed be well protected there
with Bert and the boys and Sam Neddick, the hired man who saw all,
knew all, and told only what he was of a mind to.

It was a good thing Janet hadn't yet got around to putting up the
family photographs. Mr. X nodded, all unawares. "Don't see why not,
if she feels well enough to travel. Probably the best thing for her. You
weren't planning to stay there with her, I don't suppose?"

It was an order. Madoc let Mr. X know he understood that fact.

"Oh, there's no need. She'll be well taken care of and I can always
nip over when I get some time off. Would you care for a little more of
the pie?"

Mr. X announced himself replete and in a rush to get back to the
—er—hospital. He beamed kindly on Muriel, addressed her as "gra-
cious lady," and left her pleasantly aflutter and no doubt champing at
the bit to run up and tell Janet all about it, if Nurse Nurney would
only let her. That was all right; she could help with the packing.
Madoc would ride back to headquarters with Mr. X and the deputy
commissioner, stay just long enough to tie up some loose ends, and
negotiate the loan of his own chief's Winnebago. He could then tuck
his Jenny up in a comfortable bed, make the trip without discomfort,
and have her in Pitcherville by nightfall. Tomorrow he'd take a little
run over to Bigears.

CHAPTER 7

Janet had laughed him out of the Winnebago, which was probably just as well. She'd insisted she'd be fine in the car and, as far as Madoc could see, she was.

They'd waited until morning to start because Madoc had to clear his desk first and besides, as Janet thriftily pointed out, they still had last night's supper to eat. She'd taken a trial run down to the kitchen late in the afternoon and found she could manage well enough so long as she didn't try any fancy bending or stretching. So Officer Nurney was freed to go off duty and Muriel to run home and tell Jock all about the big doctor from Winnipeg, and Janet and Madoc to spend a cozy evening and a cozier night together.

Then Janet had treated herself to a good hot soak in the tub to limber her up, got dressed with more help from Madoc than she really needed, and they were off. Muriel was going to water the plants and take in the mail. Every man and woman on the Fredericton Police Force, not to mention the local RCMP, would be guarding the property off and on as other duties permitted. Nevertheless, Janet rather hated to leave. This was the first time she'd be sleeping away from her own home since they moved in, and she wasn't keen on the idea. On the other hand, if Madoc was going to be detecting somebody over at Bigears, she'd be near him. Now she knew how Lady Rhys felt when Sir Emlyn got an invitation to conduct a chorus in Riga or Wellington.

They didn't bother to phone ahead to the farm. That would only have put Annabelle into a premature tizzy. Janet still had her door key, but she wouldn't be apt to need it. At least one member of the family was pretty sure to be around. There was also the question of security.

Madoc didn't actually think their phone had been tapped, but he did know some people in Pitcherville still had party lines. Marion Emery, old Maw Fewter, and no doubt a few more would have their ears glued to the receiver as soon as they heard two longs and a short ring. He and Janet spent a fair portion of the drive thinking up interesting explanations for her battered condition. None of them would fool Bert for long, but Bert would have sense enough not to say so. Living with Annabelle, he'd had plenty of practice keeping his mouth shut.

This was not to say Bert didn't adore Annabelle and so did Madoc, up to a point. They dawdled along so they'd arrive just before noon, timing it neatly so Annabelle could go into her whirlwind act, producing a Thanksgiving feast out of the old cookstove in about three minutes flat and getting them all sat down to it before Bert had got the top off the rum bottle to give himself and Madoc the ritual snort. They'd have been just as well fed if they'd arrived two hours earlier, but the effect wouldn't have been so exciting.

For a while there was little conversation except of the "This is delicious" and "Any more in the pot?" variety. Annabelle expected her cuisine to be taken seriously, and it was worth the attention. When they'd got down to the tea and pie stage, though, it was she herself who raised the question.

"But you still haven't told us what you're doing here on a weekday. Don't tell us you've run out of crooks to chase. You could have knocked me over with a feather when I saw your car pull into the yard."

This was a doubtful premise. Annabelle wasn't many inches taller than Janet, but three kids and a lot of good cooking had increased her girth to about twice her sister-in-law's. She amplified on this theme for a while, then Bert gave her a big kiss on the mouth to staunch the flow and give Janet a chance to start her story.

It was quite a yarn, starting out with Muriel's tale of a good pine washstand going cheap and winding up in the barn of a poor old widow with a shaky ladder up to the loft.

"And she actually let you climb it, knowing the state it was in?" cried Annabelle. "You should have sued her!"

"A poor old widow? Besides, her eyesight was so bad she couldn't have seen how rickety the ladder was. I could, and I knew I was taking a risk, so it was my own stupid fault. I figured with a heavy coat and boots and all, I'd be well enough padded not to hurt myself if it did break, which just shows you how wrong a person can be. Let that be a warning to all of us," she added with a meaning look at her youngest nephew, who was given to putting on his father's Loyal Order of Owls regalia and hurling himself off the top of the henhouse, shouting, "Owlman to the rescue!"

"What gripes me is that I still don't have a washstand and my mother-in-law's arriving a week from today. You don't suppose Marion has one over at the Mansion she wouldn't mind selling?" Janet knew the mere mention of Marion's name would set Annabelle off for at least another hour while the boys went back to school for the afternoon session and Bert and Madoc adjourned to the barn to see how the livestock were doing and maybe exchange a few words about the Grouses and the McLumbers.

On any normal day, it would be taken for granted Janet would help Annabelle clear the table and cope with the dishes. She did make one feeble attempt to pick up some teacups, then stopped, holding on to the back of a chair. "Guess I'd better go lie down for a while."

Annabelle was instantly at her side. "Do you want to go upstairs to bed?"

"Why don't you just help me into my nightgown and bathrobe? Then I can lie down here on the couch. If I can't help, at least we can visit."

So Annabelle rambled on in her warm, quick voice as she tidied the kitchen and then sat down to darn a sweater of Bert's that he'd snagged on the cream separator, and Janet smiled and put in a word edgewise now and then. Between times, she nodded off, knowing Annabelle wouldn't be a whit offended if she noticed. Being together was what counted.

Out in the barn, more serious conversation was going on.

"So that's why I want Jenny out of Fredericton, Bert," Madoc wound up. "This case is so damned hush-hush that I'm to handle it by myself and they won't even tell me what it is I'm supposed to be looking for. What matters most to me is that I don't know whether somebody's also looking for Janet, and I don't dare leave her there alone to find out."

"I should damn well think not," Bert replied. "But will she stay? You know Jen."

"It was her own idea to come here. She knew she'd be safe with you and Annabelle and Sam Neddick. If I honestly thought I was putting any of you in danger, I'd have bunged her straight into hospital under guard and kept her there. I still will if it becomes necessary, so if you see the least little sign of anything out of the way, you damn well let me know in a hurry. Do you think it's safe to tell Sam?"

Bert grinned. "Hell, he probably knows more than you do already. But Sam will keep his mouth shut, unless there's something he thinks you or I ought to know. So all you want from Belle and me is to keep Janet safe and quiet till she gets better, eh? She's not hurt bad, is she, Madoc?"

"As far as we can tell, it's mostly bruises and a few superficial cuts from the broken glass. That's part of the problem. It won't take her long to get back on her feet, and I don't want her going anywhere, not even down into the village. Maybe you can put Annabelle up to starting her piecing a quilt, or something of the sort that will keep her indoors and occupied. I may be around for a few days myself, if you can stand me."

"Tickled to have you. Matter of fact, Fred Olson was telling me just yesterday that we might have to call you out here again. Seems Pitcherville's in the midst of a major crime wave."

"Why? What's happened?"

Bert grinned. "Somebody stole Perce Bergeron's old truck."

"The one his father used to carry the stud bull around in?"

"Hell, Madoc, how'd you know that?"

"We have our methods. What color was this truck?"

"Kind of a dirty barn red, or used to be."

Janet had said the truck she saw was painted dark green. The first thing any sensible thief would have done would have been to repaint it a different color.

"Could you describe the truck for me?"

Bert could describe the bull who'd served the Bergerons, not to mention the lady Guernseys and Holsteins of the area, so long and so well. He was clear on every detail from the horns to the hooves, but when it came to what make and year the truck was, he couldn't rightly recollect. "Fred Olson could tell you better than I," he apologized. "It's more in his line of work than mine."

That was true, Fred being not only Pitcherville's town constable but also its town mechanic, and its blacksmith when there was any smithing to be done. "Then I'll take a run down there," said Madoc. "I owe him a courtesy call anyway. Does Annabelle need anything from the village?"

"I hardly think likely. If there is, one of the boys can scoot down for it after school. Young Bert, most likely. He's in love with the little Williamson girl. Or was, last I heard. Cripes, they grow up fast nowadays."

Madoc said he supposed he'd be saying the same thing himself in a few years' time, and got into the motor pool car he'd borrowed instead of the Winnebago. He hadn't wanted to shake Janet up in the old Renault. As for her own car, it was in a garage somewhere near Harvey Station and it could damned well stay there, as far as he was concerned, till his birds were safely in the bag.

Fred was glad to see him. Madoc was equally glad to see Fred. He had considerable respect for the overweight, middle-aged, one-man police force who'd braved Pitcherville public opinion—and that took some braving—to call in the Mounties on the off-chance there might be a murderer loose in the village, and thus bring him together with Bert Wadman's younger sister.

"Hello, Fred. I understand you've been wanting to call a high-level conference on the subject of a missing wedding vehicle."

"Wedding vehicle? Oh, I get it." A grin found its way with some effort through and around the jowls and wrinkles. "Yep, we got a grade-A crime wave around here. Perce Bergeron's old bull truck an' a dozen two-by-fours from Jase Bain's junkyard."

"Well, well! This is more serious than I thought. Has Bain filed suit against you yet for negligence or malfeasance?"

"No, but he's workin' up to it. Care to set a spell?"

"Thank you."

It was warm enough in the garage with a fire of wood scraps burning in the stove Fred had fashioned from an oil drum and a few angle irons. The seating arrangements weren't fancy. The chair Fred offered had a hunk of plywood roughly nailed on over the hole where the cane had let go, and that was the best of the lot, but it did well enough.

The constable picked up the teakettle that was simmering on top of the oil drum and gave it an interrogative slosh. Madoc shook his head.

"No tea for me, thanks. I've just got up from one of Annabelle's little snack lunches. Any ideas about who's waving the crime?"

"Nary a one. Sam Neddick don't know, an' neither does Maw Fewter. Sam still goes to see 'er now an' then, for old times' sake. Annabelle sends things down sometimes when she bakes. Once or twice, Sam's even paid out his own money for a bag o' gumdrops. Maw's talked herself into believin' he really meant to marry her Dottie."

"What does Sam think of that?"

"Doesn't bother him none. Let 'er think if it gives 'er any comfort, is the way he looks at it. Don't cost him nothin'. O' course he picks up all the village gossip at the same time."

"I can imagine. What's new on the grapevine?"

"Well, the biggest news seems to be you an' Janet. Anything fresh to keep the pot boilin'?"

"Plenty, I'm afraid. Poor Jenny took a bad tumble yesterday and banged herself up in grand style. I expect I'll be branded as a wife beater before the day's out."

Fred chuckled, as Madoc had hoped he would. "I shouldn't be surprised. How'd it happen?"

"I'm blaming Marion Emery, myself. If she hadn't presented us with one of those old-fashioned pitcher and bowl sets from the Mansion, Janet wouldn't have been out hunting for an antique washstand to set it on."

Madoc repeated the yarn Janet had spun to Annabelle. Fred nodded in complete sympathy.

"That's a woman for you. Whatever she can't have, that's the thing she wants most. Mine's been yammerin' at me to move all the furniture out of our Marilyn's room an' turn it into a sewin' room for herself. Marilyn's finishin' up at Acadia this year, an' be darned if she didn't announce her engagement to a nice young feller from Digby whose father runs a lobster pound. Does all right, too; sells 'em to the tourists in summer an' ships 'em down to Boston in the winter. The boy's studyin' to be a lawyer, but at least he's got somethin' to fall back on if the law don't pan out. Though I don't know's I'd want to fall back on a lobster, myself."

Fred chuckled again. "So the gist of it is, they want to be married as soon as Marilyn graduates, which means she won't be comin' back to stay and the wife wants to get goin' on the bridal gown an' the bridesmaids' dresses. Any furniture Marilyn don't want, Millie's goin' to get rid of, she claims."

"Well, before she sells any of it, ask her if there's one of those washstands with a hole in the top and a shelf underneath. I'll pay whatever she asks to keep my wife off any more rotten ladders."

"Hell, is that what Janet was lookin' for? I got one right over there in the corner. Don't ask me where it came from. I've forgotten, if I ever knew. It ain't in too bad shape, far's I can see. I could slap on a coat o' fresh paint."

"If you do, I'll run you in for disturbing the peace. The idea, I believe, is either to preserve them in a suitably battered condition or else to strip them down and then restore them, whatever that may mean. If you'd just brush off the cobwebs and let me know what you think it's worth?"

"Hell's flames, how do I know what it's worth? You better take a look for yourself before you decide whether the thing's even worth luggin' home."

Fred set aside the chipped graniteware basin that had been sitting in the top since God knew when. Together, the two upholders of law and order went over the washstand. Barring a few grease stains and too many coats of the wrong color paint, each one knocked off in spots to show the color underneath, they pronounced it sound and fit to travel. This was definitely a strip-and-restore job, and that was fine with Madoc. It would give Janet something to work off her surplus energy on, once she got some back.

"Want to take it with you now?" Fred asked. "Or shall I run it up in the truck later?"

"Why don't you take it, if you don't mind? Janet will be glad of a chance to say hello. But about the money—"

Fred gave Madoc a sly grin. "Tell you what. You get Perce Bergeron's truck and Jase Bain's lumber back for me, and we'll call it square."

"But suppose they're beyond getting? Would you settle for the thieves who took them?"

"I'd settle for anything that will get Perce an' Jase off my back."

"In that case, it's a deal. Now Fred, can you describe this truck of Bergeron's in detail?"

"I can do a little better'n that. Why don't you take yourself a run out to Bergeron's and ask Perce for a picture of it? He must have hundreds of 'em. Old Elzire, Perce's father, was a real sharp feller. He believed it paid to advertise. He'd have postcards printed up with a picture of the truck an' the bull an' some cute sayin'. 'Why wait till the cows come home? We'll throw the bull your way,' that was one of 'em. 'Service with a smile,' that was another."

"Catchy," said Madoc.

"Ayup. Elzire was a smart one, all right. It was a good idea, you know, cartin' the bull around to the cows instead o' makin' the farmer drive 'em to stud. That truck put Perce's food on the table an' clothes on his back, an' sent him to school, an' he darn well knows it, eh? Hell, he'd rather o' lost his mother-in-law. A damn sight rather, though you needn't tell 'er I said so. I used to have a few of Elzire's postcards kickin' around myself, but don't ask me what became of 'em. Anyway, I expect likely you'd as soon go get Perce's story for yourself. Straight from the bull's mouth, as you might say."

Chuckling at his own wit, Fred told Madoc how to find Bergeron and said he guessed maybe he'd better get back to lining Jim Allenby's brakes. However, Madoc was not quite ready to let him go.

"By the way, would you happen to know a chap from somewhere around these parts named either Grouse or McLumber who went into the military quite some years ago and did pretty well for himself? He'd be around your age, give or take a few years, tall and sturdily built, probably blond when he was younger but gray-haired now, roundish face, florid complexion, and bright blue eyes that look as if you could take them out and play marbles with them."

"Cripes yes, that'd be Charlie Grouse. I went to school with him. Eyeball Grouse, we used to call him. General Grouse nowadays, from what his relatives try to make you believe, but I don't think Eyeball's ever got quite that far. Colonel or major, I forget which. They say he's turned into a kind of a stuffed shirt, but what the hell, he's entitled, is the way I look at it. Yep, you got to hand it to ol' Eyeball, he didn't do so bad for a boy from Bigears. You run into him down to Fredericton, eh?"

"Yes, but please don't mention it if you should happen to run across him. I'm not supposed to know who he is."

"Huh. So he's gone in for the cloak-an'-dagger stuff now? Well, I s'pose that's all part o' the game if you want to get ahead. 'Twouldn't be my cup o' tea an' I shouldn't o' thought it would o' been Eyeball's when we was playin' one ol' cat at recess forty years ago, but that's the way it goes. If he ever lets you in on the secret, tell him Fred Olson says hello. At least I don't have to make believe I ain't me."

CHAPTER 8

Perce Bergeron was precisely where Fred Olson had said he'd be, out in his barn looking mournful. He was sitting on a high stool at a workbench built into the front left-hand corner, doing something to a piece of equipment whose use Madoc could guess the general nature of but didn't care to hear the particulars.

"Afternoon, Mr. Bergeron," he said. "I'm Bert Wadman's brother-in-law. My name is Rhys."

"Oh, the Mountie. Glad to meet you. Fred Olson sent you over about my truck, I'll wager."

"As a matter of fact, he did. I've brought my wife for a little visit with Annabelle, and Bert happened to mention your problem. I came down to ask Fred about it, because I thought it might possibly tie in with a bigger one we've run into."

"You mean there's a gang going all over the province stealing bull trucks?"

"Heavy equipment of various sorts, actually. From the way Fred describes your truck, I'd doubt very much if there are many like it around."

"And you couldn't be more right. I've never seen another one like ours. My father built that bull box himself, and had it mounted to his own specifications. Pa was a man ahead of his time, if you want my opinion. Only the time caught up with us and now it's all this goddamn artificial insemination. Hell of a way to treat animals, but what can you do?"

He threw down the instrument he'd been working on, and pulled out a drawer from under the bench. "Fred tell you about my father's advertising campaign? Now, that took imagination and enterprise. That was Pa all over, imaginative and enterprising. Damn, I miss that truck! It's like losing Pa all over again."

"You were his only son, Mr. Bergeron?"

"Hell no, I was his fifteenth. Some of them were twins, of course.

Pa was sixty-seven when I was born, and as good a man as he ever was. Sired two more after me, but they were both girls, Annette and Finette. Mama called her that because she said Finette was positively the last, and she was. Mama wasn't getting any younger herself by then, you know. 'Forty-eight's too old to be washing diapers,' I can remember her saying. So Pa bought her a new washing machine, which didn't change her mind any, not but what she didn't appreciate the gesture, you understand. Yes, Mr. Rhys, I've got brothers old enough to be your grandfather. Damn near old enough to be mine, if it comes to that, scattered from here to hell and gone. They all turned out imaginative and enterprising, like Pa. Lit out and made their fortunes in the wide world."

"But you stuck to the farm."

"Oh yes, I've never wanted to be anywhere else but here. Besides, I couldn't leave the parents. By the time I was full-grown, they were getting on a bit."

Madoc nodded. Elzire would have been pushing ninety by then. Perce must be another of Eyeball Grouse's classmates himself, or pretty close to it.

"My brother Armand stayed around, too, but Armand was never one for the bulls, unless it was a bull moose. He likes the woods. Started guiding before he was fifteen. Pa said if that was what Armand wanted, then that was what Armand ought to do. He said Armand would find his way, and Armand did. He married one of the McLumber girls from out back and started his own hunting lodge."

"Really?" Madoc wondered how many brothers he might have to work through before he could get Perce back to the bull truck. "How is the lodge doing?"

"It was going great guns, till the lakes began dying. Fishing's pretty slim around here by now, you know. It's the goddamn acid rain that's killing 'em off. Armand gets hot under the collar about those smokestacks down in the States, not that we're a hundred per cent innocent ourselves, but Armand says it's all the same because who the hell comes up here throwing money into Canadian industry anyway? Armand's real big on emission controls. Last time he was out home here, he was raising hell with me because I've never put a catalytic converter on the bull truck."

"You don't suppose Armand might have decided it was his civic duty to remove the truck from temptation's way?" Madoc suggested diffidently.

Perce spurned any such notion. "Armand would never do a thing like that! Not behind my back, anyway. He might drive her off to Fred Olson's garage in a fit of righteous indignation and make Fred fix her up. I won't say he mightn't do that, because he damn well might. Armand's pretty bullheaded, which isn't surprising, bulls being our heritage, so to speak. But he wasn't that riled up. He knows the bull truck doesn't get driven much nowadays."

"But the truck was in drivable condition at the time it disappeared?"

"For sure. I've kept her that way as an act of filial piety, clean as a whistle, tires pumped up, all shipshape and Bristol fashion. Only I've never repainted the body because Pa did that last when he was eighty-six and I felt it would be a desecration of his memory to cover up his handiwork. I do throw on a fresh coat of varnish now and then, to protect it from the ravages of the elements."

"You've never thought of building a garage for the truck?"

"Not I, no sir. She sat right out there where she'd always sat. That was Pa's way, you see. He was a good man, mind you, a kind man in his way, but he didn't hold with pampering. If she couldn't stand up and take whatever the heavens chose to dish out, then she wasn't the truck for him."

"I'm surprised she survived as long as she did, in that case."

"Oh well, you see, Mr. Rhys, she went through a few what you might call metamorphoses along the way. Sooner or later the old frame would rust out and the engine get past repair, so Pa would send for a new one and just bolt the old bull box on to the new chassis."

"Ah, then she wasn't precisely an antique in her moving parts."

"Not at all. I told you Pa was always one to move with the times. We remounted the bull box less than twenty years ago, shortly before Pa passed to his reward. I didn't honestly think he'd be taking the bull out much more, him being just hitting the century mark by then, but he said do it, so I did. No, Mr. Rhys, there are plenty of trucks on the road today that look older than she does, though damn few with so long or so distinguished a history, if I do say it myself."

"And proudly, I'm sure. Would you have a photograph of the truck in her most recent incarnation?"

"Incarnation, I like that word. Pa would have, too. Yes, I've got her right here. We had new cards made at the time, see. That was part of the tradition. I have to admit I've come to rely mostly on ads in the paper and the telephone book, but I'm sure Pa would have done the same. He was all for progress, though I'm personally damned if I see where artificial insemination falls within that category. Jesus, they're even doing it to people now!"

It was a *cri de coeur.* Madoc made no attempt to respond, but busied himself with the truck photos. Not many of the last batch had got distributed. Perce was easily persuaded to part with a number of them. He even produced a front-on shot which had an assortment of Perce's own grandchildren clustered on and around it but was reasonably clear as to detail. Janet had got a close enough look at the oncoming cab; she should be able to determine whether or not this could have been the truck she encountered on that accursed hill.

"This is exactly what I need, Mr. Bergeron. Now, you said the truck was ready to go. Does that in fact mean somebody could merely have climbed in and driven it away?"

"That's exactly what I mean. The drive was plowed, the truck was shoveled out, the gas tank was full, and she even had her battery in. You'd have had to warm her up a while before you started out, but she'd have turned over all right. I'd had her out myself just a couple of days before. I used to drive her down the road and back, you know, just far enough to loosen the old joints and keep the battery charged. She ran fine as silk, all things considered. Pa would have been proud of her. Damn it, Rhys, I can't believe she's gone!"

"What puzzles me," Madoc said quickly lest Bergeron become totally unmanned, "is how it—er—she was got out without the household's being alerted. As you say, she'd have needed to sit here with her engine running for—how long? Five minutes?"

"Three or four, anyway."

"And a vehicle of her size and age would make a fair amount of noise, one might think, regardless of how well she was maintained."

"She would and no doubt she did. Only you see, the kids were rehearsing."

"Ah?"

"As I mentioned before, my brother Armand's got this hunting lodge over on the West Branch."

"That would be somewhere in the vicinity of Bigears?"

"Not too far, depending on how you define Bigears. Pa always said

Bigears was more a state of mind than a precise geographical location. Pa had a great feeling for *le mot juste.*"

"One sees that he must have had," Madoc replied politely.

"What the guests do is, they drive out as far as the pavement goes, then they leave their cars in a big shed Armand had built. Each car has a separate stall with a lock on it, which fosters a sense of security. From there on in it's a pretty bumpy ride, but Armand's got three old army jeeps he bought surplus and painted up with pictures of moose on the side. He named his place Bull Moose Portage, you see. Armand has a flair, like Pa."

"Obviously."

"So anyway, as I said, Armand's fishing isn't what it used to be on account of those goddamn smokestacks spewing sulfur dioxide all over the goddamn North American continent with no thought to the fact that there's somebody on this planet that has a concern in the ecology even if they don't own stock in the company. Naturally, that's cut into Armand's business, so there's not much he can do except go after the tourists as well as the sportsmen. Now, to attract tourists, you've got to offer them more in the way of entertainment than a few mosquitos to swat."

"The point is well taken."

"Realizing this, Armand's worked out canoe trips, nature walks, ski trails, and so forth that the guides can run instead of loafing around bitching about the acid rain. Then he puts on a nice supper and afterward they have entertainment. None of that punk rock stuff, of course, because people who go on bird walks wouldn't be the type to care for it, but maybe a barn dance or an evening of Canadian folk songs like Ronald from Bras d'Or or the one about young Charlotte who froze to death because she wouldn't wear her winter drawers when her boy friend took her for a sleigh ride. Or Old-Timers' Night when everybody sits around and sings the same song to a different tune."

"I'm tone-deaf myself," Madoc admitted.

"Then you'd fit right in at Armand's sing-alongs, from what the kids tell me. See, what happened was, naturally Armand wasn't going to lay out good money for talent when he can get the kids to do it for fun. So he bought up an assortment of secondhand musical instruments at an auction and passed them around among the tribe. Well, some of them took to the instruments and some didn't, but there's six or eight that you can stand to listen to if you're not too particular, and the rest do what they call the vocalizing. My daughter Cecile took piano lessons, so she's the director. Every so often they like to come here for their rehearsals and I don't mind telling you that's the night I take my wife out to supper and the movies. So that's how come nobody heard the truck warming up."

"The truck was gone when you and your wife came home from your night out, then?"

"Gone as though she'd never been," Perce confirmed sadly. "And the kids hadn't heard a thing, which didn't surprise me any, I must say. We'd heard them plain enough, all the way coming up the road. They were pretty sick about it when I told them, but that didn't help us any."

"That truck was something of a local showpiece, wasn't it?" Madoc asked. "I know my wife happened to mention it just recently in Fredericton."

"I'm not surprised, her being away from Pitcherville so long. How dear to my heart are the scenes of my childhood, when fond recollection presents them to view. Cecile was trying to get the kids to harmonize that the other night, but they wanted to sing some ghastly thing about taking a space walk with a little green girl from the moo-hoo-hoon. 'Autres temps, autres moeurs,' as my grandpère would say."

"I don't suppose he's still around?" Madoc ventured. Among the Bergerons, he felt, it might be possible.

But Perce Bergeron said he wasn't. He also said in response to Madoc's further query that neither hide nor hair of the truck had been seen since that fateful night, not that Madoc supposed it had, but asking questions to which he knew he wasn't going to get satisfactory answers was part of his job. Then Perce's eyes began wandering mistily from the workbench over which his father's postcards were strewn to the drive outside where his father's bull truck ought to have been sitting but was not; and Madoc took his leave because he hated to see a grown man cry.

CHAPTER 9

The next step, and he took it gladly, was to get back up to the farm and show Janet those pictures of the old bull truck. He arrived just in time for a cup of tea, as would have been the case no matter when he got there. He didn't need tea now any more than he had at Fred Olson's, but he took it. A yes was always easier than a no with Annabelle. Furthermore, the tea was better and the cup no doubt a damn sight cleaner.

Janet was resting comfortably. She'd had a good nap, she told him, and was thinking seriously of getting up for a while.

"I tell her she'd better take it easy while she has the chance," said Annabelle.

"And how right you are," Madoc agreed. "Stay put, Jenny. You're going to have company. Fred Olson's bringing you a present."

"Such as what?" Annabelle demanded. "A secondhand spare tire?"

"I'll grow a firsthand one of my own if I stay here much longer." The thought didn't hinder Janet from accepting another of Annabelle's neatly shaped, lightly browned madeleines, though.

"Don't worry about that now. You've got to keep your strength up," Annabelle reminded her. "Madoc, you're not eating a thing. Let me go cut you a piece of fruitcake. You always like my fruitcake."

"I do, but would you mind wrapping it in a paper napkin or something so I can take it along with me?" he asked in self-defense. "I just popped in to check on my wife. I still have another call to make, and I'd like to get it over with before dark."

"But you'll be back in time for supper?"

"If I can."

"Honestly, Janet, I don't know how you stand it, never knowing when to light the oven."

Annabelle bustled off, no doubt to pack a hamper in case Madoc should faint from hunger along the road and disgrace her before all

Pitcherville. Madoc took advantage of her brief absence to show Janet the pictures he'd brought from Bergeron's.

"What do you think, love?"

She rubbed her cheek against his coatsleeve. "Oh yes, no doubt about it. They must have slung on a coat of green paint, but they couldn't disguise that funny-looking grill. Poor Perce! He'll be sick as Aunt Prudie's cat when he finds out."

"He's none too happy now," Madoc told her. "Nice chap. You might try thinking up a way to break the news gently."

"I don't suppose there is one. Where are you off to now?"

"To see your old pal Jason Bain. He's been robbed of some valuable lumber."

"I'll believe that one when I see it. Anyway, what's lumber got to do with Perce's truck?"

"Quite possibly nothing."

"Then why are you going?"

"Because I made a deal with Fred Olson."

"About the present he's bringing me?"

"No sacrifice is too great, love."

"You don't mean to tell me the present's coming from Bain's place? I can't picture myself ever giving houseroom to anything he'd got his grubby old mitts on."

"Your present is not coming from Bain's place. Now go back to sleep like a good little wife so you'll be fresh and rested for later."

"Don't get your hopes up. Annabelle's put us in the room with the squeaky bedsprings."

"It's a poor detective who can't track down an oil can. Farewell, mine own. I'm off on my perilous mission."

Madoc kissed his wife once more for luck, thanked Annabelle for the sandwich, the hunk of fruitcake, and the thermos of tea; all of which would come in handy should he happen to get storm-stayed out at Bain's. It was only a five-mile run each way and there wasn't a cloud in the sky at the moment, but one never knew.

Once off the road, he found the drive in to Bain's as he'd expected, abominable at the start and worse as he went along. Rather than tax the pool car's springs to the breaking point, he pulled over to the side at the first reasonable opportunity and hiked the last quarter-mile or so. He deduced Jason Bain would be at home from the fact that he could see no fresh oil spots among the bumps and ruts. Fred hadn't mentioned anything about Bain's getting a new truck, as he surely would have if so incredible a happening had in fact occurred, and Madoc knew the old one leaked like a punctured tin. Unless Bain had managed to promote himself a free crankcase somewhere.

No, he hadn't. When Madoc reached the end of the lane, he found the truck sitting there with a glistening black pool underneath. One might surmise the old coot was spending more on oil than a new vehicle would cost him, provided one didn't know Jase Bain. The logical explanation was that he'd managed to swindle somebody out of a few cases and didn't give a hoot how much the old wreck spewed, so long as the oil wasn't costing him anything.

One might also think Bain would invite a person in to warm himself, but Madoc had expected no such amenity at the end of his trek. Nobody else would get to soak up any heat Jase Bain was paying out good money for, even though in practice he undoubtedly wasn't. He'd be burning scraps he'd scrounged from somewhere, if he was burning anything at all.

In any event, the interview took place on the doorstep, with the lord of the manor bundled into a bearskin coat that had lost most of its hair. His turtlish head was protected by a rakish red and green wool tam o'shanter. Some member of a ladies' curling team must be wondering what became of her cap, Madoc thought. Bain wouldn't actually have stolen the tam, but found it lying about somewhere and carefully refrained from making any inquiries as to who might have mislaid one. Old Jase seldom committed an outright crime. Therefore, he was in a position to take a righteously militant stand against the miscreants who'd had the wicked audacity to boost his two-by-fours.

"One hundred an' twenty feet o' prime studdin' an' what are you goin' to do about it, eh?" he demanded.

"That's a very good question, Mr. Bain," Madoc replied with due solemnity. "Suppose you give me some particulars about how the two-by-fours were taken. Were you here when it happened?"

"What kind of a dumb fool question is that? O' course I wasn't. If I'd o' been here, I'd o' loaded their pants with buckshot."

"Thereby perhaps laying yourself open to a charge of grievous bodily harm. You may be thankful, then, that you were away. At what time did this alleged robbery occur?"

"On the fourteenth o' March, like I told that jeezledy fool Fred

Olson. Sometime between ha'past eight in the mornin' an' six o'clock at night."

"In broad daylight, then. Bold fellows, weren't they? And you say nothing was taken except those two-by-fours."

"That's all I know about right now. I can't be sure, can I? Come the spring thaw, I might find a lot more stuff missin', mightn't I?"

"I shouldn't advise it, Mr. Bain."

Madoc was looking over the junkyard. This was no doubt the cleanest he'd ever see it, with nothing but oddly shaped bumps showing instead of the piles of stowage, salvage, and wreckage he knew were strewn all over the lot. Bain was a packrat on the grand scale. The stuff was supposed to be for sale and there were plenty of signs of digging around the piles, but Madoc doubted that Bain ever sold much of his scavenging. Most people knew better than to try striking a bargain with old Jase.

Madoc didn't suppose for one second the two-by-fours had been prime new wood, or that they'd run to anything like the footage Bain claimed he'd lost. The odds were they'd been bean poles instead of studding, for that matter. Any story Bain told tended to contain a grain of truth, but perhaps not a great deal more than a grain.

"Precisely where were these two-by-fours taken from, Mr. Bain?" he asked. "I assume that long, rectangular bump over there is your lumber pile?"

A few brown stumps were bared in a grin of contempt. "You ain't assumin' very good, Inspector. That ain't my lumber pile. It's seventeen o' them travelin' privies from a construction company, laid on their sides so's no smart-aleck kids'll come whoopin' in here an' try to shove 'em over. The lumber's behind them bushes."

Bain pointed to a lump that didn't look like anything in particular, half-concealed by a clump of bowed-over saplings. "Anybody that happened to have eyes in their head might o' noticed where the snow's been dug out fresh at the end an' them two-by-fours hauled out from under the tarpaulin I had coverin' the pile. I spotted it soon as I druv into the yard."

"Sharp of you, Mr. Bain."

Madoc strapped on the snowshoes he'd been carrying slung over his shoulder and made his way to the lumber pile. Bain didn't follow, but stayed on the doorstep watching him like a hawk as he hitched up the frozen tarpaulin and took a peek underneath.

At least the old devil hadn't amused himself by sending the Mountie on a wild goose chase. It was in fact a lumber pile and there was a gap among the boards where something that might as well be assumed a group of two-by-fours had been snaked out rather cleverly without toppling the rest. Judging from what he could see, Madoc doubted more than before that the studding had been either new or prime.

Could that explain why the top-heavy truck had fallen over? Suppose Bain's vanished studding had been stolen to make a cradle for Mr. X's unknown quantity, and suppose the wood had been too rotten to sustain so much weight when a real strain was put on it? That would mean the thieves had more confidence than skill in their carpentry.

So that let out all the local handymen, not to mention the ones who worked in the lumber mill. Fred Olson would know who they were. Meanwhile, on with the detection. Madoc went back to the steps.

"Since you noticed the intrusion right away, Mr. Bain," he said, "I assume you immediately began looking for tracks in the snow."

Bain made a strange noise through his nostrils.

"And what did you find?" Madoc was a patient man.

"Not a jeezledy goddamn thing. Looked to me like what they done, they come in draggin' a big toboggan behind 'em an' went out the same way so's it would wipe out the marks where they stepped. They must o' stood on the toboggan when they was gettin' the two-by-fours out, too. I couldn't find nothin' but a wide levelin'."

"You say 'they.' Would this necessarily have been a two-man job?"

"Don't see why it should. I said 'they' 'cause I don't know if 'twas one or two or a whole goddamn pack of 'em, an' I ain't puttin' myself out on a limb. Seems to me one could o' done it in a pinch. Don't take a whole hell of a lot o' strength to pull a toboggan over hard crust."

"Even with a heavy load of two-by-fours." Madoc made the statement and let it lie there. "Let's assume one reasonably healthy person, then. Two might have had a hard time keeping their feet inside the toboggan's track, don't you think? They'd have been on snowshoes, I expect."

"Dumb fools if they wasn't. Never know when you might hit a soft spot."

"Oh, I'd say whoever did this was no fool."

Maybe not so clever as he or she thought, but hardly a fool, and definitely no stranger to Jase Bain's junkyard, since the toboggan had made a beeline for the right one of those many deceiving snow-covered mounds. And perhaps no stranger to Bain, either, since he'd known March 14 would be a safe time to excavate without risking that load of buckshot.

"And you were gone that entire day, Mr. Bain. Wouldn't that have been a somewhat unusual thing for you to do?"

"I had important business," Bain snapped.

"I'm sure you did. Can you tell me if it was private business or what might be termed public business?"

"Huh. Name me one thing that ain't public business around this goddamn village."

"You have a point there," Madoc conceded. "In fact, though, you're pretty well outside the village here, aren't you? If you really wanted to, I should think you might be able to come and go more or less as you pleased without anybody's knowing."

And often did, no doubt. "What I'm driving at is whether this business was something that would have been impossible for you to keep quiet. Such as an auction or a court case, for instance, that might have been announced in the papers."

" 'Twa'nt a court case," Bain growled. "Not yet, anyways."

"Then it did involve a dispute of some kind, news of which might well have got around. Did it take you out of the Pitcherville area?" Over toward Harvey Station, for instance? Madoc didn't ask him that.

"Could of," the maddening old goat admitted after thinking it over.

Madoc had had enough of this. "Mr. Bain, if you want to play guessing games, you'll have to find another playmate. Either give me a straight answer or I'll wish you a very good afternoon and be on my way."

That did it. "You don't have to be so goddamn hotheaded," Bain yelled. "A man's got a right to mind his own business, ain't he? All right, I was over to Woodstock, lookin' up some stuff in the county records an' talkin' to a few people out around there. I had to call 'em up the day before to tell 'em I was comin' so's I wouldn't waste the gas gettin' there an' not findin' 'em home. So it was a matter o' public record, if you want to call it that."

"Why? You're not on a party line out here by yourself, are you? I don't see any wires."

"I ain't got no phone. They'd o' made me pay a fortune to run the line in an' I wasn't goin' to stand for it. I druv into the village an' used the one at the Busy Bee. Bunch o' good-for-nothin' bastards settin' around there as usual, flappin' their ears so's they wouldn't miss nothin'."

"Couldn't you have used the pay phone at the drugstore?"

Bain gave him a sideways look and said nothing. The one at the drugstore wouldn't take slugs, perhaps. Anyway, if he'd called from the Busy Bee, it was a safe bet the news had been well spread. That was Maw Fewter's hangout.

So perhaps the raid on Bain's junkyard had been an inspiration born of opportunity. Since Bergeron's truck had been used in the hijacking plot, and since a cradle had to be built inside to hold the hijacked object, it followed as the night the day that the materials to build it with had to come from somewhere. Armand and his home-grown floor show came to mind. Why spend money for what you can get without paying?

Swiping a few old boards from Jase Bain was not a crime anybody around these parts was going to take seriously. They'd either assume some kids did it for a bonfire at the skating pond or to build a hut in the woods or some such trivia, or else that Bain was lying for some deep and devious reason of his own. On the other hand, if anybody was seen going to the lumberyard for new studding, a natural curiosity would arise as to what was going to be built, and where, and why, and wouldn't the builder maybe like a hand in the building of it? Odd-jobbing was a major industry around here, especially in the cold weather when there wasn't all that much doing around the farms. Eyeball Grouse would see the logic and so, no doubt, would his relatives and former neighbors.

"I see the toboggan tracks have been pretty thoroughly tramped over," Madoc remarked.

"That was Fred Olson, mostly."

Like hell it was. It was Bain marching back and forth counting his boards after the fact. Not that it mattered. Fred wouldn't have gone to any special pains to preserve the tracks, because Fred wouldn't have taken the matter seriously. Neither would Madoc, under different circumstances.

"Well, no matter," he said. "I gather they simply came out here to the driveway, or whatever you call it, and got lost in the general confusion."

"Seemed like."

"You didn't notice any unfamiliar tracks as you drove in?"

"It's pretty dug up."

It was, though far from pretty. Madoc didn't pursue the matter. Whether the lumber thieves had come in by jeep, snowmobile, or flying saucer was not particularly germane to the issue. What did matter was where they'd taken the two-by-fours after they got them. There was also the problem of what they'd done with the hijacked van after they'd transferred the stolen object to Bergeron's bull box.

If Mr. X did indeed come from Bigears, and Janet would never have taken so positive a line if she weren't sure of her ground, then he must have grown up knowing all about Elzire Bergeron's historic landmark. If there'd been a war on and no other suitable vehicle at hand, he might conceivably have requisitioned the old truck for military purposes. If he'd been on the enemy's side, he might have looted it as a trophy. Neither being the case, he or whoever was in charge of odd vehicle procurement had probably done the sensible thing and rented a milk truck or a moving van or one of those big drive-it-yourselfers. Or a circus wagon or a gypsy caravan, assuming there were any left around.

The first news of the hijacking had been the discovery of the van with the two retching drivers locked inside. If Madoc's deduction about Perce's bull box and Bain's two-by-fours was correct, that meant there'd been three vans involved. The first and probably largest of the three, which had contained the object that was transferred to the bull box, must not have been found by the time Mr. X appealed to the RCMP for help.

No, that didn't necessarily follow. Mr. X had been too carefully ambiguous on that point. He'd told them the drivers were transferred to a different van—Madoc had envisioned a small one—and kept there incommunicado while the hijackers made their getaway. Madoc and perhaps the deputy commissioner also had inferred that the second van was the one they were found in, but was that in fact the case?

Might they not have been put back into the first one after the object of the hijacking was transferred to the bull box?

If they were in the second van, couldn't it have been traced? Perhaps it had, and turned out to have been stolen from a little old lady who'd been selling pot holders at a church fair during the whole period while the outrage was being committed. In that case, why couldn't Mr. X have said so? Had it been funk, orders from above, or general cussedness that rendered him so overwhelmingly uncommunicative? Or had it been a pretty strong hunch that some Grouse or McLumber was involved in the hijacking and that the less he told of the facts, the less likely the case was to be solved. And the failure would be Madoc Rhys's, not Eyeball Grouse's. Very neat.

Madoc walked back to the car, opened the thermos, poured himself a cup of Annabelle's tea, tasted her sandwich and found it good, realized after some minutes' cogitative chewing that he'd finished the sandwich and was well into the fruitcake, poured out the rest of the tea to wash down his snack, pondered whether the next leg of his expedition should be over to Armand's or out to Bigears, made his decision, stoppered the thermos, stuck the rest of the fruitcake into the glove compartment for a rainy day, turned the car around, and drove back to the farm.

CHAPTER 10

Perhaps he'd have been well employed tracking down each and every member of Armand Bergeron's vaudeville troupe and questioning them one by one. Madoc deemed it a far, far better thing to be lounging here on the old daybed in the corner of the kitchen with Janet curled up against his chest and Julius the cat perched on the cushions behind him, purring down the back of his neck.

Bert had the pieces of Annabelle's toaster spread out on the kitchen table, trying to figure out why the damned thing had started hurling pieces of bread all over the kitchen lately. Sam Neddick was sitting across from him whittling a wooden duck decoy which he would later stain with tobacco juice, rub down with wood ashes, and peddle to some ecstatic tourist as having been carved by his great-grandfather. Annabelle was mending a pile of shirts and socks belonging to the three young replicas of Bert who were allegedly doing their homework while in fact eating popcorn. All six were assisting Madoc with his inquiries, though at least four of them didn't know it.

Neatly docketed in his mind at this point were various pieces of information, among them that Cecile Bergeron wasn't much on housekeeping (Annabelle) but sure was a good-looker (Bert, trying to get Annabelle's goat) and that she read too damn many books and got funny ideas (Sam Neddick). Pressed to explain what sort of funny ideas, Sam was not clear. In his opinion, any female that sat around with her nose in a book all day was bound to get funny ideas. Goaded to the defense of her sex, Annabelle demanded to know who could blame a woman for seeking romance and adventure in books, there being darned little of it to be got from the men around Pitcherville.

Bert Junior volunteered the information that Cecile had a new boy friend who thought he was pretty hot stuff because he could throw a hunting knife up in the air and catch it in his teeth. This led to a digression of some length, with young Ed and young Charlie saying young Bert ought to try it in front of his girl and their father retorting that he (Bert Junior) damned well hadn't better and that he (Bert Senior) would tan the pants off any kid of his he caught handling a hunting knife or any other knife in a reckless and irresponsible fashion and didn't they realize what dentists' bills ran to nowadays?

Janet roused herself enough to tell Julius to get his tail out of her mouth and demand that the rest quit yammering about hunting knives and tell her about Cecile's new boy friend. Who was he and where did he come from?

That stopped them. Not even Sam Neddick knew much of anything. His name was Pierre. He'd wandered into Armand's place one Saturday night, done his hunting knife trick to wild applause, hung around the piano a lot while Cecile was playing, offered to buy her a beer and been turned down because Cecile wasn't that kind of girl, at least not in front of so many Bergerons. Thereupon he'd shown up at Mass the following morning, wily cuss that he was, been permitted to walk Cecile home and invited by Perce's wife to stay for Sunday dinner so the family could look him over and decide whether he was halfway reasonable husband material, since Cecile wasn't getting any younger.

The family's decision was still pending, Sam believed, but there could be no doubt that Pierre's being a man of mystery appealed to Cecile's sense of romance and adventure and that Armand didn't mind having Pierre around on Saturday nights now that his hunting knife trick had proved a surefire crowd pleaser.

"But what does he do when he's not catching knives in his teeth?" Janet demanded.

"Good question," Sam grunted, squinting along his duck to see whether he'd got the two sides reasonably symmetrical. "Claims he's a guide an' a nature writer."

"What's a nature writer?" Ed wanted to know.

"A person who writes pieces about nature for the magazines, I suppose," said his mother. "Birds and flowers and—"

"Watch it, Belle," Bert teased. "Ed's kind of young for that stuff."

Ed said he was not and what stuff? His mother said never mind and asked Sam where Pierre got his pieces printed. Sam shrugged and went on shaping his duck.

"Well, what's his last name?" Annabelle prodded.

"Dubois, he calls hisself."

And why wouldn't he? Madoc thought. Peter of the Woods was a fine name for an alleged guide and nature writer who could catch a hunting knife in his teeth, not that he'd have many teeth left before long if he didn't quit showing off in front of the fair though unhousewifely Cecile. Pierre Dubois sounded promising. But what of the other members of the band?

Well, Raoul was steady enough but Etienne was wild as a hawk. In Sam Neddick's considered opinion, Blaise wasn't a damn sight tamer, for all he could play the guitar and the trombone with equal felicity. Sam didn't say felicity. He didn't say trombone, either, because he couldn't think what to call them cussed brass things that slid in an' out an' made such a god-awful blattin' noise.

Young Charlie could. He was himself taking lessons on the trombone and practiced every afternoon out in the barn, to entertain the cows on these dull late-winter days. For this act of charity he was loudly praised and much encouraged by his entire family. He offered to play right now for Aunt Janet and Uncle Madoc. Janet suggested instead that they come out tomorrow afternoon and listen along with the cows, provided she felt up to it and Uncle Madoc didn't have to go off detecting somebody.

Getting back to the Bergerons, as Madoc gently insisted they do, Marie-Claire was her Aunt Cecile all over again. If she didn't stop mooning around over books and music and that Clarence McLumber from Bigears, she was going to wake up one of these days and wish she had, was Annabelle's none too humble opinion. Sam, however, had it on good authority that Clarence McLumber seemed to be less interested in Marie-Claire these days than he was in hanging around with Blaise and Etienne and the enigmatic Pierre Dubois.

"Where do they hang around?" Madoc wanted to know.

"Out in the woods, mostly. Admirin' nature with a sixpack o' Moosehead apiece, though I guess they cut a little cordwood for Armand now an' again when the spirit moves 'em," Sam answered.

"Any more in their crowd go with them?"

"Shouldn't be surprised. Lyon Grouse an' his cousin King McLumber was over to the Busted Antler with Dubois a couple o' nights ago."

"Sam means the Deerhead Restaurant," Janet explained to Madoc. "The one with all those dozens of deer horns nailed all over it. We stopped there once on our way here, remember?"

"Whatever for?" cried Annabelle. "Didn't you think I was going to feed you?"

"You weren't here. It was that time your mother was sick and you went down to take care of her. All we had was a sandwich and a piece of pie, as I recall. It wasn't too bad, for restaurant food." Actually it had been quite good, but Janet wasn't about to praise anybody else's food in Annabelle's kitchen. "What happened to that pretty grand-daughter of Perce's, the one with all the curly hair? Yvette, wasn't it?"

"Yvette's okay," said young Bert gruffly, his voice by now having completed the change that had sent it careening from squeaks to rumbles for the past year or so.

"Not so okay as the little Williamson girl, eh?" said Bert Senior.

"Aw, Dad, cut it out before the brats start on me again."

As umbrage was being taken by the brats and quelled by the parents, Fred Olson showed up with Janet's washstand, scrubbed and made as presentable as possible. She of course was delighted and Annabelle only a few degrees less so for Janet's sake. Fred was made a great fuss of and Bert urged to get that silly toaster out of the way so Fred could sit up to the table and have a piece of pie, not that he needed it as he himself remarked and as the overstrained seams of his trousers attested.

"How you doin', Madoc?" he asked with his mouth full.

"Well, I've visited the scene of the crime." Madoc gave his wife one of his sad little smiles. "I may as well come clean, Jenny. That washstand isn't exactly an outright gift. Fred made me do a dicker for it."

"Aha, the great two-by-four robbery," said Bert, neatly picking up the cue. "Was Jase Bain surprised you've called in the Mounties, Fred?"

"Haven't asked him. I expect he'll take it as his natural due. This is mighty good pie, Annabelle. Why thanks, I don't mind if I do. What'd he say, Madoc?"

"About what you'd expect." Madoc gave them a somewhat embellished account of his interview with Bain, knowing full well the boys would spread it all over school and their friends would take it home to their parents. That was fine with him. It looked as if he might be around Pitcherville for a while, so the locals might as well know he had a reason for staying, even if it did lead them to assume he was using Bain to wangle a paid holiday with his in-laws out of the RCMP.

"So I may be here a bit longer than I expected, if that's all right with you and Bert, Annabelle."

It couldn't have been righter. Annabelle said so at considerable length. So did the boys, who felt their prestige greatly enhanced by having a Mountie for an uncle. Bert only gave Madoc a grin and a nod, and went on screwing the toaster back together.

"There, by Jesus. Want to get me a piece of bread, Charlie, and we'll give her a try?"

Much to the boys' disappointment, the toaster worked fine. "Aw Dad," Ed protested. "It was more fun the other way."

"Never you mind," snapped his mother. "If you think it's any fun standing over a hot stove first thing in the morning frying bacon with hunks of toast flapping past my ears, you've got another think coming. Now get along upstairs, the pack of you."

"Aw, Ma, tomorrow's Saturday," Bert protested.

"I don't care. I'm not having you sprawled out in bed all morning when your father's got chores for you to do. Janet, you'd better go, too. Your eyes look like two burnt holes in a blanket."

Fred Olson said he guessed he'd better mosey along before his wife sent out the bloodhounds. Madoc neatly pocketed Bert's oil can. After half an hour's sorting out, the party was over.

While Janet was washing her face and brushing her teeth, Madoc de-squeaked the bedsprings, but a fat lot of good it did him. Between the long ride and having so many people around her, Janet hadn't had much chance to rest. She was asleep almost before she got through kissing him good night. After that, there wasn't much for Madoc to do but go to sleep himself, so he did.

CHAPTER 11

Even the rooster slept late the next morning. It was half-past eight before Annabelle got them all gathered around the breakfast table for fried eggs, fried ham, hot biscuits, and a few other things. Bert and the boys had been out to the barn, of course, because the livestock always came first, and Julius had got his saucer of cut-up ham, not that Julius exactly counted as livestock.

"Ol' Jule's just one of the farmhands like the rest of us," Charlie was arguing. "You spoil him, Ma. Go filling him up with ham and he won't want to be bothered catching the mice."

"How'd *you* like to get stuck with a cold mouse for breakfast?" Ed yelled back.

"Could we please change the subject?" Janet asked her nephews. "I feel a bit queasy."

"You do?" exclaimed Annabelle.

"It's not that kind of queasy," Janet protested, knowing full well what was in her sister-in-law's mind. "But I think I'll skip the ham and eggs all the same, if you don't mind. In fact, I think I'll go on back to bed for a while."

Madoc leaped up so fast he upset his chair. Bert grinned.

"Don't panic yet a while, Madoc. You'll have plenty of time for that later. Sit down and eat your breakfast."

"I don't see why Uncle Madoc's flapping around like a wet hen just because Aunt Janet's got a bellyache," Ed remarked, helping himself to about half a jar of strawberry jam. "You going to be like that when you get married, Bert?"

Annabelle and Bert Senior had stern rules about fisticuffs at the table, but they were still trying to enforce them as Madoc helped Janet back to their bedroom. "I'd like to know what people have kids for anyway," Bert was roaring, plenty loud enough for Madoc to hear and take warning.

"Good question," Madoc murmured into his wife's ear. "Do you want to reconsider, Jenny love?"

"I just want to get back to bed," she told him. "I think it was the smell of that ham frying that put the kibosh on me."

"I wish you'd let me take you to a doctor."

"Madoc, I'd know if there were anything really wrong with me. I overdid it a little yesterday, that's all. Now go back and finish your breakfast before you start a panic."

"If you say so."

But Madoc was back in the bedroom as soon as Bert and the boys had gone about their chores and Annabelle had shooed him out of the kitchen because she wanted to put her bread to rise and that was one thing she never cared to do and talk at the same time. When he slipped into the room, though, he found Janet fast asleep, breathing normally and not looking as if she were about to develop any alarming symptoms. He stayed there watching and wondering for a while, then went off to the hardware store and bought a can of stuff to strip paint off washstands with.

The stuff smelled awful and looked worse, but it did the trick. Madoc worked out in the woodshed for the rest of the morning. By the time Annabelle rang the dinner bell, he'd got all six layers of paint off. The washstand looked worse than before, in his opinion, but no doubt Janet had some plan afoot to turn it into a thing of beauty, or something near enough to satisfy herself and his mother.

After he'd cleaned up, he went to check on Janet, who was awake and not queasy any more. "I think Julius and I will take it easy today, though," she told him. "What have you been up to all morning? Not out to Bain's again, I hope?"

"No, I've been stripping your table for you."

"That was sweet of you." Janet grabbed a fistful of his hair, which was black and almost but not quite curly, and pulled him down to be kissed. "How does it look now?"

"Queasy."

"That's all right. I'd decided to paint it regardless. It's nothing so very special, you know."

"I never supposed it was."

"But you went ahead and bartered your soul to Fred Olson for it anyway."

"Well, darling—"

"I know, you don't have to tell me. A poor excuse is better than none. Have you decided how you're going to weasel your way in with the Grouses and the McLumbers?"

"I thought I might begin by stepping out with another woman. How do you think Bert would take it if I invited Annabelle over to Armand's lodge tonight to enjoy the floor show? For that matter, how do you think Annabelle would react?"

"I think they'd both be tickled silly. So would Maw Fewter and a few more around town."

"Yes, well, there's that. Have you a better idea?"

"Nope. Go ahead and let 'em talk. But why don't you want Bert along with you?"

"Because I want him here keeping an eye on you. He doesn't have his Owls' meeting on Saturdays, does he?"

"Thursday, if they haven't changed the date since we were last here. We'll be home by then."

"What makes you so sure?" Madoc growled into her neck. "Going psychic on me like Aunt Blodwin?"

"Nope, just thinking about all we've got to do before your mother comes. You might just mention to one or two people that Bert and I had some family business to hash over so you and Annabelle decided the pair of you might as well clear out and leave us to it. That ought to start them wondering if Uncle Sid out in Saskatchewan's finally kicked the bucket and left us his fortune. Or if Cousin Henry scooped the pot and we're trying to figure out a way to claim undue influence. I'll be interested to know how much they run it up to before they find out he's still alive and kicking. So will Uncle Sid, I expect. He's never had two cents to rub together in his whole life, that I know of. I don't suppose you'd care to drive back over to the hardware store before you leave me in the lurch, and pick up a can of dusty blue paint in case I feel up to finishing that washstand tomorrow?"

"And how will I know which shade of dusty blue paint to get?"

"How many shades do you think they'll have, for pity's sake? Get whichever one they've got. A pint should be plenty. The satin finish, not the shiny. Mr. McLumber will help you pick it out."

"Ah, I see. You're being clever again."

"Well, there's no sense wasting the afternoon, is there? I can't imagine he's the man you're after, but he's pretty easy to get into a conversation with. Tell him you bumped into Eyeball Grouse yesterday in Fredericton and see what he says."

"Darling, Eyeball Grouse is not a name to be bandied about in hardware stores. I'm not supposed to know he even exists."

"Then couldn't you say you met a relative of Mr. McLumber's but you can't recall offhand what his name was?"

"Why don't I simply ask him which of his male relatives has fallen in with evil companions and developed a knack for felonious assault?"

"Well, you're the policeman. I'd try sort of wiggling my way around to it myself. Not that I'd get far, I don't suppose. They're a pretty clannish bunch out in Bigears. Still, it never hurts to try, as Great-aunt Winona said when she put mittens on the cat so he wouldn't scratch up her new chesterfield."

"Are you two coming down to dinner or not? Ma wants to know so she can dish up the stew." That was Ed, clattering up the stairs three at a time. "Ma says she'll fix you a tray if you'd rather stay abed, Aunt Jen."

"How about it, Jenny?" Madoc asked her. "Could you eat something?"

"I'd love a cup of tea," she admitted. "Run back and get me one, would you, Ed? No sugar, remember. Tell your mother I wouldn't mind a piece of that bread she baked this morning and about half a teaspoonful of stew, but I'd as soon wait for that till she can come up and talk to me while I eat. You go along with Ed, Madoc. No sense in your keeping the rest of them waiting."

So Madoc went. He'd barely got a foot inside the kitchen when everybody was asking, "How's she feeling?"

"She's clamoring for hot bread and dusty blue paint," he reassured them.

"She going to paint the bread?" Charlie wondered.

"It's for the washstand," snapped his mother. "Stop trying to be funny and eat your dinner if you're so wild to get to the hockey rink. Bert, you make sure your brothers stay up at the shallow end of the lake. This is a treacherous time of year."

It was as good an opening as any. "Speaking of treachery, Annabelle," said Madoc, "how'd you like to sneak out on your husband tonight?"

"Madoc, whatever do you mean?"

"I thought you might like to go out to Armand Bergeron's lodge with me and catch the show. It's rather the in thing with Pitcherville society these days, isn't it?"

"Such as it is, I suppose you might say so. It appears to be respectable enough, from what I've heard. But it's mostly the young crowd that go there for the dancing."

"And what are we? Come on, Annabelle, be a sport."

"Go ahead, Belle, do you good," said Bert. "You know damn well you've been yammering at me to take you. Now I won't have to."

"Serve you right if I happened to meet somebody more obliging." Annabelle could still charm when she tossed her curls and turned on her over-the-shoulder smile. "But what's Janet going to say if we go off and leave her alone, in her condition?"

"What do you mean alone?" Bert retorted. "The boys and I'll be here, won't we?"

"I don't know, Madoc, it doesn't seem right. Why can't we wait till next Saturday when she's feeling better, and all go together?"

"Because next Saturday you're all coming to Fredericton to meet my mother."

Annabelle still wasn't ready to give in. "Couldn't you bring Lady Rhys out here instead?"

"Mother will only just have arrived. We'll have to give her a while to admire the new washstand before we start gallivanting, don't we? Furthermore, we've already given her a faithful promise you'd be on the welcoming committee. Annabelle, is it yes or do I have to deputize you?"

"Hey, I get it," shouted young Bert. "Uncle Madoc's detecting somebody and Mum's supposed to be the beautiful lady spy that gets the bad guy on the spot so the good guy can grab him. Right on, Mum!"

Annabelle turned the color that used to be known as Schiaparelli pink. "I don't know where you kids get such crazy notions. Watching too many of those trashy television programs, eh."

"Nope. Reading those paperbacks you've got hidden down in the preserve closet," Bert Junior replied sweetly.

"I do not have them hidden! I stuck them there for want of a better place to put them because there's so darn much junk of yours and your father's all over this place. And furthermore, why couldn't you have been doing some homework for a change instead of stuffing your head with that kind of nonsense?"

"Annabelle," said Madoc, "I want you to be the beautiful spy who lets the dumb cop know who's who and what they're up to. I can't take the boys because they're too young to be hanging around a dance hall on a Saturday night. I can't take Bert because it would look too strange for the pair of us to go off by ourselves and leave you sitting here with my sick wife. Janet suggests you and I pretend she and Bert had some family business to talk over so we decided to clear out and leave them to it."

"What family business, for instance? Why couldn't you and I be in on it?"

"No doubt we could, if there were any. Our story is that it was too utterly dull and boring and we didn't want to be bothered."

"Nobody's going to believe that."

"Jenny doesn't think so, either, but she figures we'll be doing an act of charity by giving the village something fresh and juicy to chew on. The thing of it is, Annabelle, Jason Bain's been giving my distinguished colleague Fred Olson a rough time over that lumber he claims was stolen. He's been threatening Fred with a lawsuit, impeachment, and six or eight other things. Fred doesn't know yet whether Bain's actually been the victim of some crime far more serious than he's admitting to, or if the old man's setting Fred up as the pigeon in one of his swindles. If it's the former, we'd like very much to know what it's all about. In the latter case, Bain ought to be stopped before he pulls it off, and I should take a personal pleasure in stopping him."

"Oh well," said Annabelle, "if it's a case of spiking Jase Bain's guns, of course I'll do anything you want me to. Why didn't you say so in the first place?"

"Mainly because I was a bit nervous that some one of the persons present might drop a careless word in the wrong ear and upset the applecart. Listen here, you lads. You can joke about old Jase and his two-by-fours if the other kids bring it up, but if any one of you so much as looks as if he thought Fred and I might be taking the old coot seriously, I'll chuck you all in the slammer. Is that clearly understood?"

"You bet!" was the consensus of the gathering.

"What are you going to do now, Uncle Madoc?" Charlie asked before his brothers could shut him up.

"I'm going back to the hardware store and buy your aunt a pint of dusty blue paint for her washstand. Can I drop you at the hockey rink?"

He could, and did. Then he went on to McLumber's and selected a shade called Loyalist Blue with a good deal more assistance than he needed from a remarkably chatty young clerk. Madoc tried to get the young fellow switched off to more interesting subjects, but had no luck. Roughly half of Pitcherville was in there clamoring for attention, and Mr. McLumber appeared to expect, not unreasonably, that the clerk go and do what he was getting paid for.

Madoc hung around for a while, picking out a paintbrush, admiring various gadgets, and getting elbowed out of the way by shoppers of more serious intent, but didn't get another crack at the garrulous youth. After a while he gave up the struggle and took his small purchases out to the farm. He found Janet sitting up in bed, talking clothes with Annabelle. She agreed Loyalist Blue was just the ticket, and went on talking clothes. Madoc went back to the woodshed and painted the washstand Loyalist Blue.

CHAPTER 12

Annabelle had done him proud. She was wearing the Frenchwoman's ultimate chic: a well-fitted black dress and matching pumps. A Liberty scarf Janet had brought her from London was deftly twisted at the neck and pinned with a golden brooch in the shape of a cow with a ruby eye Bert had given her to remember him by when he was out milking the herd. She'd used a discreet amount of makeup and smelled deliciously but not too strongly of the toilet water the boys had clubbed together to buy her for her birthday. When Madoc complimented her on her appearance, she laughed.

"It's all my family's doing. Bert, you make sure the boys get to bed at a decent hour, eh."

"Never you mind us," her husband retorted. "Just remember you're there on official business and don't go whooping it up with Armand and his crowd. If any of those guys get fresh with you, have Madoc take their names so I can bust their jaws for 'em sometime when I get around to it."

Madoc promised he'd do any necessary busting. They went off in a flurry of last-minute orders from Annabelle and hypocritical assurances from her husband and sons that these would be followed to the letter. Janet, who'd come down in her bathrobe to see them off, waved from the kitchen window. Everybody else hollered from the doorstep. Annabelle settled her coat, fussed with her scarf, and hoped she'd do all right. She was nervous as a partridge in hunting season and relieved her tension as Annabelle naturally would, by a running monologue on everything from crime to patchwork, punctuated by an occasional "What's old Jase really up to, Madoc?"

"We'll know when we've winkled out the facts," he told her, and kept on driving. He didn't mind Annabelle's flow of conversation. In fact, as the son of a choral director, he found it both natural and comfortable. Annabelle had an agreeably low-pitched voice, as well as a clever way of turning a phrase which one seldom found in the lyrics of oratorio and anthem. Nor did she keep repeating the same few words with trills and variations for page upon page.

It took them the best part of an hour to get out to Bull Moose Portage, not because the distance was so great but because the driving was so slow once they left the main road. They hadn't had to wait at the big shed Perce had mentioned for a jeep to take them in; a big sign had told them, somewhat optimistically: ROAD OPEN. GO AHEAD TO LODGE. Probably it had been smooth enough when it was plowed out, but traffic must have been brisk since the last snowfall, for the ruts were deeply carved. The number of cars around the lodge when they finally got there confirmed Madoc's deduction. Armand and his home-grown talent were really packing them in.

The lodge itself was pretty much what Madoc had expected, deliberately rustic on the outside and barny on the inside. Its most outstanding decorations were two stuffed bears standing on their hind feet, one wearing a hunter's cap and fluorescent vest, the other demure in a frilly apron and flowered headscarf. A small stage had been knocked up of rough planking at one end of the room, and a good many small tables with chrome underpinnings and red plastic tops were clustered around it. He led Annabelle to one of the few that were unoccupied, and ordered them each a vin blanc.

It was a middle-aged woman who took their order, and Madoc would have been willing to bet she was at least a cousin of Eyeball Grouse. She turned her hyperthyroid gaze thoughtfully on Annabelle before she went off to the bar, which was far and away the most popular spot in the room.

Annabelle was amused. "That's Armand's wife's sister Prissy. Doesn't know whether to recognize me or not. I suppose they have to be careful in a place like this, not to scare off the customers. I'd better say my little piece when she comes back, not that she'll believe me."

She said it, and Prissy smiled and nodded, but Madoc doubted whether she'd been able to hear a word. A gaggle of young Bergerons were onstage now with their secondhand instruments, squeaking and banging and hooting and thumping their feet and flapping their elbows in the approved manner of modern dance bands. To Madoc's tone-deaf ears they didn't sound much worse than his sister Gwen used to when she was starting her clarinet lessons, though they were certainly making a lot more noise.

Nobody else seemed to be minding the racket, either. Couples were out on the floor doing something that involved putting their thumbs to their foreheads and spreading out their fingers, bending at the hips to an approximate right angle, and doing even stranger things with their legs. Armand, with his penchant for home talent, must have conscripted the game warden as choreographer, Madoc thought. He leaned over to Annabelle.

"How do you like it?"

"It's nice. The curtains are pretty." A typical Annabellian reply. "Bernice must have run them up."

"Which is Bernice?"

"Oh, you'd never catch her in a place like this. Bernice is awfully religious. But naturally she'd want to help out her brother. Doesn't Cecile look pretty tonight?"

"Which is Cecile? The one at the piano?"

"No, that's her niece Yvette. Cecile must have been giving her lessons. Cecile's over at that table in front of the stage with Basil McLumber and some man I don't—ah, I'll bet that's the new boy friend. Cecile's not done so badly for herself, *hein?*"

So that was the fabled Pierre Dubois. Annabelle's enthusiasm was justified, Madoc supposed, if a woman went in for tall, broad-shouldered types with curly beards and hawkish dark eyes. He himself had dark eyes, but they were rather more like those of a scolded spaniel. That was irrelevant to the issue at hand; anyway, Janet liked them. Janet wouldn't be impressed by Pierre.

The man had got himself up like an old-time *coureur de bois* in fringed buckskins and a wide sash handwoven in a mélange of bright colors. He'd even perched a scarlet toque with a pompon atop his overlong black curls. The toque looked brand-new. Madoc wondered if Cecile had just finished knitting it for him, possibly comparing herself to Elaine of Astolat embroidering the cover for Sir Lancelot's shield as she murmured, "Knit two, purl two."

Cecile was dressed in a long gown of some softly draped material in a pale shade Madoc couldn't make out in the dim light. Annabelle would tell him later, no doubt. Anyway, she was a wispy, big-eyed little thing with slender, fluttery hands that fluttered fairly often in the direction of Pierre's buckskin thrums. She looked like the type who could picture herself floating down the river in a funeral barge with a lily on her bosom. Only it would have to be a birchbark canoe to maintain Pierre's image, and where would you find one these days? And what would happen when she got to the rapids?

Regardless of all that, Cecile appeared in lively enough spirits tonight. She was smiling up at Dubois, who in turn was smiling down at her. He showed a fine set of teeth unchipped by the hunting knife he carried strapped to his hip and would perhaps do his celebrated trick with before the evening was much further spent. The secret, of course, was to catch it with the lips before it ever got to the teeth; which was not to say the stunt didn't require nerves of steel, the reflexes of a mountain cat, and a penchant for silly deeds of meaningless derring-do intended to impress moony young women like Cecile and harebrained youths like those who were clustered around Pierre.

Sure enough, they were urging him to do it. He was flashing his teeth and shaking his head, either being modest or stalling until the band stopped playing and he could have everybody's undivided attention. Madoc suspected the latter, and was right. No sooner had the dancers quit their mooselike antics and left the floor than Pierre shrugged, flung out his hands in a fine Gallic gesture of surrender, threw back his picturesque head, pulled the famous knife from its well-worn sheath, for which Cecile might secretly be embroidering a cover, and flipped it nonchalantly into the air.

Then the bright steel blade was quivering upright with its point hidden in the exuberant mass of his beard. Everybody applauded except Madoc and Annabelle, Madoc because he suspected Pierre was pulling a fast one and Annabelle because she thought that man was setting a dreadful example and some kid would be darned lucky if he didn't wind up with a hunting knife down his gullet from trying to copy that crazy stunt.

She said so to the waitress, who only smiled and reached for their empty glasses. "And furthermore, a person might think a man his age would know enough to take off his hat indoors in the presence of ladies. I'm surprised Cecile hasn't dropped him a hint."

That at least brought a reply. "Oh, I don't think there's much Pierre Dubois could do wrong in Cecile's eyes. That was two white wines, right?"

"Unless he's got a bald spot he's trying to hide," Annabelle finished defiantly. The waitress smiled again and hurried off. Annabelle could think what she pleased; Armand's sister-in-law's job was to keep the drinks going.

Nobody was going thirsty tonight. They were three-deep around the bar now. Madoc excused himself to Annabelle and meandered to the men's rest room, mainly so that he'd have a chance to see whether anybody was paying any attention to the impressive array of brand-name bottles stacked behind the bartender. He'd have been willing to bet most of them were either empty or illegally refilled with something other than what their labels advertised. As far as he could tell, no matter what anybody ordered, it all came from the same under-the-counter source and sold for a dollar a slug. Madoc wondered if perhaps Armand was relying on home talent in the booze department, too. Bootlegging was still a thriving industry in certain parts of Canada, and the RCMP had had some interesting times determining which parts.

As he was pondering this interesting subject on his way back, Madoc noticed Annabelle had acquired tablemates. These proved to be a couple name Flyte from downriver a way. Maybe Flyte was the man's real name, though it could well have been a *nom de guerre*, since he made no bones about having been a draft dodger from Boston during the Vietnam War.

"Didn't they declare an amnesty some years ago?" Madoc asked him.

"Yes, they did. I could have gone back, but I decided I'd rather stay in New Brunswick. It's a better way of life, to my thinking. Besides, I'd met Thyrdis here, and she was none too keen on leaving her own people."

"They've turned their house into a lovely gift shop," Annabelle put in. "Janet and I have been down there a couple of times. That's how we happened to recognize each other. Let's see, you're Donald, aren't you? And you're the one who makes those cute mugs shaped like pigs and chickens?"

"I'm a potter," Donald replied rather stiffly. "I make a great many things. Most of my designs are more serious attempts to interpret the medium, but we've found we have to bend a little if we want to stay in business. I guess you farmers don't have that problem, eh, Madoc?"

"Oh, we do plenty of bending." Madoc was quite willing to be a farmer for the evening. "Potting business pretty good, is it?"

"Not so bad." Donald picked at the frayed cuff of his tweed jacket. "Of course, this is our slow time of year."

"Not that we care," said his wife staunchly. "It gives a breather to prepare for the tourist season."

"Thyrdis does some beautiful things." Donald abandoned the cuff as a bad job and began running his fingers through the fringe of a woven sash he was wearing. It was similar to the one around Pierre Dubois's waist except that it had a blue stripe down the center instead of a red one, and might have made more sartorial sense with something other than that ratty but respectable suit.

Madoc nodded over toward the piano, where Cecile was evidently getting ready to play. Pierre was standing ready to turn her music for her. "I see there's another of your customers."

"'Cecile?" said Thyrdis. "She bought one of my shawls a while back, but she isn't wearing it tonight."

"I meant the chap with the sash."

"Oh no, that's not one of mine. I never work that pattern."

In a pig's eye you don't, thought Madoc. He'd seen enough Welsh tapestry weaving to have an eye for a pattern. Having verified his suspicions about the whiskey from a surreptitious sniff at Donald's glass—rotgut with a dash of caramel, obviously, though Donald didn't seem to be minding—he let Annabelle carry the conversational ball while he took inventory around the room.

It intrigued him to note how many of the men in the room were wearing those same woven sashes. Most of them had the blue stripe like Donald's, five went in for a shade like spruce green, but only Pierre Dubois had a red one. The greens included Blaise Bergeron, his brother Etienne, their cousin Achille, who was obviously much the eldest of the trio, and a couple of other men around Achille's age, one of them called Jelly McLumber—short for Gilles, Madoc supposed—and the other Clarence Grouse. Several more Bergerons were in the blue stripe squad, along with a fortyish Jelly Grouse and a young Clarence McLumber, a pair of Fewters who were connected somehow with the old woman from Pitcherville, another McLumber who turned out to be the popeyed youth from the hardware store, Fred Olson's wife's cousin Henry Skivins and his nephew Bartlett, though what they were doing together in a place like this was more than Annabelle could fathom, and that odd Mr. McAvity from over by the Forks who collected butterflies. There were a couple more whom she'd never set eyes on before. Madoc counted twenty-three in all, and these out of a crowd of maybe a hundred at the most, including the women and the staff, if such they could be called.

Of course it was by no means unheard-of for young fellows to copy the style of some man they admired. Pierre Dubois was a charismatic type, not that Canadians went in much for charisma, as a rule. But these weren't all kids by any means, and they weren't actually trying to ape Dubois. Madoc didn't see another buckskin thrum in the place. The men were wearing pretty much what anybody would wear on a Saturday night to a hunting lodge in the boondocks: anything from a sports jacket like his own with a light pullover under it to a red-and-black checked flannel shirt or a snowmobiling outfit. Only the sashes were uniform. Madoc wondered if "uniform" might possibly be the operative word.

He knew better than to ask. Flyte would no doubt say they were trying to reaffirm the ethnic spirit of the region, or something equally high-minded and obscure. If there was any such movement afoot, why wasn't anybody talking about it? Or peddling sashes for the good of the cause?

Cecile had been strumming rather aimlessly on the piano keys. Warming up, Madoc had supposed, to warble some cheerful ditty about unrequited love or untimely demise. Instead, she suddenly whipped into a jiggy barn dance tune. A Bergeron kid with a concertina stepped forward to help her out, and another of the tribe stepped to the microphone.

"Oh super," cried Thyrdis. "Etienne's a fabulous caller. Come on, everybody."

She made sure her woven dirndl was firmly hitched, flung her long woven scarf backward over her woven blouse so the ends could swing wide as she pranced and twirled, and ran with Donald on to the floor. Annabelle turned to Madoc with such a look of pleading that he couldn't have resisted if he'd wanted to, which in fact he didn't. In the first place, he'd far rather be hopping about than sitting here swilling whatever this stuff was that Armand called wine. In the second, he was intrigued to find out why not only Donald Flyte but every single blasted one of those twenty-three sash wearers—young, old, or in between, with or without a partner—was leaping out to join the sets like a bullet from a gun.

Etienne was indeed a first-rate caller, and Annabelle an adept partner. Madoc didn't get to keep her to himself much, however. Etienne went in for a lot of intricate switching about. Madoc could swear he'd had a swing around with every woman on the floor and half the men before they'd been at it ten minutes. It was like being one of the little pieces of colored glass in the kaleidoscope he'd played with as a kid.

Lots of the dancers were good, but the beau of the ball was Pierre Dubois. He was everywhere, thrums flying, feet stamping, white teeth flashing from behind that curly black beard, never missing a figure. He was also up to something. Madoc didn't know what, but he watched the red toque systematically bobbing its way to each and every one of the men wearing the woven sashes. On one pretext or another, Dubois would take that man's hand. Often as not, especially if the man wasn't one of the better dancers, he'd leave the floor soon after he'd been touched.

Was this some part of a secret ritual, a mystic laying-on of hands, a grip of brotherhood? Or was Dubois passing on a message? He couldn't be handing out notes, not in that number and not at a gallop, with so many people around and so many chances to fumble the passing. Maybe he squeezed their hands in Morse code, but how much could he convey in those brief contacts? Enough, apparently, or he wouldn't be taking the trouble.

The kid from the hardware store was among the last to receive the magic handshake. Madoc was clear across the dance floor at the time, and he had a feeling Dubois had made sure he was before approaching young McLumber. Somebody must have tipped him off that the Mountie was present. If Dubois was any judge of men at all, he might be having a qualm or two about this particular recruit. The kid had impressed Madoc as a know-it-all just in that brief transaction over the Loyalist Blue paint. Get a few beers under his belt and he'd be shooting his mouth off right and left. Most of the men touched had shown more sense than to let on anything of importance had passed between them and Dubois. Young McLumber was looking so damned guileless that any policeman worth his salt would have collared the fellow on general principles.

Well, this wasn't Madoc Rhys's collar to make, but at least he now knew whom to lean on should it become necessary to unravel the tangled web of those multicolored sashes. The caller was out of breath; the dance was winding down. Madoc bowed to his partner of the moment, who happened to be an elderly man in a lumberman's plaid, found his panting but joyous sister-in-law, and escorted her back to their table.

CHAPTER 13

After the dance, the band played a couple of more or less recognizable golden oldies while Cecile and the concertina virtuoso refreshed themselves, Cecile with a *petit verre* and the kid with a Pepsi-Cola. Dubois was all over Cecile again, gallantly pulling out a chair for her, fetching her wine from the bar, getting himself a beer to keep her company. It was only his second or third drink of the evening, Madoc noticed, and nobody could say the man hadn't earned it.

Annabelle didn't want any more wine. She had a *café noir* and a slice of *gâteau* that wasn't up to her own standard, then began to fidget.

"Madoc, don't you think it's about time we started back? Bert will be wondering where we've got to."

If Madoc knew Bert, Bert was pounding his ear quite peacefully and had been for some time. But Annabelle was right about leaving. They wouldn't be the first, by any means. Some of the early dropouts from the dance floor were already gone. Others were getting ready to brave whatever might be happening outside. Madoc dropped money on the table, got their coats from the rack over by the stuffed bears, and helped Annabelle on with hers.

As they made their way to the door, followed by a good many pairs of thoughtful eyes, Annabelle got stopped by various acquaintances wanting a final word. While Madoc was standing patiently in the background trying to look like a brother-in-law who'd taken out his sister-in-law merely from a sense of family duty and intended to take her straight home from the dance, as in fact he did, he noticed young McLumber being given a polite but firm *congé*. Pierre Dubois was doing the talking. Armand Bergeron was standing with his arms folded, making it clear just by being there that McLumber needn't try to put up an argument.

And that was interesting, too. The hardware clerk had a pretty full load aboard, no question about that, but so did almost everybody else in the place. No doubt the cheap drinks were the main reason why many of them had come. This wasn't a rowdy crowd, but it wasn't what you'd call subdued. The kid hadn't been acting any more boisterous than a good many others, including some of his fellow sash wearers. But perhaps he'd reached the limit of what he could handle and Armand knew it from previous experience. Or perhaps that innocent act he'd put on during the dance had alerted Pierre Dubois to what he ought to have realized before he let McLumber become a member of the sash society, or whatever the hell it was. Anyway, the kid was going, on a snowmobile to judge from the outfit he was wearing, and Madoc was still left standing.

Not for long, though. Annabelle was really anxious to get back to her family, and kept working her way toward the door. They made it, and none too soon. A snow squall was just beginning to splat wet flakes into their faces.

"I hope we get home before the worst of it," Annabelle said nervously.

"We'll make it, never fear," Madoc reassured her. "This won't amount to anything."

A few other cars were already on the narrow lane. A couple more pulled out while Madoc was letting his engine warm up. These made it poky going. They were snug enough in the car once the heater began to function, but the sticky snow soon coated the windows until Madoc had hardly any visibility except for the two fans kept clear by the windshield wipers. He didn't much like that, but putting on the defroster would mean freezing Annabelle's legs, so he just kept poking.

"It won't be so bad once we get out on the road," he remarked to Annabelle.

She, to his surprise, didn't answer and he realized she'd fallen asleep. The wine and the workout on the dance floor must have done her in, not to mention the lateness of the hour. She'd been up since half-past five or thereabout, most likely, and would be again in the morning, which was closer than he'd realized.

He let her sleep and wished he could do the same, with Janet beside him instead of Annabelle. To keep himself alert, he thought about those twenty-three woven sashes. Armand Bergeron hadn't been wearing one, but it was dollars to doughnuts he knew why the rest were. If he didn't, he was a rotten innkeeper.

Why were two of Armand's young relatives involved and not the others? There'd been a lot of Pepsi-Cola floating around the bandstand, maybe that meant some of the boys were too young to qualify. And the girls would be out just because they were female. The feminist movement still hadn't made much headway among the Bergeron clan, obviously, if a woman of thirty or more still had to bring her male friends home for the family to check out, and didn't dare drink a beer in public.

Cecile was too restful a topic. Madoc was beginning to nod when he was startled wide awake by a sharp crack not far off. It brought Annabelle upright, too.

"Madoc, what's that?"

"Sounded to me like a rifle shot."

"Huh. Somebody jacking a deer, I'll be bound."

Madoc didn't contradict her, but his own thought was that this would be one hell of a time and place to commit the illegal act of startling a night-feeding animal with a sudden flash of light and shooting it down as it stood momentarily paralyzed by the glare. Maybe if the lead car happened to catch a deer with its headlights and there was a rifle handy and somebody drunk enough to yield to temptation —but the headlights wouldn't be bright enough, not tonight. This damned sticky snow was coating the glass, reducing their beams to a gentle moonlight glow.

Now what? They could hear clashing and strong language up ahead. Madoc stopped just in time to avoid rear-ending the car in front of him, and prayed the car behind would do likewise.

"Stay here, Annabelle. Sounds as if there's been a pileup ahead of us. I'd better go see what's happening."

"Oh, Madoc! What are we going to do?"

"Sit tight till Armand gets a wrecker out here to clear the road, if we have to. It's probably nothing much, though. Don't worry. There's a blanket in the back if you get chilly."

"But you won't be long."

"No no."

Madoc put up the hood of his parka and braved the storm. It didn't take all that braving, actually. Those big splatting flakes were more a nuisance than a threat.

As he passed the car in front of his, its driver rolled down the window. "What's the matter up there? We heard a shot."

"Could have been a tire popping," Madoc told him. "I suppose the driver stopped short and the next one plowed into him."

The man said, "Hell," and rolled up the window again. Madoc picked his way forward. There were more cars ahead than he'd realized. He counted six before he got to the pileup. Three cars were involved here, none of them seriously. None of their passengers appeared to be taking any interest in their smashed taillights and caved-in bumpers. They were all up ahead, standing around something Madoc couldn't see. Was it the dead deer?

No, it wasn't a deer. It was the young fellow from McLumber's in his snowmobile, with a hole in one side of his parka hood and a corresponding one coming out the other side. The hood was still on his head, or whatever might be left of it. The head was resting on the handlebars. There didn't appear to be any blood to speak of. It must all be inside the hood.

"Damn good shooting," somebody remarked. Nobody answered him. They must all be in shock. No wonder. Madoc stepped forward.

"I am Detective Inspector Rhys of the RCMP," he said softly. "Could you tell me, please, which of you was driving the car just behind him?"

"I was. Name's Grouse. Harold Grouse." He was one of the older, sashless men who'd been sitting at a table up near the bar, chatting with his companions, taking no part in the dancing, not punishing the whiskey. "My cousin Si here was with me, and my wife Enid."

"That's right," said a middle-aged woman in red nylon boots and a muskrat coat. "We were all three sitting in front together. Closer to the heater. You feel the cold, coming out of that warm hall."

Maybe she was feeling it now. Her teeth were chattering. Once she'd got started talking, though, she couldn't seem to stop. "It was such a lovely time, the music and all. And now this. I never thought to see such a—"

"But you did see," said Madoc. "Exactly what did you see?"

"Why, I hardly know what to say. We were just driving along, you know, slow and careful as you'd naturally expect, and Buddy was up ahead of us."

"Buddy. You knew this chap, then."

"Lordy, yes. Known him all his life and then some. Buddy McLumber. His real name's Elwood. Was, I suppose I ought to say. But I don't believe I've ever heard anybody use it. Maybe his toullers, I don't know. His uncle runs the hardware store. Buddy was named for his uncle. He just started working there a few weeks back. You must know Ed."

"I was in there today, as a matter of fact," Madoc confessed. "Buddy here sold me some paint. He seemed like a friendly young fellow."

"Friendly." She made a funny little sound. "Friendly isn't the word for it. He'd talk the ear off a brass monkey. Poor Buddy."

She started to cry. Madoc tried to shut her off. "You still haven't told me what happened. You saw Buddy on his snowmobile. Was he going fast or slowly?"

"Wasn't going fast." That was the man called Si, taking up the tale Enid couldn't finish. "He'd o' shook the guts out of 'er if he'd tried to speed up over these here ruts. I dunno why Bud was in the road at all. Seems to me with a snowmobile he'd o' done better to get off an' run acrost the snow."

"Buddy never did have no sense," said Harold Grouse.

"Hal! That's a fine way to talk about somebody that's sitting here dead right in front of your face," Enid scolded.

"Well, he didn't. Anyway, Inspector, what happened was, I was driving along, taking it easy the way my wife said. There was Buddy up ahead of us leadin' the parade, as you might say. I shouldn't be surprised if that was why Buddy stuck to the road, so's he could be first in line. It would have been like him. Never missed a chance to show off. Anyway, all of a sudden we heard a rifle crack and over he went, like you see him now."

"And the snowmobile stopped dead?" Madoc demanded.

"Right in her tracks. So I hit the brakes myself, naturally, and the fellow in back o' me didn't, which was understandable enough and I don't hold it against him in the circumstances."

"Wait a minute, Hal," said his cousin. "I'm not sure but what Bud stopped just before he was shot. Seems to me he might of. You'd been keepin' a proper distance behind, but you were darn near on top of him when he keeled over. Unless he'd been slowin' down. Hard to tell, and I suppose I wasn't paying much attention anyway, if the truth be known. But there he was, so we all piled out an' came to see what was the matter."

"You didn't move the body?"

"Well, of course we did," said Harold Grouse. "I did it myself.

Didn't know if he'd been hit or just passed out from too many beers. I took hold of his hood by the top. But then I saw the holes in the sides an' got a glimpse of—God! I hope I never see the like again. So I let it fall back the way it was. Didn't know what else to do."

"You saw nothing of whoever shot him?"

"Hell no," said Si. "You couldn't see a damn blasted thing except straight in front o' the windshield wipers. Not on the side he was shot from. You can tell from the size o' the hole in the hood. I remember that from the war." He swallowed hard.

"All I can say is, whoever did it must have been either drunk as a skunk or one hell of a good shot," added one of the other spectators.

"No doubt," said Madoc. "Now, if you'll just give me your names and addresses, perhaps we can get this line moving."

He wouldn't gain anything by keeping them here. Probably nobody in the line had seen anything on account of the snow plastering their windows. The sharpshooter would have taken this factor into account. And be over the hills and far away before Madoc could go after him, but first things first. He copied down the information they gave him, then performed the revolting task of shoving Buddy McLumber's body to one side so that he could squeeze himself into the snowmobile with the corpse and drive it up on the bank.

The damned thing wouldn't start.

Si and Harold and the rest offered a fair amount of useless advice, then Madoc thought of checking the gas tank. It was bone dry. Luckily, Harold had a spare can in his trunk. Madoc cleared the way, waved on the three front cars, none of which, fortunately, was mangled badly enough to be inoperative. Then he worked his way back down the line.

He hadn't expected any luck in identifying the sniper and he had none, but he did find one couple from Pitcherville who said they'd be more than willing to take Annabelle home with them. When he got to his own car, he said, "Annabelle, I've got a bad one. Buddy McLumber's been shot and I'll have to stick around. The Phillipses are just ahead and they're going to take you back with them. Do you think you could drive this car out to the road and leave it there for me?"

"I don't see why not." She slid over into the driver's seat. "I'll leave the keys under the seat, shall I?"

"Good girl."

"Is Buddy going to be all right?"

Madoc didn't answer that, just said, "Thanks, Annabelle," and headed back to where he'd left the snowmobile. Buddy McLumber's condition hadn't changed.

CHAPTER 14

Madoc took Buddy around to the back of the lodge. As he'd expected, he found a special parking area out there reserved for snowmobiles, and a reeking hole in the lumpy ice covering one of the vacant spaces.

So it hadn't even been a difficult shot. The sharpshooter had merely drained all but a few drops of gas from the tank, followed along within sight of the road, and waited till Buddy was sitting there wondering why his vehicle had stopped all of a sudden. It would be absurd to think there'd been a mistake in identity. Buddy's was the only cockpit-type snowmobile here, and certainly the only one painted bright magenta with BUDDY in staring white letters along the sides. Nicely planned and faultlessly executed. Madoc found a door, went in, and tracked down Armand opening another case of Pepsi-Cola.

"I need some help outside. One of your customers has been shot."

"Huh? Who?"

"A young fellow named Buddy McLumber. The one you got Pierre Dubois to bounce."

All Armand said was "How did it happen?"

"Somebody picked him off, most likely with a deer rifle, as he drove his snowmobile up the land."

"Picked him off? You trying to give my place a bad name? Who the hell are you, anyway?"

Madoc told him, and Armand simmered down a little. "How bad is he hurt?"

"He's dead. Shot through the head."

"Oh Jesus. Wait here."

He left the door into the dance hall open. The crowd had thinned out considerably by now, but Madoc could see a few Grouses and McLumbers clustered around the piano with Dubois.

Armand selected one who didn't appear to have too much of a load aboard and steered him out back.

"Sorry to drag you away, Alf, but the inspector here tells me Buddy's had an accident."

"Goddamn snowmobiles. Dumb kid ought to know better. Where is he?"

"Just outside." Madoc jerked his head and stepped to the door by which he'd come in. Armand and Alf, who must be a McLumber, followed.

"Hey, Bud, what the hell'd you do now?" Alf said, and waited for an answer that didn't come. "What's wrong with him? Out cold, is he?"

"Let's get him inside." Madoc didn't add: "Before he starts to stiffen."

"Maybe we shouldn't be lifting him." Alf was sounding worried now. "If it's a broken back or something—" He pushed back the hood, and started to retch.

"I'll get a blanket." Armand practically ran away from the snowmobile, but he was back again, gritting his teeth, in a minute or so. Together, he and Madoc got the body into what he called the rec room, and laid it out on the Ping-Pong table. The place was cold as a barn.

"He'll do till morning," Armand remarked, not irreverently. "Must have been a rifle, all right. Anybody see who shot him?"

"No, the snow was coating everybody's car windows. The sniper would naturally have kept his back to the wind, especially if he was using a telescopic sight. I asked all down the line, but had no luck."

"Natural enough. Driving in snow, you keep your eyes glued to the road in front of you."

"What I can't figure out is who the hell would want to kill Buddy," Alf burst out. "Didn't have much sense and you couldn't shut him up with a sledgehammer, but there was no more harm in him than a kitten. What am I going to tell his mother?"

"Don't ask me," said Armand, "but you better go tell her fast before somebody beats you to it and starts a family feud. Could you try to get out of here without broadcasting it in the bar that there's a crazy sharpshooter loose on the hill?"

"There isn't," Madoc assured him.

"What makes you so cussed sure?" Alf demanded.

"Because I can show you evidence the gas was drained out of Buddy's tank. That indicates to me the snowmobile was deliberately caused to stop when its rider didn't expect it to, and thus make him a sitting target. According to one person's testimony, this appears to have been what in fact happened. You're quite sure nobody was out to get Buddy?"

"Hell no. Who'd want him? I guess you must know what you're talking about, Inspector, but it don't make no sense to me. All right, Armand, I'll just sneak out the back here and go on out to Bigears. If any of the boys come looking for me, tell 'em I left because I wasn't feeling well, which is no more than the God's honest truth. Lord a'mighty, what next?"

"Next," said Madoc sadly, "I request the loan of a hand lantern and a pair of cross-country skis and see if I can track the killer down."

"All by yourself, in the dark?"

"Unless you'd care to help me."

"Huh. Pretty damn funny, aren't you? What you want done about Buddy's snowmobile, Armand?"

"I'd suggest you run it into a woodshed, if there is one handy, and throw a tarpaulin over it, Mr. Bergeron," Madoc said. "I'm sure you don't want people noticing it and asking questions. Some of his friends out in front there might be inclined to take umbrage if they knew you'd chucked him out into the path of a bullet."

"What the hell are you talking about? I had Pierre tell him to go home because he'd had all he could handle and was starting to act up. Buddy could make a pest of himself when he got drunk, and I didn't want my customers bothered. I've got a right to run a decent place, haven't I?"

"Not only a right but an obligation," Madoc agreed. "So why didn't you tell him yourself?"

Armand shrugged. "I thought it would come easier from Pierre. He's got this jollying way with him, you know. The kids look up to him. I'll get your skis and lantern, Inspector."

"And I'll get myself out of here," Alf grunted. "Christ, I hate the thought of telling Nella."

"She's—er—not your wife?"

"Hell no. She's my second cousin and my sister-in-law and a few other things, that's all."

"What about the father?"

"Oh, him. He was over the hills an' far away before Bud was ever born. Married six or eight more by now, for all I know. That turned out to be a hobby of his. Nella got a divorce and took back her maiden name, but most likely they were never legally married in the first place."

"And the boy became the apple of her eye, I suppose."

"Ayup. She made a cussed fool of Bud, not that he couldn't of done it himself without any help from his mother. Bad blood there. Maybe it's all for the best, but I guess I won't say that to Nella. 'Night, Inspector."

He left, and Armand came back with the skis and battery lantern.

"I think these ought to be about your length, Inspector."

"Just fine, thank you."

"Oh, no problem. We keep them to rent. Anything else you need?"

Armand was awfully anxious to please all of a sudden. Madoc shook his head. "You might just tell me whether you noticed a pair of skis missing when you went to get these."

"Eh? No, I'm sure they were all there. The rack was full. I'd have noticed. Have to be careful the kids don't use 'em and forget to put them back. Look, Inspector, we'll be closing here pretty soon, but I can give you a key to one of the cabins if you want a place to come back to sleep. Leave the light on, turn up the heater, put in a thermos of hot coffee, sandwiches, anything you say."

"Thank you, but I don't expect to be back tonight. I'll return your skis as soon as I'm through with them."

Armand waved his hand. "No problem. By the way, is it okay if I let them make arrangements about the body?"

"I'll be back in the morning to take some pictures for evidence."

"I can do that for you now if you like," said Armand. "I've got a color Polaroid camera. People are always wanting their pictures taken with fish they've caught. When they can find one to catch," he added somewhat bitterly. "Just a second, it's right behind the bar."

The camera was a good one and the photographs were all too clear. Madoc thanked his obliging host and stuck them in an inner pocket for safekeeping. "These will do fine. You can go ahead and let the family claim the body whenever they want to. Good night, Mr. Bergeron."

Madoc refastened the parka he'd unzipped when he'd gone back inside the lodge, tilted the skis and poles over his shoulder, and trudged out to the parking lot, the red lantern swinging from his other hand. If he turned it on, of course, he'd be an easy target should the sniper still be around. If he didn't, he wouldn't be able to see any tracks in the snow.

Down here it was pretty hopeless. The snow near where Buddy's vehicle had been parked was packed into a solid gray mass, nor could he see any sign that the person who'd drained the tank had climbed up over the bank to get to the hillside. Maybe there'd been two: one to drain and one to shoot. Maybe there'd been a whole string of them stationed along the way in case Buddy chose a different route or the gas didn't give out at the right moment. A real military operation.

With Eyeball Grouse at the head of it? He must be groggy. He began checking along the edge of the parking lot, found a spot where he could persuade himself there were signs somebody had clambered up over the wall of frozen chunks, took the same path, strapped on his skis, and turned on his lantern.

After a wearisome and fruitless stint of zigzagging across the open hillside near the lodge, Madoc moved on to the stand of evergreens that followed along above the lane. Here, where the thick spread of the boughs had caught much of the snowfall, he had a bit of luck. His lantern beam easily picked up a branch that had just recently had its load of snow knocked off, and then another.

After that, it wasn't too hard. He found the place where the sniper had stood waiting long enough to dislodge a fair number of the crusted lumps and trample among them. Trying to keep his feet warm, Madoc supposed. There were prints to be seen, but it looked as if strips of sacking had been wound around the boot soles, either to provide better traction on the glazed-over slope or else to blur any tracks. So the sniper was familiar enough with the terrain to realize he could manage without snowshoes.

This wasn't where the sniper had fired from, it was where he'd spied Buddy beginning to have trouble with his vehicle, and realized the gas was giving out. From here, he'd run hell-for-leather, parallel to the lane, heedless of the trail he was leaving in his wake. He hadn't had far to go. Madoc could see exactly where the shot had been fired from, a neat crease cutting across the frosting on a fir bough directly in line with the emergency flare he himself had stuck into the bank to mark where the stalled snowmobile had been found with its dead driver still aboard. It hadn't been more than coincidence, probably, that the sniper had timed his run so perfectly and been able to get a side-on shot just as the vehicle stopped. He wouldn't have cared. At this range, a shot from ahead or behind would have been just as easy and just as deadly.

Madoc saw no spent casing lying on the snow, and no sign the killer had gone pawing around to find one. He wouldn't have been using one of the illegal semiautomatic rifles, then; more likely a single-shot with a telescopic sight. He'd have seen for a certainty that he'd stopped his man with the first shot, left the casing in the gun, and got the hell out of there.

He'd been cagey about it, though. He must have dropped down on his hands and knees or maybe even wormed his way along on his belly until he was far enough back among the trees so that nobody could possibly spot him from the lane. This was clear enough from the fact that only branches right down against the snow line showed any sign of having been brushed against. Then he'd got to his feet again and made a beeline for—as Madoc had pretty much expected—the big shed where people who didn't care to risk their springs on Armand's apology for a road had left their cars and waited for a lift in to the lodge. There, no doubt, he'd had transport waiting and simply driven away. If he'd hung around behind the shed till the coast was clear, it would have been a cinch to get out without being seen.

Maybe he hadn't had to. Maybe those brothers of the belt who'd been trickling away during the dance and shortly thereafter had been waiting for him drawn up in solid phalanx to applaud the execution of a silly young fellow who couldn't keep his mouth shut. About what? Madoc kicked off Armand's skis, stuck them and the poles inside his borrowed car, and drove himself back to the farm.

Janet was waiting to let him in. "I couldn't sleep, so I came down and made myself a pot of tea. Want some?"

The offer was welcome as her kiss. "Please. Did Annabelle get home all right?"

"Yes, ages ago. The Phillipses dropped her off. She told me you'd been kept behind because that McLumber boy who works in the hardware store got shot on his snowmobile. What was it, some drunk with a rifle trying to be funny?"

"No, I don't think so. Where is she now?"

"Sleeping the sleep of the just. You wore her out. She said she had a perfectly lovely time, all but the last of it. She was worried about Buddy McLumber."

"She might as well save her sympathy for his mother. Thanks, love." Madoc took the mug of tea Janet handed him, pulled the rocking chair close to the stove, and set her down on his lap. "Come and warm me up."

"You could stand warming," she murmured into his neck. "You're cold as a frog. Madoc, are you trying to tell me Buddy's dead and you went out there alone at night after the one who killed him?"

"That's my job, dear. Naturally, I waited to make sure the bird was long flown before I started out. Keep this under your *chapeau*, Jenny, but I doubt very much Buddy's death was an accident. I have a hunch he'd been recruited by some secret society before they found out Buddy couldn't keep a secret."

"You mean like the Owls? Madoc, what were you drinking at Armand's place?"

"I wondered that myself, love."

"All right, be that way if you want to. But people don't go shooting each other over that kind of nonsense."

"You'd be surprised the silly stuff people get shot over. Actually, though, I was thinking of something more like the IRA or the Ku Klux Klan. Perhaps I'm all wet, but there was something decidedly cloak-and-daggerish going on at Bull Moose Portage this evening."

"Annabelle didn't say anything about it."

"I'm sure she didn't notice. It was all pretty surreptitious."

He told her about the varicolored woven sashes slung around unlikely bellies, about the passing of the handgrip during the so conveniently choreographed country dance, keeping his voice to a thread in case any of the Wadmans should be astir and coming down to see what was going on.

"And not long after the dance was over, Bergeron shut off young McLumber's drinks and got Dubois to give him the push, or so he claims, because McLumber was beginning to make a pest of himself. I hadn't noticed it myself, and I've had a fair amount of professional experience with drunk and disorderlies, as you know. He hadn't got half a mile from the place when his snowmobile stalled because someone had drained his gas tank in the parking lot, or so the evidence indicates. At that point, somebody who'd been stalking him along the lane potted him like a sitting duck. If that doesn't point to an organized conspiracy, maybe you'd like to tell me what does."

Janet rubbed her forehead against his by now somewhat stubbly chin, thinking it over. "So you think this new boy friend of Cecile Bergeron's is the head of it. Where was he when Buddy got shot?"

"Still in the lodge, to the best of my knowledge. At least he was there when Annabelle and I left, and in pretty much the same place when I got back with the body. That doesn't mean much, you know. If he's any sort of leader at all, he'd know better than to let any breath of suspicion blow his way. Several of the brethren had already left while the dance was still on. Any one of them would have had time to drain the tank and get himself posted for the ambush before McLumber got his walking papers. I assume they all hunt, like most of the men around here. That was as clean a shot as you'd ever want to see."

Janet shuddered. "I'd never want to see any. Poor Annabelle! She didn't see it happen, did she?"

"No, love, not a peep. We were well back in the pack and the snow was sticking to the car windows on that side anyway. We heard the shot, that's all, and then the commotion when the lead car stopped short behind the snowmobile and a couple of others piled up into it. I was dim enough not to hop out right away and go to see what happened. I just sat there hoping the blasted line would get moving again."

"It's as well you did. That sniper might have taken a potshot at you."

"I hardly think he hung around long enough for that. Anyway, there were targets enough if he'd wanted another. The chaps who'd banged into one another got out, of course, and discovered Buddy was dead. Naturally they assumed it was an accident, either a crazy drunk or somebody jacking a deer. I'm sure they were meant to think so."

"If the gas hadn't been let out of Buddy's tank, you might have come to the same conclusion, mightn't you?" said Janet. "Don't you think that was sort of extra frosting on the cake? And what about the rifle? It seems to me if a person wanted to hit a moving target at fairly close range, a blast from a shotgun would be just as effective and harder to trace because there'd be no bullet. Of course it wouldn't have been so spit-and-polish. What you're telling me sounds more like an army maneuver."

"You know, love, that's a damned good point. Well thought out, faultlessly executed, and a lot of extra fuss for no good reason from a civilian point of view, unless the killer wanted it made known that McLumber had in fact been deliberately murdered."

"Wouldn't that be pretty crazy?"

"Not if you meant the killing to serve as a warning to somebody else. I'll have to get back out there first thing in the morning."

"Then you'd better hike yourself up to bed right now," said Janet. "You'd also better watch yourself around that lodge. Maybe the warning was meant for you."

"I can't buy that, Jenny. You don't try to scare off a law officer by murdering somebody right under his nose. I'm more inclined to think they didn't fully realize I was one. I was just Bert Wadman's brother-in-law, out for a mildly clandestine good time with Bert's wife. Annabelle's a marvelous dancer, by the way."

"I'm not so bad myself, in case you're ever interested enough to try me."

"Yes, Jenny."

Madoc got into his pajamas, did what he had to in the bathroom, and climbed into bed with his wife. He fell asleep at once, and stayed asleep. He didn't even hear the telephone when it rang at a quarter to four.

Janet did. So did Bert. She let him take it, and lay there listening to him swear as he stumbled over various things, trying to get to the goddamn thing before it woke everybody in the goddamn house. A minute or so later he was back upstairs, shaking Madoc by the shoulders.

"Bert, quit that," Janet hissed. "He's only been asleep a couple of hours. They had a murder out at Bull Moose Portage."

"Well, now they've had a bombing at Jase Bain's. Fred Olson's on the phone having conniption fits. He wants Madoc to get over there as quick as the Lord will let him."

CHAPTER 15

Madoc was awake and out of bed before Bert finished his message. "All right. I'll talk to Fred."

"At least put on your bathrobe and slippers."

Janet might as well have saved her breath. She got out of bed herself, wincing a bit from her bruises, followed him downstairs with the warm robe, and wrapped it around him while she tried to listen in. What Fred had to say was pretty horrendous and mostly profane. It boiled down to the fact that he'd never seen such a jeezledy mess in all his born days and hoped to Christ he never would again. Every goddamn piece of junk in that jeezledy yard was scattered from here to hell and gone.

"What about Bain?" Madoc asked him.

"Cripes, for all I know that poor old bugger's scattered, too. There ain't nothing left of the house but a cellar hole and a pile o' kindling."

"I'll get on to the bomb squad, and then come out. Where are you calling from, Fred?"

"Jim Badger's place. It's the nearest to Bain's. He got woke up by the explosion. Shook the house an' busted a window, he says. He went to find out what it was, and then called me. Then we went back together an' when I seen what happened, I figured I better get hold of you."

"Did you try searching the wreckage for Bain?"

"Best as we could with just a couple o' hand lanterns. Jim couldn't stay long. He's a traveler, he tells me, an' he's got to get on the road pretty soon. I don't know what to do, Madoc."

"Stay where you are and have a cup of tea to warm you up, if there's one going. I'll be along as soon as I can. Jenny, do you know where Jim Badger lives?"

"She wouldn't know Jim," Olson interrupted. "Tell her it's the old Henry Fewter place. You know where it forks off to get out to Bain's?

There's a little brown house with an old boat in the yard just beyond."

"Yes, I know where you mean," said Madoc. "See you in a while, Fred."

By the time Madoc had put in his call to the bomb squad and got his clothes on, Janet had ham and eggs and warmed-up biscuits waiting for him. He saw no reason not to stay and eat them. There wasn't really much point in his going at all until after sunup. Janet was all for calling Fred Olson back and reminding him of that fact.

"What's the sense in poking around out there in the dark?"

"It won't be dark much longer, and poor old Fred's in a swivet, as well he might be."

"All right, Madoc, if you feel you have to. I'll wrap Fred up a few doughnuts. They'll calm him down fast enough, I shouldn't be surprised."

Janet was already filling the thermos Annabelle had lent him yesterday, and looking a good deal perkier than when she'd arrived, thank God. Madoc kissed her at some length, took the bag she'd packed, and went out into what was left of the night.

He found the place easily enough. Fred Olson's car was in its well-plowed driveway and a light was on over the front door, illuminating a painted sign that read BADGER'S HOLE. No Badger came to his knock, but the door was unlocked, so Madoc went on in and found Fred asleep in a maple platform rocker that had been cheap to begin with and hadn't aged gracefully. He opened the doughnut bag and held it under Olson's nose.

"Eh? Mpf? Oh hi, Madoc. What time is it?"

"Getting on toward five. No Badgers in the hole?"

"Eh? No, only Jim, and he left a while back. Told me he batches it when he can't get a woman to move in with him. He claims he's been tryin' for the past year, but they all want to get married first. Don't sound likely to me, the way they are these days."

"This wouldn't be a terribly exciting place to live, I shouldn't think."

Madoc looked around the small shabby room. It could have stood a woman's touch, all right, though Badger had made one or two clumsy attempts to smarten up the place. He'd lined up a collection of beer cans, each a different brand, across the mantelpiece. Over them he'd tacked a cardboard advertising poster showing a racing skater, and nailed a pair of crossed hockey sticks above it. A deep-sea fisherman's rod stood in the corner with a dapper little Red Coachman dangling from its line. More dry flies were stuck into the band of a felt hat that lay on a badly ringed table, beside a lamp made from a duck decoy. There was a sofa that matched the chair and a dinky maple coffee table that must have been thrown in with the set, and that was it for the decor.

"Doesn't look as though Badger spends much time here," Madoc remarked to Fred, who was calming his nerves with a few doughnuts, as Janet had predicted. "What do you know about him?"

"Seems a decent enough feller," Fred grunted, spraying a few crumbs. "I never see much of him, to tell the truth. He tells me he's a traveler for a sportin' goods company an' he has to be on the road a lot. This here's what he calls his camp. He says he's always had the notion of gettin' a little place somewheres in the woods so's he could do some huntin' an' fishin' an' the like. Says his wife left him some years back 'cause she couldn't stand him bein' away so much. Prob'ly a few other things about him she couldn't stand, but Jim didn't go into that. Anyways, he says he batted around in cheap hotels an' roomin' houses for a few years, then he found out about this place an' bought it. Seen an ad in the papers somewheres. You know how they write 'em up: picturesque woodsy retreat amongst the beauties o' nature with a pair o' moose in the yard an' a wolf at the door. Must o' been goin' cheap. You want one o' these doughnuts, Madoc?"

"No, Janet stuffed a big breakfast into me before she'd let me out of the house. She meant the doughnuts for you."

"Might as well finish 'em up, then. Thank her for me, will you? Don't look as if I'm goin' to get much chance to do it myself. Guess we ought to be gettin' back out to the scene o' the crime, eh?"

"In a minute. Does this picturesque retreat have a bathroom?"

"Through there."

Fred jerked his head and went on eating his doughnut. Madoc found the facility with no difficulty—the whole house wasn't much bigger than a breadbox—and noted with some surprise how clean Badger had left it, and how bare. He'd even taken his toothbrush and razor away with him. Odd that a man who traveled so much wouldn't keep extra ones in his luggage. Unless, of course, he was bearded and toothless.

The bedroom was neat, too. Badger had made up his bed, or rather his cot, with knife-sharp boxed edges and the blankets tucked in tight as a teenager's jeans. Here again there were attempts at homey touches: a couple more sporting posters tacked up on the walls, a brand-new tennis racquet without a press hanging by its frame from a nail driven into the wall, and various implements of Badger's trade arranged like a store display in one corner. Madoc inventoried a golf bag with an assortment of woods and irons but no putter, a pristine fielder's glove he'd have bartered his soul for when he was ten lying beside a catcher's mask, cross-country skis about the right length for Janet paired with men's downhill ski boots size eleven or twelve.

The sky was lighter now, he observed through the uncurtained window. Fred had polished off the doughnuts and was showing every sign of wanting another nap. They'd better get out in the air fast or they'd both be asleep.

The marshal had come in his tow truck, so they took that in to Bain's place, leaving the pool car as a landmark for the bomb squad. The junkyard was a mess, all right. Madoc stood watching the sun come up over total devastation, wondering which of the fragments might be Jason Bain.

As he studied the terrain, though, Madoc realized it was in fact not so messy, considering. He himself was no demolition expert, but it wouldn't surprise him to find out whoever set off this explosion had been one. There was relatively little scatter, yet nothing appeared to have escaped the debacle.

"Did Badger mention how many bangs he heard?" he asked Olson.

"Can't say as he did, not to my recollection. He just told me the rumpus woke him up an' he wondered what the heck was goin' on. Took him a while to get his head workin', I should think, what with the windows rattlin' an' him not knowin' if he was goin' to wind up wearin' the roof for a muffler."

"Did he say when he'd be back from his trip, or where we might be able to get hold of him?"

"Hell no, an' I plumb forgot to ask. I ought to turn in my badge an' stick to fixin' cars."

"Never mind, Fred. I expect we can pick him up if we need him. What does he drive, do you know?"

"Big Chevy station wagon. Dark green, 1982 model." Fred reeled off the license number and the approximate mileage, which was high.

"I've had it in the shop a few times. That's how I come to get acquainted with Jim."

"He certainly must do a lot of driving."

"On the road more than he's off, from what he tells me. That don't do a car much good, not in the kind of winters we have up here. He was kiddin' me he'd like to get transferred to Florida, only they don't play much hockey down there. That's the backbone of his business, Jim says."

Madoc was not passionately interested in the bulk of Jim Badger's business. He was regretting the fact that he'd taken time to eat before coming here, and wondering if he'd be justified in putting out a call for a 1982 green Chevy wagon. "He didn't happen to mention the name of the company he travels for?"

Fred thought it over. "If he did, I don't remember."

"Well, it probably doesn't matter." Madoc looked over the vast jumble in front of him, and sighed. "I see what you meant about not knowing where to look for Bain. I suppose we ought to have another go at the house, though the chances of his being trapped alive in the rubble are roughly those of a snowball in hell, wouldn't you say?"

"I'd put 'em a little slimmer'n that, but you never know. Jim an' me tried shiftin' some o' the boards an' yellin' to see if we could raise any answer, but we didn't. Be a hell of a note if Jase was down there someplace unconscious, I s'pose. At least it ain't been long enough to freeze a person. That's somethin'."

It wasn't much. Madoc and Fred both knew they were wasting their trouble, but they edged the tow truck as far in as they dared and did the best they could with its meager help, tugging and sweating among the debris as mightily as though they believed it would do any good.

"At least the exercise keeps you warm," Madoc grunted after a while.

"Cripes a'mighty, I'll say. Must be about seven below* an' I'm sweatin' like a pig. Hey, listen, you hear somethin' comin'? Would that be your bomb squad?"

"Not this soon, I shouldn't think. More likely somebody local coming to see what—wait a minute!"

* Canadian temperatures are given in Celsius. This would be equivalent to 20° above zero Fahrenheit.

Madoc dropped the fragment of wall he'd been trying to drag free and started running. Fred took after him.

"You think it's him?"

"Or somebody driving his truck. There can't be another that makes such a racket."

"Ain't nobody else could keep it goin', either. It's got to be him."

It was. With a hideous screeching of brakes on mangled drums, Jason Bain brought the wreck to a standstill and jumped down, yelling. "What's that tow truck doin' here? This is private—"

He never did get to say 'property.' He just let his jaw drop and stood there staring.

"Honest to God," Fred said later, "I thought Jase was goin' to drop dead on the spot."

But he didn't. He only stood and stared. After a long, long time he whispered, "What happened?"

"We don't know yet," said Madoc, "but we believe you've had a deliberate bombing. An explosion was reported to Marshal Olson here at approximately half-past three this morning by Mr. Jim Badger who, I believe, is your closest neighbor."

"I don't hold no truck with neighbors," Bain managed to croak.

"Then you got a damn sight better one than you deserve," Fred snapped back. "Jim was out here in the dark strainin' his guts out tryin' to see if you was trapped in the rubble."

"I been away." Bain's voice was absolutely without inflection. "On business."

"The hell you have. Where you been?"

"Away. On business."

"You'll have to do better than that, Mr. Bain," said Madoc.

That broke the freeze. Bain went straight up in smoke. "Goddamn you! Druv my own son away from me, now you're comin' in here an' throwin' your weight around like you owned the place. You got no right!"

"Yes, I have. Marshal Olson requested my assistance."

"Then why didn't he request it soon enough to do me some good? I told you, goddamn it! I filed a complaint of robbery. I asked for police protection, an' what did I get? Look at this! Everything I own gone. Gone like a—damn your souls to hell, somebody's goin' to pay for this."

Ah, that old black magic had him in its spell. As a baby turns to its mother, as a lover to his mistress, Jason Bain turned to his only stay and solace. "I'll sue!"

"Whom will you sue, Mr. Bain, and why?"

"You know cussed well why. I demanded my rights and didn't get 'em. I showed you the pile where my lumber was robbed from. I reported the crime right an' proper, an' where did it get me? Sabotage, that's what it is. If this ain't grounds for a lawsuit, there ain't no justice anywheres. As to who's goin' to pay, you'll find out fast enough, Mountie."

"Threatening a police officer, Mr. Bain?"

"Now Jase, take it easy," said Fred Olson. "You don't want to get into any more trouble than you're already in."

That stopped him again. Bain went a sickly yellow, swaying on his feet. He was scared, that was what, scared clear through to the bone.

"Who's after you, Mr. Bain?" Madoc asked gently. "And why?"

For a while—it seemed a long time—Bain only kept that blank, unwinking stare. Then, slowly and deliberately, he drew off with one filthy boot and landed Madoc a kick in the shins.

CHAPTER 16

There wasn't much force behind the kick. It was mostly surprise that threw Madoc off guard, though only for a split second. Then he was whipping out his notebook.

"I'll have to take you in, Mr. Bain. The charge is assault and battery on an officer of the Royal Canadian Mounted Police. Marshal Olson will take you in custody and deliver you to the lockup, where you will be held pending due process of law. You will please accompany the marshal and myself to his vehicle. It is my duty to warn you that any further attempt at violence will be severely dealt with."

He was not concerned about a further attempt. Bain had already got what he wanted: free board and room at the public expense and protection against whomever he was so deathly afraid of. You really had to hand it to the old bugger.

As for making him talk, Madoc wasn't going to waste any more breath this morning. Let the bird sit in the cage for a while and see how he liked having his wings clipped.

Appearing somewhat bemused by this strange turn of affairs, as well he might, Fred Olson got the tow truck turned around and moved Bain's junk heap clear of the path. Then they boosted the prisoner aboard and drove out to where they'd left the pool car, one on either side of him. Madoc got out and fished a pair of handcuffs out of the car's trunk, not that they'd be necessary, but just to let Bain know it wasn't going to be all roses. As he secured the old man's wrists to the hook that held the seat belt, Bain snarled something about cruel and unusual punishment. Madoc assured him sweetly that this was by no means unusual, but that Marshal Olson would be happy to discuss genuinely cruel punishments with him should Mr. Bain care to consider the various options available.

"Surest thing you know," said Fred. "Always glad to oblige. You comfortable in those bracelets, Jase, or would you like 'em screwed a little tighter?"

"Go ahead an' have your fun, you goddamn tub o' lard," snarled the prisoner. "You'll be squirmin' soon enough."

"Be scratchin', more likely, sittin' next to you. I better warn you, Jase, first thing they're goin' to go down at the jail is make you take a bath. Ayup, the way of the transgressor is hard, an' we don't aim to make it any easier. You won't be comin' with us, Inspector?"

"No, I have to wait for the bomb squad. I'm sure Mr. Bain won't give you any trouble."

Bain's parting shot was "What's goin' to happen to my truck? Leave it there to get blown up, I s'pose."

"No, I expect we'll want to impound so it can be examined for possible evidence," Madoc replied.

"Evidence o' what?"

"Perhaps you'd like to save us a little time by answering that question yourself."

That shut him up. Madoc had thought it would. He might as well let the experts give the truck a thorough going-over at that, just for the record. There might be some scientific interest in finding out what was keeping that old heap of rust still running.

He and Fred had killed more time than he'd realized pawing through the wreckage. Madoc didn't have to wait long for his reinforcements. He explained the situation to the corporal in charge of the squad, headed them in the direction of the exploded junkyard, and went on back to the farm.

Janet gave him a pleasant surprise by being up and dressed, sitting in the rocking chair with Annabelle's mending basket on the floor beside her and the button box on her lap.

"Hello, Jenny love," he said. "Back at work, are you?"

"Yes, I'm trying to detect a few pajama buttons," she told him. "What happened out at Bain's?"

"Quite a lot." Madoc described the scene of devastation while his wife and sister-in-law listened, spellbound.

"Going to all that trouble to blow up a pile of junk?" Janet shook her head. "It doesn't make sense. Whatever's behind it, do you think?"

"Spite," said Annabelle, fetching the freshly filled teapot and the doughnut crock. "Sit down, Madoc. Lots of people have a down on old Jase for one reason or another, as you well know. Though that's carrying a grudge pretty darn far, I must admit. Sounds to me as if they must have used a ton of dynamite, considering the size of the mess out there."

"I don't know if it was dynamite or something else," he answered, "and it looked more like small charges carefully placed, but I'll be able to tell you better after a while. I left a squad from headquarters out there poking around to see what they can find."

"Haven't found anything of old Jase himself, I'll bet. I shouldn't be surprised if he did it himself, for the insurance. He'll turn up yelling for his rights, you mark my words."

"He already has," said Madoc.

"There, what did I tell you? You should have arrested the old coot."

"As a matter of fact, I did."

"No fooling! What did you charge him with?" Janet asked.

"Assault and battery with a not very dangerous weapon, namely a filthy old boot." Madoc hiked up his trouser leg and displayed the rather puny bruise. Janet was unimpressed.

"That the best he could do? Oh well, if you play it right, maybe it'll get you a few days off for being wounded in line of duty. But whatever do you suppose got into him? Could it be having his seventeen traveling privies blown up that shoved him over the edge? Or was he actually asking to be locked up?"

"Well," said Annabelle practically, "I don't know how else he'd get bed and board without having to pay for 'em. You going to press charges, Madoc, or throw an aged widower out in the cold to fend for himself on his own money for a change?"

"I thought I'd give him time to get over the shock, if it was one, and see what develops. Is Sam Neddick around?"

"If he isn't, he ought to be. Try the big barn."

Madoc did. Somewhat to his surprise, Sam was there.

"Mornin', Inspector. Lookin' for rustlers?"

"No, I'm looking for a deputy. Do you think Bert could spare you for a while?"

"How long a while?"

"Your guess is as good as mine. Do you ever go out to Bull Moose Portage?"

"I been."

"Got dressed up for the occasion, did you?"

Sam thought that one over for a second, then allowed his lips to twitch. "Not me, Inspector. I always stuck to galluses myself." To prove his point, Sam snapped the broad khaki webbing of his braces.

"What's it all about, do you know?"

Sam shrugged, which meant either that he didn't know or that he didn't care to say. Madoc tried another tack.

"Is Dubois running the show, or fronting for somebody else?"

Sam's eyes, clear crystal like a malemute's, met Madoc's for an instant. "I been wonderin' that myself."

"Would you care to help me find out?"

Sure he would. Finding out was Sam Neddick's one passion in life, as far as Madoc or anybody else had ever been able to determine. The hired man didn't come right out and say he'd be tickled pink, but he didn't try to act as if he'd rather stay and commune with the cows.

"What you got in mind?"

"A point of information I was hoping you might be able to help me put to use." Madoc described what Dubois had been up to during the dance. "Would you have any idea what it might mean? Aside from the fact that Buddy McLumber was shot directly afterward. I don't know whether he was still wearing his sash at the time."

Sam did, of course. "He'd took it off an' stuck it in 'is pocket. Must o' got in the way when he was puttin' on his fancy snowmobilin' suit. His Aunt Cecile's all for buryin' it in the coffin with 'im, but his mother wants to keep the fool thing to remember 'im by. God knows why."

After this burst of information, Sam fell silent. Madoc waited. Protocol having been observed, Sam went on.

"What Dubois done didn't have nothin' to do with Buddy gettin' shot, I wouldn't think. Means a meetin', more likely."

"Any idea where or when?"

"Same as usual, I s'pose. We might's well get started. Snowshoes in your car?"

"I've a pair of cross-country skis I borrowed from Armand Bergeron last night. I meant to return them this morning."

Sam twitched his nostrils, went to the woodshed, and came back with two pairs of snowshoes. "I stuck my head in the door and told 'em we was goin'. Annabelle gimme this."

A lunch and a thermos, of course. Annabelle must keep them lined up in a row on the pantry shelf. Madoc got into the car and shoved Armand's skis aside to make room for Sam. Receiving no instructions to the contrary, he headed for Bull Moose Portage. They weren't more than halfway there, though, when Sam ordered abruptly, "Turn in here."

"Here" appeared to be nowhere in particular, but it had been dug out after a fashion and looked more or less navigable, so Madoc turned. After a hundred feet or so, the turnoff petered out to a snow-bank on one side and a sheer drop on the other. Guided solely by the instinct of self-preservation, Madoc pulled as close as he could get to the snowbank.

That proved to have been the right move. Sam hopped out, taking both pairs of snowshoes with him. He pawed around under a spruce that grew down over the side of the bank, dragged forth a vast sheet of whitish plastic, and draped it over the car. Commando tactics, by thunder. Madoc waited for Sam's next move, and was not disappointed when the hired man fished again among the branches of the spruce and came out with a long rope that had a noose tied in the end of it.

"Stick your foot in the loop, grab holt of the rope, an' swing your-self across the ditch," he ordered. "Aim for the bare limb o' that big oak that's stickin' flat out behind them little seedlin' firs on the other side of the ditch. See it?"

Madoc saw it, got himself adjusted, shoved off from the bank, and made a perfect landing. The rough bark gave a good grip and wouldn't show footprints. He sent the noose whizzing back across the ditch, and lowered himself gingerly to the crust. By the time he'd got his snowshoes strapped on, Sam was beside him, tucking the noose into a fork of the oak.

"We'll find it there easy enough on our way back," he grunted. "Whole thing's prob'ly a waste o' time, but it never hurts to muddle your trail. Don't matter if we leave a little sign from here on in. Ain't nobody likely to notice."

He glanced up at the sun that was trying to break through the overcast, and set a course roughly west-southwest. Madoc followed, avoiding the snow-laden evergreens as best he could. That light fall of new snow last night hadn't penetrated this thicket much, but he and Sam both watched out for soft patches and steered clear of them whenever possible.

They didn't talk at all. Madoc had never tracked with Sam before, and he respected the work of a master. A timber wolf would have seemed clumsy beside the elderly man. Just how old Sam was, none of the Wadmans could say. Maybe Sam didn't know, either, but whatever his age was, it hadn't slowed him down any. Madoc almost wished it had. He was musing on that de-squeaked bed he'd got to spend so little time in and wondering how much farther they'd have to go when Sam flopped down on his belly, slid his snowshoes under his body, and snaked himself in under a low-spreading spruce.

Madoc did the same, and just in time. He found they were directly behind a good-sized lean-to made of overlapping fir boughs over a framework of saplings. In fact, they were so close it was possible to burrow with one finger into the needles and make a tiny peephole while keeping themselves well screened from those inside.

Pierre Dubois was kindling a small fire just outside, where the heat would reflect back to warm the lean-to while the smoke drifted the other way. The chap was a woodsman, whatever else he might be. His cohorts were straggling in by twos and threes, each with that woven sash tied around his mackinaw or parka. Some were tying the sashes as they came, Madoc noted, and he could understand why. They wouldn't be the sort to whom anything in the nature of fancy dress came naturally.

He was recognizing faces and voices. These were the men who'd got the secret handshake, no doubt about that. They were crowding into the lean-to, hunkering down, talking to each other in low tones, like hunters on the stalk. None of them looked out of place in so rustic a setting. Like as not they were most of them guides or pot hunters, who depended on their guns to keep meat on their family tables.

They weren't here for fun, that was plain. Their voices were harsh, their faces grim. There was none of the fraternal joshing Madoc had run into the night Bert took him to the Owls' Club. Strange as it might seem, he got the distinct impression that this was a business meeting.

When everybody was present—and they all were, because Madoc had been keeping count as they arrived, deducting one for the murdered recruit—Pierre stood in front of the lean-to with his back to the fire, and made his opening remarks. Gone was the bon vivant, the insouciant *voyageur*. Today Dubois was a man with a mission.

"I don't have to tell you, brothers, why our number is one short today. One of us—perhaps not the most important to our cause, but still one of us—was murdered last night."

"What do you mean murdered?" demanded one of the older men. "He got shot going home from the dance. How do you know it wasn't an accident?"

"I know because it's my business to know, Brother G. You men have trusted me to be your leader. I aim to honor your trust by looking out for your interests. To do that I need everybody's full cooperation. If any one of you knows anything about the shooting of Brother W, he'd better tell me now."

There was a shifting of bodies and a clearing of throats, but nobody spoke. Dubois looked from one to another, his black eyes glinting.

"I think you all understand what I'm asking. We don't have to know who shot him, but we do have to know why he was killed. Naturally we're all outraged and grieved by the loss of our young brother, and extend our sympathy to those members of his family who are present"—he didn't put quite so much punch into this last—"but what we absolutely must know is whether his being shot had anything to do with the fact that he'd become a member of our group. Because if it did, that means every one of us could be in danger."

"We knew that when we signed on," grunted one of the men.

"We knew that when it came to carrying out our avowed purpose we'd be exposing ourselves to certain risks, yes. You have to admit, though, that it's one thing to get fired at by a security guard when you're performing an act of sabotage, however justified, and something one hell of a lot different to get potted like a rabbit on your way home from a dance."

"Damn right!" From the way he pronounced his final *t*, that must be either a Grouse or a McLumber. "What's the sense in lettin' ourselves get killed before we done the job?"

"Okay then," Dubois had to raise his voice over the chorus of agreement. "Keep your eyes and ears open. If anybody picks up any scrap of information, however small, I want it reported to me at once. By the way, does anybody know anything about an RCMP man who showed up at the Portage last night."

"Married Bert Wadman's sister Janet from up on the hill in Pitcherville," somebody replied promptly. "He come with Bert's wife, Annabelle. Fine-lookin' woman in a black dress that fit pretty good. Cecile knows 'er."

"I'm s'prised you didn't ask to get introduced, Pierre," said somebody else.

Dubois wasn't interested in kidding around. "What about the Mountie? What does he look like?"

"Scrawny little black-haired runt with baggy britches an' a red mustache."

"No mustache," someone contradicted. "Janet made him shave it off. Smartened him up some, too."

"That so? I never noticed."

"He ain't the kind you'd notice."

"Did anybody happen to notice what his name is?" Dubois didn't sound happy.

"Reed? Royce? Rhys, that's it. Welsh name. His folks live in Wales mostly. Got money, they say, but you'd never know it to look at him."

"Nice-spoken feller. Talks so soft you can hardly hear him."

"Wait a minute," said Dubois. "You're not by any chance talking about the Inspector Madoc Rhys who tracked down Mad Carew single-handed?"

"Well, he had to, didn't he? A Mountie does whatever he's sent out for. That's the rule. Always has been."

"It's different these days. They wouldn't be likely to send a single man out on an assignment like that. They use modern methods."

"What the hell kind of a modern method you goin' to use against a crazy lumberjack seven feet tall with a double-bitted ax who's already killed God knows how many people an' won't come out o' the woods so's a posse can get at 'im, eh?"

"The meeting will come to order," barked Dubois. "Does anybody know why Rhys took his sister-in-law to the Portage?"

"Sneakin' a night out while his wife's laid up," said either a McLumber or a Grouse. "That's the way them rich aristocrats act. My wife's always readin' about them in books she gets at the paperback exchange. Has to keep 'em hid in a closet where the kids can't find 'em."

Dubois was trying hard not to lose his temper. "Anybody who has any real information on what Rhys is doing around here will also funnel it back to me as fast as possible. Now let's get on with the business of the meeting. How are we progressing with the transport situation, Brother F?"

"Well, I been scoutin' around, and I come up with two possibilities. There's a school bus we could get for five hundred dollars, but she'd need an awful lot of work. You know how they drive them things till they tear the guts out of 'em. The other one's a delivery truck I thought we might be able to fit up with seats in the back from that old movie theater they're tearing down over at the Fort. She'd be kind of a tight squeeze and we'd have to figure out some way to ventilate the back, but she's not in too bad condition, considering."

"How much?"

"Owner's askin' twenty-two fifty, but I think I could beat him down. The engine's in pretty good shape, and the tires still got some tread on 'em."

"But would we have room enough for our equipment?"

"I figured we could put racks up around the sides."

"Sounds like you'd have to build the goddamn thing over before we could use it," objected a brother wearing a sealskin cap that must have been his grandfather's. "I move we keep looking. If only we'd commandeered Perce Bergeron's bull box before some jeezledy bastard beat us to it!"

"That bull box wasn't Uncle Perce's." A young Bergeron, obviously. "It was a family heirloom and Uncle Armand would have raised holy hell and queered the whole expedition if we'd tried to lay a finger on it. You know that as well as I do, Jock. I mean Brother Q."

"But Armand's in sympathy with our aims. Hell, he's suffered as much as anybody and a damn sight more than some, hasn't he? Havin' to turn a decent huntin' lodge into a goddamn honky-tonk because the goddamn acid rain's started to kill the goddamn lakes and the goddamn trees so the goddamn fish an' the goddamn animals can't live in 'em. He knows it's got to be stopped, same as we do. And he knows those goddamn bastards down there won't ever do a goddamn thing but sit around on their backsides claiming they got to do another goddamn study because they don't want the goddamn bastards that's running the factories and financing their campaigns to get mad at 'em. Why the flamin' sweet Nellie can't we just pile into our cars and go down there and drop our bombs down those goddamn stinking smokestacks and be done with it?"

"Because we'd fail in our mission and be a damn sight worse off than we are now, that's why," Dubois insisted. "We've been through this time after time, Brother Q. We're not trying to start a border war, we're trying to call attention to the plight of our environment in a way dramatic enough to show the entire North American continent that we mean to get something done about saving it while there's still time. But there's no sense in making martyrs of ourselves for nothing, and that's what will happen if we go off half-cocked and defeat our own purpose. If we go in separate vehicles, some of us are bound to get stopped at the border, found to be carrying concealed explosives, and arrested as terrorists. That will blow the lid off for the rest of us, and you know it as well as I do. We stick to our plan. We all go together, or we don't go at all. Is that clear?"

"What about Jase Bain's junkyard?" yelled somebody in the hindmost row. "I wasn't in on that."

"Jase Bain's junkyard?" Dubois sounded genuinely astonished. "I don't know what you're talking about, Brother P."

"Seems to me there's one hell of a lot you don't know for somebody that claims to be runnin' the show. You tryin' to tell us you didn't sneak over there last night an' blow the place up to test out what we was goin' to do at the automobile plant?"

"*Nom de Dieu,* no! What would be the point? A junkyard's not a factory or anything like it. We have no explosives to waste and I don't need the practice. I told you I learned demolition in the army. So did Brother J and Brother K, they tell me. Where were you two last night, if it comes to that?"

"Look, I got no time to sit here listenin' to foolishness," either Brother J or Brother K called back. "I promised to drive Buddy's mother into town. She's hell-bent on talkin' to Ben Potts about the funeral."

A wise leader knew when to give in gracefully. "Right, brothers. I think we've accomplished as much as we can here today. I'm sure every one of us will want to attend the funeral of our fallen comrade. Keep up the good fight, and for God's sake try to get a line on the person who felled him. I'll look into the matter of the bombed junkyard personally as soon as I get my next week's article into the mail. It's a real zinger this time, I promise you."

"Ayup, and it'll do about as much good as the last one did," muttered the malcontent Brother Q. "What a goddamn waste o' time this turned out to be."

CHAPTER 17

"They was pretty quiet today."

Sam had led Madoc in an unerring beeline back to the camouflaged car. They'd stowed the tarpaulin back under the tree and were warming themselves up with Annabelle's hot tea and gingerbread. "Usually they do a lot more rantin' an' cussin' about them jeezledy sons o' bitches that run the gov'ment, not that I blame 'em none. You goin' to run 'em in for conspiracy?"

"Oh, I hardly think so," said Madoc. "I might just drop a word to the customs people at Windsor about keeping an eye out for a school bus loaded with grown men wearing fancy sashes and carrying hand grenades. How long has the Brotherhood been in existence, Sam?"

"Last couple o' months, since Dubois blew into town. Ice fishin's been no damn good this winter, an' I guess they figured they might as well do somethin' to entertain theirselves."

"Who are they, do you know?"

"Yup."

"Perhaps you'd oblige me by writing down their names, then."

Madoc held out his notebook and pencil. Sam shied away from them.

"I ain't much for writin' things down. Ain't much for squealin', neither, as a rule. If it wasn't for that McLumber kid gettin' shot—"

"I understand, Sam. Do you know where they're getting their explosives?"

"Ain't got none yet, between you an' me. That was just bletherin'. Dubois is waitin' till he gets his master plan worked out, whatever the hell that's supposed to mean. He snuck over to Detroit an' took some snapshots an' swiped a handful o' street maps out o' one o' them tourist information places. They been passin' 'em around at the meetin's an' jawin' about strategies of attack."

"Diabolical," Madoc murmured, pouring out the last of the tea.

"Oh, it's all that an' then some." Sam squinted down the mouth of the thermos to make sure none was going to waste. "They can get their hands on some dynamite easy enough. Swipe it from a construction site, maybe, or get six or eight o' the brothers to buy a few sticks each, claimin' they want it for blastin' out stumps or whatever. Funny thing, though, last time I looked in on 'em, that McLumber kid that got killed was gassin' to Dubois about how he knew where to lay 'is hands on somethin' better than dynamite."

"What do you mean he was gassing to Dubois? Didn't the rest hear him, too?"

"Nope. The kid got there before anybody else. Then Dubois showed up an' Bud begun tellin' him about it, real excited. He wanted it announced with a great foofaraw at the meetin', but Dubois told 'im this was top secret stuff just between the two of 'em an' they wasn't to breathe a word of it to nobody. So Bud was pretty tickled at that an' set there the whole time smirkin' like a dern fool Chessie cat."

"Did you hear Buddy explain to Dubois why this explosive was so superior?"

"Hell, he didn't know 'is ass from 'is elbow. He claimed it was somethin' brand-new that made one hell of a big bang, then set a fire that was hotter'n the flamin' blue hubs o' Tophet. He said it was sure top secret all right, that there wasn't hardly nobody that knew about it. Dubois says then how come Bud knew, an' for once in his life, the kid clammed up. So I reckon Dubois caught on that it was just a bunch o' hot air an' wasn't goin' to make a fool of hisself takin' Bud at 'is word."

Sam grinned, but Madoc didn't. "You say the kid told him the stuff exploded with unusual violence and then burned with intense heat?"

"That's what he said. Melted steel, burned brick an' concrete right down to a powder. Wasn't a damn thing it wouldn't do, to hear him tell it. An' it was easy as pie to use an' you didn't need more'n about a teacupful to wipe out a whole goddamn factory."

"And you doubt that Dubois believed him?"

"Would you?"

"As a matter of fact," said Madoc, "I would. Sam, has Bert told you what really happened to Janet?"

"He kind o' hinted that she'd run into a gang o' toughs an' had 'er car stole, but he didn't want Annabelle an' the boys to know 'cause

you're out to get 'em an' you don't want any talk goin' around that
might tip 'em off who she was."

"That's the general drift. Here's the rest."

Madoc told Sam the whole story, beginning with Perce Bergeron's
bull box and ending with Eyeball Grouse's stolen object. Sam listened
without saying a word. Then he nodded.

"Them names. You want to write 'em down?"

"If you'd rather I did." It dawned on Madoc that Sam had likely
never learned to read and write with any facility, if at all. He wiped
off the gingerbread crumbs on the paper napkin Annabelle had fur-
nished, picked up his pencil, and said, "Go ahead."

Sam began reeling them off in alphabetical order, giving each one a
pithy character reference as he went. They seemed a worthy enough
bunch on the whole, though there were some who couldn't be trusted
with a bottle, a surprising number who couldn't be trusted with another man's wife, and a few who couldn't be trusted with anything
whatsoever. Two of these were McLumbers and one was a Grouse.

"That lot come from Bigears, I assume," said Madoc. "Do any of
the others?"

"Nope."

"Does any of the rest speak with that odd little Bigears twist to the
ends of his words?"

"Nope. You got to be born to it, seems like."

"Then let's concentrate on those three. Does any of them go off for
overnight or longer without letting on where he's going?"

"Hell yes. They all do."

"Together or separately?"

"Depends."

"Was one or more of them away night before last, when Janet had
her car stolen?"

"I can find out."

"Do that, will you? Also, do you know of anybody from Bigears
who's left the village and gone to the bad?"

"Well, there's one in jail an' one in Parliament."

Madoc awarded this quip one of his sad little smiles. "Give me
their names and I'll run a check. One never knows. Do you think
Pierre Dubois is using this Brotherhood thing as a cover for some kind
of scam?"

"Nope. Ain't got sense enough to make it work. Look at all that goddamn foolishness about Brother A an' Brother B when they all know each other as well as I know you an' a damn sight better. An' yammerin' about secrecy an' then gettin' em to wear them damn fool sashes in public that Thyrdis Flyte weaves for 'em."

"She told me she didn't," said Madoc.

"Don't s'prise me none. She'd lie in what she figured was a righteous cause an' feel like a hero-wine for doin' it. Her an' Brother E, they go in for high thinkin'. Fine people, but they just can't help trustin' that anybody who's on the right side knows what the hell he's up to. Far as bombin' them cussed factories that's spewin' acid all over the Northeast is concerned, I don't say as I'd mind havin' a go at it myself if I thought it would do any good. Trouble is, there's so cussed many of 'em, an' it ain't just the Yanks, neither. An' it's more than the factories, too. Take that poor young jackass Bud McLumber, for instance, yellin' about pollution while he was drivin' that goddamn snowmobile lickety-split through the woods he was so friggin' concerned to protect. Time you got through bombin' 'em all, you'd o' made such a mess we'd never get dug out from here to doomsday. If we get a move on, we ought to make it back in time for dinner. Annabelle might have some o' that there stew left we had yesterday. Always tastes better warmed up, to my way o' thinkin'."

It had tasted pretty good the first time around, Madoc remembered. Bert was no doubt wondering when Sam would be back to finish the work he was getting paid for. Besides, Madoc had a few projects of his own. He started the car, backed very carefully away from the gully before he turned, and concentrated on his driving till he'd got them safely out to the paved road. Then he asked Sam, "What do you know about that man Jim Badger who bought the house out near Bain's?"

"Not a jeezledy goddamn thing," said Sam with palpable disgust. "He comes an' he goes, an' that's the best I can tell you. Claims to be a traveler for some sportin' goods firm."

"Why do you say he claims to?"

"Well, I ain't never seen his paycheck. Can't be doin' too bad for hisself, anyhow. He paid cash on the button for the house. 'Bout twice what it was worth, too. Don't ask me what he wanted it for in the first place. He ain't in it more'n two or three times a month, far's I've ever been able to make out. Comes in with a bagful o' them frozen dinners an' holes up for a day or so, then he's off again. Drives a big dark green Chevy station wagon full o' hockey sticks an' the like."

"Yes, Fred Olson told me about that. Does Badger ever have company?"

"Not to my knowledge."

"Fred Olson says Badger told him he'd been trying to find a woman to move in but hasn't had any luck so far."

"Then he's either hellish fussy or he ain't been lookin' very hard. There's men older an' poorer than him that don't have much trouble," Sam replied somewhat smugly. "He'd have to get one that's already got 'er own car, I s'pose. Time was when you could set a female down somewheres an' she'd stay where you put 'er, but now they all want to be out runnin' the roads."

"I must have a few words with Janet on that subject," said Madoc. "Badger can't be much to look at, then?"

"Well hell, neither am I. I wouldn't call 'im no ravin' beauty, but it ain't the kind o' face that would scare a person on a dark night."

"Just what does he look like?"

" 'Bout like a bowl o' rice puddin' if you stirred it up some an' stuck in raisins for the eyes an' mouth. Nothin' what you'd call outstandin' about his looks. He's middlin' height an' prob'ly peels down to about a hundred an' seventy."

"He'd be a bit on the hefty side, then?"

"Ayup, you might say so. Squabby, you know, not hard fat like Fred's. Don't s'pose he takes much exercise himself for all he peddles them sportin' goods. Spends most of 'is time behind a steerin' wheel, from what Fred says o' that wagon."

"How old a man is he?"

"Forty, forty-five, somewheres around in there, I'd say. His hair ain't gray, what I seen of it. Kind o' what they call mousy, though God knows why. You can catch a mouse pretty near any color you're o' mind to."

"What color are his eyes?"

"Come to think of it, I ain't never seen 'em. Badger wears them big dark drivin' goggles all the time like they was glued to 'is face. To find out, seems to me I'd have to pick a fight with 'im an' knock 'em off."

"Yes, well, you might do that," said Madoc absently. "If you don't mind, I think I ought to swing around past Bain's and see what the bomb squad chaps have picked up. Would you like me to drop you off first?"

Sam wrestled silently for a moment between Annabelle's cooking and his innate reluctance to miss out on anything that was happening. Curiosity won. "Go ahead. I'll stick with you."

They found the junkyard more thoroughly junked than before, and the men from the bomb squad just packing up to leave. The place had been thoroughly explored, they reported, and no undetonated explosives discovered. Their verdict was that the demolition had been wrought by a series of small dynamite charges placed at strategic spots, wired together, and detonated probably all at the same time.

"A professional job, then," said Madoc.

"Oh yes, quite professional. We couldn't have done it better ourselves. By the way, your Mr. Bain must have been pretty broadminded about what he collected, wouldn't you say?"

"He'd take anything that wasn't nailed down, according to local opinion. Did you find anything interesting, other than the fragments of seventeen used chemical toilets?"

"Is that what they were? We were rather hoping for flying saucers. Anyway, there were a good many bits and pieces of old automobiles, fencing, and other jagged metal. Nasty stuff. A lot of wood, and an incredible amount of broken glass. No trace of man or beast except a number of dead rats. We've put up a 'Danger—Keep Out' sign, as you see, and heartily recommend the site be bulldozed as soon as possible so that it doesn't become attractive to kids and scavengers. As it stands, the place is an open invitation to a mass epidemic of blood poisoning."

"I'll pass the word. Have you had a chance to check out the Badger house?"

"We did, and found nothing in the way of explosives. Nor a great deal of anything else, for that matter. Goes in for the simple life, does he? We lifted some readable fingerprints from a pair of shin guards and a glass in the kitchen."

"Good. Let me know if you turn up anything on them. And thanks for coming."

"Our pleasure. Here's Badger's key back. Regards to your wife. How's she feeling, by the way?"

"Much improved." Madoc knew Annabelle would be tickled pink if he brought the crew back for Sunday dinner, which would assuredly not be warmed-over beef stew, but decided against doing so. There was a pretty good restaurant on their way back, and he didn't want to get involved with playing host, even to his own colleagues. "We'll see you back in Fredericton, then."

"You'll be at headquarters tomorrow?"

"No, I hardly think so. Not till we've got a better line on this bombing."

"Haven't you already bagged somebody?"

"Yes, but I'm not sure what for. The official charge at the moment is kicking me in the shins."

Laughing, the men went off. Sam cast a hopeful glance at Madoc, but got a shake of the head. "Sorry, but I want to stop at Badger's for just a moment."

"How come? I thought they done it. What was they sayin' about checkin' for explosives?"

"I wanted to make sure his won't be the next place to blow."

Sam chewed that one over for a while, then nodded. "But how come you had 'em take fingerprints?"

"General principles. Since nobody around here appears to know a great deal about Badger, it occurs to me the RCMP might. Running a trace is no great job nowadays, you know. Somebody just pops them into a computer. After making those poor chaps drive all this way on a Sunday morning, I thought we might as well make them feel loved and needed."

Sam didn't ask why Madoc felt an urge to stop at Badger's again, but he was right there when Madoc turned the key in the lock. Once inside, he sniffed from room to room like an old setter on the trail.

"Anything strike you?" Madoc asked him.

"Too damn neat. Ain't natural for a man alone."

"It makes me wonder if perhaps he's spent a fair stretch of time either in the military or in jail," said Madoc. "That's one of the reasons I find him interesting."

"Well, like as not you could get to meet 'im tonight."

"Do you think so? It seemed to me that his clearing off so early with his shaving tackle and suitcase suggested he was either doing a vanishing act or facing a long drive that would get him to an early appointment tomorrow."

"S'pose he ain't runnin', he might get to thinkin'. I mean, hell, here's a man that's sunk a pretty good hunk o' money in a house he claims he's been wantin' for a long time. He's been shook out o' bed by his nearest neighbor's place gettin' blown to hell an' gone. If 'twas me, no matter how big a deal I had on, the farther away I got, the more I'd start wonderin' whether the place would be standin' when I got back. That bein' the case, I might decide to hell with the appointment an' turn around an' head home."

"Unless Badger happens to be on a plane heading for Vancouver."

Madoc didn't believe it. A mere traveling salesman wouldn't be covering so vast a territory, and a man high enough on the company ladder to be sent on that long a trip would be pulling down enough money to afford a less shabby home than this. Sam might or might not be clairvoyant, as some people claimed he was, but he did have an almost infallible animal instinct about which way any cat was likely to jump. Madoc finished checking around to make sure no telltale dabs of fingerprint powder had been left for the finicky Mr. Badger to spot and wonder about, then picked up the key again.

"All right, Sam, let's move out."

"Where to?"

"The farm. It looks to me as if the next thing on our agenda ought to be a damned good dinner and a nice long nap."

CHAPTER 18

Madoc felt by now as if it ought to be somewhere around the middle of tomorrow night. In fact, though, they got back to the hill in time to get washed up and share the ritual snort with Bert before Annabelle called them to the table.

"Sorry I didn't have something better to give you," she apologized as they helped themselves to fricassee of fowl with dumplings so light it was a problem keeping them on the plates. There were carrots and turnips from the root cellar, homemade hot rolls, a crisp salad to cleanse the palate for a superb dessert of *pommes en belle vue* with whipped cream Charlie claimed to have produced by playing Sousa marches on his trombone to a musically inclined cow. After that there was coffee with chicory, ground fresh in the old box grinder that had been kicking around the pantry since before anybody could remember, and after that there wasn't much a person could do but crawl upstairs and fall asleep.

Madoc did just that. Janet joined him for a while after she'd helped Annabelle clear the table and put the food away, not that they'd left much to put. At some point during the afternoon, Madoc drifted close enough to consciousness to hear one of the boys complain, "Uncle Madoc still asleep, for Pete's sake?" and his wife reply in the low, sweet voice his father admired so greatly, "Don't you dare wake him or I'll skin you alive."

He patted that portion of her most conveniently to hand under the comforter she'd pulled over them both, and sank back into oblivion. When he woke again, he had to go looking for Janet and found her downstairs helping Annabelle get supper.

"Well, you finally decided to rejoin the human race?" Bert put down the Sunday paper and took off the reading glasses that made him look so oddly scholarly.

"Madoc didn't get more than two hours' sleep last night," Janet defended.

"That'll teach him to run off with another man's wife. By the way, Madoc, Sam was looking for you a while back. He said to tell you your bird's a grouse. That make sense to you?"

"All the sense in the world. Where is he now?"

"Down helping Ben Potts, I suppose. He generally does. Chances are he'll turn up soon as Belle gets the grub on the table. Need a hand there, woman?"

"You might offer Madoc a *petit verre*. It's just onion soup tonight, so I thought we'd have a glass of white wine with it."

Janet said, "That sounds good to me," but Madoc said none for him, thanks. It would put him straight back to sleep again and was there any official word on the funeral arrangements for young McLumber?

"Oh yeah, it's all arranged. They're having visiting hours tonight, seven to nine, Sam says. Would you like to go, Madoc?"

"Can you think of any legitimate reason why we should?"

"What the hell do we need a reason for?" Bert snorted. "What else is there to do in Pitcherville on a Sunday night?"

"Anyway, I'm acquainted with Buddy's mother," said Annabelle. "We met at the shower for Armand Bergeron's oldest daughter just last month."

"And I went to school with his cousin Isabelle," Janet added.

"Do you feel up to it, though, love?"

"Oh, I think so, if it's not too much of a crush and we don't stay long."

"You gonna pinch the guy that wasted him, Uncle Madoc?" cried Charlie.

"What kind of gangster talk is that?" snapped his mother. "Go wash your hands and comb your hair. You're not coming to the table looking like the Wild Man of Borneo. Madoc, you haven't by any chance found out who it was?"

"Sorry, Annabelle. I wish I had."

"You don't think it could be the same one who blew up Jase Bain's place?"

"Aw, Jase did that himself, for the insurance," said young Bert in a worldly wise tone.

"What insurance?" his father asked him. "You don't think any company in its right mind would sell a policy to Jase Bain? Aside from the fact that he's about as reliable to do business with as a greased eel, the house can't have been insurable. Miles out from anywhere, and not worth the powder to blow it to hell in the first place."

"Somebody thought it was," his son argued.

"Have you ever stopped to figure how many nuts there are in this world? It's my guess we've got one running loose in the woods. I want you boys to watch your step till we find out who he is."

"Maybe it's a she."

"An abominable snow woman," Charlie suggested solemnly. "I get to sit next to Pop tonight."

"Who cares? I'm sitting beside Uncle Madoc," Ed retorted. "Have you ever pinched an abominable snow woman, Unc?"

"No, but I've had my face slapped for trying. Annabelle, after that marvelous dinner, I thought I'd never want to eat again, but I must say your soup smells awfully good. I might just change my mind about the glass of wine, too, if you don't mind."

"I knew you'd say that," said Janet. "Here you are, it's already poured. We don't have to dress up when we go to Potts's, do we, Annabelle? We can keep our coats buttoned."

"If you do, you'll swelter."

Janet had put on a pair of wool slacks and a bulky green sweater with a high rolled neck to hide her bruises. "I suppose you're right," she admitted.

"Wear what you please," said Bert, taking the lid off the big white ironstone tureen and starting to ladle out the soup. "Pass your bowl, Jen. You know darn well if you dress up they'll say you're putting on airs and if you don't they'll rip you up the back for not showing more respect. You're licked before you start, so what difference does it make?"

"Can we go?" Charlie begged.

"No," said his mother. "You can stay home and do your homework, which you were supposed to finish Friday night and never touched."

"I was showing respect for Aunt Jen and Uncle Madoc."

"They weren't here then," Ed reminded him.

"You think you know everything, don't you?"

"Well, I know something," Bert thundered. "There's to be no fighting at this table. Either you two straighten up and fly right or take you suppers out to the pigsty and eat with the rest of the hogs. Hand your aunt the biscuits and try to act halfway civilized for a change."

"Yes, Dad," said Charlie with temporary meekness. "You want a biscuit, Aunt Jen?"

"Thank you." Janet didn't, particularly, but she knew better than to interfere with Bert's efforts to civilize the fruit of his loins. "Where's Marion Emery these days? I haven't seen her all weekend. Don't tell me she's started living off her own cooking?"

"No, she still freeloads when she's around," Annabelle replied, "but she's got a new wrinkle. She's bought herself an old flivver and gone into the antique business, peddling odds and ends out of the Mansion at the weekend flea markets. She's not doing too badly at it, either. Marion's shrewd, you know. Besides, it gives her an excuse to get away from Pitcherville. She's finding it a lot duller being Lady of the Manor than she thought she would."

"It'll be even duller with Jase Bain in the cooler, I expect," Janet observed. "Weren't they a red-hot twosome there for a while?"

"Oh, that blew over once Jase found out Marion's almost as crafty as he is. He was all set to marry her, or claimed he was, till he found out she had no intention of giving him a clear title to the house no matter what. Marion had just been stringing him along, of course, till something better showed up. She's got this antique dealer on the string now, though frankly I think it's that horsehair parlor set of Mrs. Treadway's he's really in love with."

"Good luck to the pair of 'em," Bert grunted. "Pass the butter, Ed."

"You didn't say the magic word, Pop."

"Oh cripes. Please. How do you like that, my own kids teaching me manners."

"That's what comes of overcivilizing them," said Janet. "What's new at school, fellows?"

The conversation flowed agreeably and more or less peaceably while Madoc, who'd always tended to get outshouted at family gatherings anyway, sat and pondered over his soup. Janet looked to be in excellent fettle. Rest and her family were doing her good; he'd been right to bring her here. He hoped he wasn't about to give her a setback by taking her to view Buddy McLumber's corpse. The coffin would assuredly be open; Pitchervilleites would tolerate none of this newfangled nonsense about not getting to see how natural he looked.

He'd just have to stick to her like paper to a wall. That shouldn't be too hard. Madoc finished his biscuit and allowed his sister-in-law to serve him a sliver of mince pie. It was venison mincemeat, the venison supplied by Sam Neddick. Where, when, and how Sam had bagged the deer was a question that never got asked. Madoc finished his sliver—all forty-five degrees of it—and drank his tea. He and Bert got the kitchen put to rights and the boys settled around the table with their schoolbooks while the women rested. By then it was getting on for seven o'clock and time to leave for the funeral parlor.

It did cross Madoc's mind that because of the unexpected development at Bain's, the meeting in the woods, and the frailty of human flesh, he'd never got back to Bull Moose Portage as he'd planned. There'd be no point in going tonight. Armand Bergeron would surely be involving himself with Buddy McLumber's funeral, for the credit of his reputation as well as his family connection with the McLumbers through his wife. Perhaps they'd have a chance to talk down at Pott's, or at least make an appointment for tomorrow.

As they were getting their coats on, he murmured to his wife, "Jenny, this may be rough on you. I don't know what could happen down there."

"Don't worry, Madoc. I'll be all right as long as you're with me."

There was only one answer to that. Madoc was making it until Bert yelled, "For Christ's sake save a little of that for later. Let's get this show on the road."

The Wadman farm was just two miles out from the village, on a considerable rise. "Remember how Daddy used to tell us how he tobogganed the whole length of the road when he was a boy?" Janet remarked as they were going down the hill.

"He sure as hell wouldn't want to try it tonight," Bert grunted. "I haven't seen such a mob since the day we buried Doc Druffitt. Looks to me as if we'd be better off to park around by Fred Olson's place and walk the rest of the way. Think you can make it, Jen, or shall I drop you and Belle off at Potts's first?"

"If you don't grab the space while you can, somebody else will beat you to it. I can manage all right, if you don't expect me to walk too fast."

"You couldn't if you wanted to," said Annabelle as they left the car and joined the throng. "Everybody and his grandfather's out here tonight, from the look of it. I suppose there's nothing worth watching on television. Well, maybe it will be some gratification to that poor boy's mother that her son got such a big turnout. I suppose I ought to have taken her something this afternoon."

"I don't see why, Annabelle," said Janet. "You don't know her all that well, and I'm sure everybody in Bigears has been deluging her with cakes and pies. Why don't you have her over to tea some day, with Cecile Bergeron and maybe a couple more? Not right away, but later on when she needs something to take her mind."

"That's a good idea. Of course Marion Emery will crash the party unless she's off flea-marketing, but that's no tragedy. Marion can be fairly good company now that she's not whining around all the time. Some of the stories she tells about the people she meets are downright laughable, though I suppose I shouldn't be thinking about laughing just now. Watch out here, Janet, it's slippery."

"I've got her," said Madoc, as indeed he had.

He was wondering how they were ever going to make their way into the jammed funeral parlor and accomplish whatever purpose Sam had got them down for, but he might have known Sam would have the situation well in hand. Somehow or other, a path was opened and a chair found for Janet. Annabelle didn't want one; she was over comforting the grieving mother and all the Grouses and McLumbers with whom she was in any degree acquainted. Bert, having paid his respects, got off into a corner with some of his lodge buddies. Madoc stayed with his wife, effacing himself as he well knew how and curious to see when it, whatever it might be, was going to happen.

Sam didn't keep him waiting long. The odd-job man had collared three or four of the men Madoc recalled having seen through his peephole at the rear of the lean-to. He was edging them over toward Janet's chair, maneuvering them around so Madoc could get a good look at their faces. Madoc, pretending to be absorbed in a chat Janet was having with one of her former schoolmates, reached down and took a firm grip on her hand.

The men were swapping hunting stories. One of them was in full cry, with Sam egging him on. "So then this city feller seen the bear. Before I could stop 'im, he drew a bead on 'er an' landed a shot in the shoulder. The bear dropped down behind some bushes an' the damn crazy bugger run up to 'er without even makin' sure she was dead."

Janet's hand bit frantically into Madoc's. Her face went dead-white. He bent over her. "It's all right, darling. Come on, we'll get you out of here."

She wet her lips. "Madoc, that's—"

"Yes, I know. Sam will understand. Don't you worry about a thing. Perhaps your friend would do us a great favor and round up Bert and Annabelle. Would you mind, Virginia? Tell them Janet's not feeling well and we've had to leave. We'll meet them back at the car. Nice to have met you."

He knew better than to suggest having Janet wait till he brought the car around. What she needed was space between herself and the man whose voice she'd just recognized: the man who'd wanted to make sure she, like the bear, was dead.

CHAPTER 19

"It was just that he used the same identical words as when he was talking about m-me."

"I'm sorry, darling." Madoc had both arms around her. Even with two thick coats between them, he could feel her shivering. "I couldn't warn you in advance because it wouldn't have been such a positive identification."

"I understand, Madoc. I'll be all right. But you are going to take him in?"

"Oh yes. He won't get another chance at you, never fear. He hasn't the faintest idea who you are, you know."

"Yes, I realize that. How could he? He never laid eyes on me. He thought I'd been—"

"But you weren't, because you're a brave and clever little Jenny."

"And you've got brave and clever Sam Neddick back there running the show for you." Janet was getting herself back under control. "You primed him for that, didn't you?"

"Since when did Sam need any priming? I told him the story, yes, and that was all it took. Sam's as good as a commando unit without even trying. Ah, here come Bert and Annabelle."

"Do they know?"

"Bert does. Annabelle hasn't a clue, I hope."

Janet had just time to say, "I'll watch my step," when they were up to her, full of anxious questions.

"It's just that I got this awful cramp in my thigh from sitting on that darned tin chair of Ben's," she lied gallantly. "I knew if I didn't get out of there fast, you'd have to carry me feet first."

"You want to stay here and I'll bring the car around?" her brother was asking.

"No, it feels better when I keep moving. I expect it was partly the heat and the crowd in there. Remember, Annabelle, the time you took the kink in your leg at the church concert while you were expecting Charlie?"

Annabelle remembered, and that took care of any further conversation until they got back to the car. Once they got her stretched out on the back seat with a lap robe over her legs and the rest of her propped up against Madoc, Janet was comfortable enough. As soon as they got her home, Annabelle insisted on helping Janet upstairs and putting her to soak in a hot tub with Epsom salts. Madoc didn't try to interfere. Fussing and coddling were just what Janet needed at this point, and maybe Annabelle needed the doing of it. He'd known there was a close tie between his wife and her only brother; he hadn't realized until now that Bert's wife loved Janet, too.

The three boys were still at it around the kitchen table. Young Bert was explaining something to Ed out of a math book. Charlie was writing a paper, his tongue stuck out to assist the labor. Bert asked Madoc if he'd like to go along to check the cows.

Madoc didn't mind. He found it pleasant out there among the friendly smells of cows and hay, with Julius the cat rubbing around under his feet, hoping he'd squeeze a handy teat and send a stream of fresh milk straight into a wide-open pink mouth. Madoc picked up the cat and tickled his jowls.

"Sorry, Julius, the milk train doesn't run on Sundays. Bert, I suppose you're curious to know what happened back there?"

"Well, I do know Jen's not one to make a fuss. What got into her all of a sudden?"

Madoc told him.

"Big fellow in the red-and-black shirt, eh? That'd be Jelly Grouse. Short for Jellicoe. Can't say I'm too surprised. He always was kind of a bad apple. Got kicked out of school for swiping the principal's car and wrapping it around a tree, blind drunk on bootleg whiskey."

"Has he ever done time?"

"I shouldn't be surprised. He disappeared for a few years. Don't think anybody missed him much, not even his mother."

"How long has he been back?"

"Cripes, I couldn't tell you that. Sam could, no doubt. He set Jelly up for you tonight, eh? I wondered why you were so all-fired anxious to go mourning for a kid you'd never laid eyes on till last night."

"It did occur to me that Pierre Dubois's little troop of happy warriors might furnish a convenient cover for somebody actually bent on more serious business. It also occurred to me that only somebody pretty well acquainted with the Bergerons would think to steal the old bull box. And it further crossed my mind that the reason Eyeball Grouse was so damned obfuscating during our interview might have been that he was afraid some of his own tribe were involved in that hijacking. Now it looks as if he had good reason to worry. What relation is he to Jelly, do you know?"

"Hell no. The way that bunch interbreed out there, they could be each other's grandfathers. Whatever he is, I can see where Jelly might put Eyeball in a ticklish position. What are you planning to do about it, Madoc?"

"Sam hasn't told me yet. Can you tell me, with all respect to yourself, why a man of Sam's capacities ever wound up as somebody else's hired hand?"

Bert shrugged. "Easy enough, I guess. You ever read that poem of Robert W. Service's, 'The Men That Don't Fit In'? That's Sam. He can't stand being tied down too tight, and he'd rather tend to anybody else's business than his own. I tell him he ought to write his life's history, but he says what's the use? Nobody would believe it."

"Probably not," said Madoc, "and possibly with good reason. Furthermore, I doubt whether he can write. In any event, he's doing valuable work for me right now. Have you any suggestions on how I might repay him?"

"Hell, don't fret yourself over it. If I know Sam, he's having the time of his life. Give him a slap on the back, eh, and buy him a fancy plaid shirt to go girlin' in. Sam's hell on wheels with the women, you know, or thinks he is. I noticed him eyeing Bud McLumber's mother Nella down at Ben's. Shouldn't be surprised if he winds up comforting the afflicted, once the shouting's over. He's got a weakness for pudgy blondes."

"As I recall, he had one for rangy brunettes a while back."

"I expect these days he takes what he can get. You in for the night, then?"

"No, I wish I were. Sam has a theory Badger will come home to roost tonight and we thought we might drop over and pay him a visit. Which reminds me, I asked Fredericton to run a check on him, and they haven't called back. Are you still on a party line?"

"No, they changed us over just last week. I'm surprised Belle didn't mention that. It's meant a few busted hearts around town, I can tell you. Maw Fewter has to get her kicks out of the soap operas now, and she says they're damn dull by comparison. Go ahead and make your call."

"I'll reverse the charges," Madoc promised.

They went back to the house, Julius tagging sulkily at their heels. "All right, Gander-Gut." Bert went to the refrigerator and took out a piece of leftover chicken. "Couldn't one of you kids have fed this critter?"

"I did," said Charlie.

"Me, too," said Ed.

"So did Mum," said Young Bert. "You ought to know what a con artist he is, Dad."

"Let's get Uncle Madoc to run him in," Charlie suggested. Julius merely gave him a look, finished off the chicken, and set about grooming his handsome whiskers.

Julius, it appeared, was not the only con artist Madoc might have occasion to confront tonight. The man who called himself Badger—and Beaver—and Bearhound—and occasionally Bandicoot—had a record longer than a pickpocket's fingers. Both civilian and military police in an impressive number of places all over the North American continent were eager to extend him the hospitality of their maximum security facilities. There were even several rewards out for his apprehension.

Madoc could hardly claim any of these, but he saw no reason why Sam Neddick and Fred Olson couldn't. When last seen, Fred had been down by Ben Potts's, trying to unscramble the mess of traffic. One might question how helpful Fred would be when it came to arresting anybody as vicious and resourceful as Badger had shown himself to be under a staggering variety of circumstances. It could, however, be argued that Fred had already served the cause by keeping Badger's car in good repair and thus lulling him into a state of relaxed vigilance.

So Madoc went upstairs to kiss his wife good night, kissed Annabelle, too, for good measure although in a respectful, brother-in-lawish manner, and went downstairs to wait for Sam Neddick. By now it was getting on for nine o'clock and he didn't have long to linger before Sam manifested himself in the doorway like the Ghost of Nixon Hollow, beckoning him out to the woodshed.

"You ready, Inspector?"

"Whenever you are, but don't you want some supper first?"

"Nope. Miz Potts fed an' drunk me, such as 'twas. Badger's come back."

"How do you know? Don't tell me he dropped by Potts's to pay his respects?"

"Close enough as made no nevermind. Fred seen 'im down on Queen Street. Said he come back 'cause he got to worryin' about the house." Psychic, beyond a doubt. "He stopped to ask what the crowd was doin' there, an' sent his sympathy to the mother. You find out anything?"

"Quite a lot. I ought to warn you, Sam, the man's a killer."

"Don't s'prise me none. How's Janet feelin'?"

"Better. She got a rather bad shock back there. You were right about Jellicoe Grouse."

"Ayup. He won't be goin' nowheres till after the funeral. You can pick 'im up tomorrow easy enough. We might as well git movin'. Badger didn't mention how long he was plannin' to worry. You want to take Fred along?"

"If you think we can keep him from getting shot. I'd rather, actually. Since he's acquainted with Badger, he'd probably have better luck getting him to open the door." And thus assure his fair share of the reward money. Fred still had two in college. "Do you think we can pry him away from downtown?"

"Sure. Most of the mourners have gone home by now. Hockey game's on at nine."

"Let's go find him, then."

"He'll be in Ben's embalmin' room, havin' a nip to warm 'im up. Ben keeps a jar in there."

Sam was right, needless to say. Fred came out wiping his mouth, shivering a bit as the raw air hit him. "Cripes, I thought I was off duty for the night."

"Hell no," said Sam. "The fun's just startin'."

"We're going out to call on your friend Badger," Madoc explained. "We'd be grateful if you went along to perform the introductions."

"Don't know if he'll be much in the mood for company," Fred demurred. "Badger told me he was almost up to Edmundston when he got to worryin' an' decided he better come back. He'll be dead beat, wouldn't you think?"

"Oh, I don't know," said Madoc. "He's used to long drives. With any luck this won't take long." He knew Fred was no coward, but he doubted if the marshal was any great actor, either. Fred might have trouble carrying off his part with nonchalance if he knew what was actually happening. "It's just a matter of going through some necessary formalities, you can tell him." How true that was!

"I get you. Then we might as well do it tonight an' get it over with. He'll prob'ly sleep better once he knows we're really takin' an interest."

Madoc thought he'd let that remark pass quietly. He motioned Sam into the back seat, waited till Fred had stowed his paunch in front on the passenger's side, and they were off. Sam knew a shortcut, naturally, so Madoc got them to Badger's sooner than he'd expected. Their man was at home. They could see him through an uncurtained window, sitting in the sagging spring rocker in front of the little old television set, watching the hockey game and sipping from a beer can, the picture of contentment. When Fred knocked on the door, Madoc saw Badger jump up and reach for the coat he'd thrown down on the sofa. Sidearm in the pocket, no doubt. But he didn't take it out.

"Who's there?"

"Fred Olson, Jim. Thought I'd better stop by an' make sure you found your place okay before I turn in my report."

The man scowled, but there wasn't much he could do except open the door. "That's mighty nice of you, Fred. Come in and have a beer. I was just watching the game."

"I wasn't aimin' to stay," said Fred. "Got a couple o' friends with me. You know Sam Neddick? He helps out at Wadman's farm."

Sam nodded and somehow insinuated himself around behind Badger and over to the sofa.

"An' this is Bert Wadman's brother-in-law, Madoc Rhys."

"Inspector Rhys of the RCMP, to be precise," said Madoc softly and sadly. "I'm afraid we'll have to take you in, Mr. Badger. There are several warrants out for you, we've found. No, don't bother reaching for your coat. Mr. Neddick has already taken out the gun, and I'm afraid he has the bad manners to be pointing it at you, Mr. Beaver."

Madoc seldom resorted to firearms himself, but he wasn't about to stifle an initiative like Sam Neddick's. "I should perhaps explain that Mr. Neddick is an even keener marksman than you are, Mr. Bearhound. Perhaps you'd be good enough to put your hands over your head while I explain the formalities to you? Tedious I know, Mr.

Bandicoot, since you've heard all this so often before, but we don't want you to get off on a technicality as you did on June 17, 1962, in Akron, Ohio."

Badger made the foolish mistake of losing his temper. He railed, cursed, and tried to take a swing at Madoc. Fred Olson, trained on skittish horses in his father's forge, put a quick stop to that. Even if he did have a belly like Santa Claus, the muscles of his brawny arms were indeed strong as iron bands. Sam stood by, helpfully offering to star Badger's kneecap, but there was really no need. When Badger's violence got out of reason, Fred merely wrestled him to the floor and plunked his own body down on top. Madoc finished his oration and snapped on the handcuffs. Sam found a piece of rope and demonstrated how to hobble the prisoner's feet Indian-style so that he could walk to the car under his own steam but wouldn't have the ghost of a chance if he tried to run away.

"Thank you, gentlemen," said Madoc. "Well, this has been a pleasant and instructive visit. Let's see, we mustn't forget to shut off the lights and the television before we go. We don't want to add to Mr. Bandicoot's difficulties by running up his light bill. First, however, I suggest we look around for the rifle that matches the bullet Buddy McLumber was shot with. It's sure to be here somewhere. He's too experienced a rogue to have carried it in his car, and too cocky to have thrown it away."

That shook Badger a little. He couldn't know for sure they hadn't found the bullet, and he couldn't quite suppress the flicker of alarm that contorted his undistinguished features when Sam said, "Up the chimbley" and proved, of course, to be right.

"I have a right to call my lawyer" was all he said.

"And so you shall, Mr. Bearhound," Madoc replied, "but not from here. We don't know what sort of signal you may have rigged up with Jelly Grouse or some other of your henchmen, you see, and we shouldn't care to run into an ambush because it's getting late and you've caused us quite enough trouble already. Now, if you will just walk quietly and sedately between myself and Marshal Olson, Mr. Neddick will lock up the house you were so worried about leaving, and follow along with the confiscated handgun."

Madoc took the rifle in front with him. Both Fred and Sam got in back with the prisoner between them. It made for a tight squeeze but a first-class deterrent against any of the shenanigans for which this one-man zoo had become so widely known and so ardently sought.

The village clock had struck eleven by the time they got down to the lockup. This in truth wasn't much of an affair, being only a room stuck on behind the old forge and fitted up with an iron cage. It was used mostly on Saturday nights for keeping unruly townsfolk in pickle, as the late Mrs. Agatha Treadway had once been heard wittily to remark, until they were sober enough to drive themselves home. It had two cots with warm blankets; it had plumbing of a sort; it had a stack of old magazines and mail order catalogs with which the temporary residents could beguile their enforced leisure. Millie Olson was wont to supply lavish meals to those in any sort of shape to eat, and Jason Bain had no doubt fared much better today than he ever had at home. Nevertheless, as soon as he heard the forge door open, Bain started yelling about his rights.

"Pipe down, Jase," Fred told him. "We've brought you a roommate."

"What do you mean roommate? I ain't havin' no goddamn drunk pukin' all over—"

Bain stopped short. He'd looked horrified this morning when he saw his ruined junkyard; he looked worse when he caught sight of Badger.

"You ain't puttin' him in here with me! I demand my rights. You got to take me straight off to the county jail an' lock me up where I'll be safe."

CHAPTER 20

"Then you do know Mr. Badger?" said Madoc. "I thought you told me you didn't bother with your neighbors."

"I don't care who he is," the old reprobate tried to bluster. "I ain't havin' him in my cell. I'm entitled to my privacy."

"You're not entitled to anything except what Marshal Olson says you're entitled to, Mr. Bain. Now why don't you come clean about who blew up your house and yard, and what business it was that kept you safely out of the way while the explosions were taking place?"

"I was just doin' a friend a favor," Bain mumbled.

"Who, for instance?" asked Fred Olson. "I never knew you had one." He was unlocking the disproportionately heavy hand-forged iron door as he spoke. "You want to come out here an' tell us about your friend?"

"What you intendin' to do with Badger, eh? Long as he's out, I'm stayin' in."

"By God, Jase, if ever there was a prize pain in the ass, you're it. Badger's goin' into that cell soon as Sam an' the inspector get through fishin' the knives an' razor blades an' cyanide pills out of his pockets, an takin' away his shoelaces. Then I'm goin' to phone down to the county hoosegow an' tell 'em to send up their brand-new Black Maria with a half-dozen armed guards to cart 'im away. You can either ride down with 'em or else make up your mind to act like a goddamn human being for once in your life an' tell us the truth."

"What truth? You got nothin' to charge me with."

"How about obstructing justice?" Madoc suggested gently. "You're not a man to scare easily as a rule, are you, Mr. Bain? Yet you're as terrified right now as though we were holding your bare feet to an open fire. What's Mr. Badger done to frighten you so?"

"He's a criminal, ain't he? You wouldn't of arrested 'im if he wasn't."

"We arrested you, Mr. Bain."

"Yes, an' you're damn well goin' to pay for it good an' proper."
Bain reeled off the words as if he'd got them by heart but had no
feeling for the role.

"But if you're a victim of false arrest, why can't he be the same?"

" 'Cause I know damn well he's—"

Bain caught the look Badger was giving him, and stopped as if he'd
been slapped across the mouth. "All right then," he growled. "I'll
come out. But you got to keep 'im back from me."

They didn't have to, actually. Badger just stood there regarding
Bain with mild amusement while the old man shuffled through the
cell doorway, keeping as far to the other side as he could in that little
space.

"Your turn, Mr. Badger," said Madoc.

The new prisoner balked for a second, then caught those clear-glass
eyes of Sam's, and went in. Fred slammed the door on him, and
locked it from outside. Sam settled himself in the old padded rocker
where Millie was wont to sit and chat with the prisoners while they
ate their suppers. He had Badger's rifle across his lap and Badger's .45
in his hand, and a few extra rounds of ammunition tucked into his
belt just in case.

"You go ahead an' call the wagon," he told Fred and Madoc. "I've
handled tougher men than this bugger. Just take Jase Bain with you is
all I ask. I can stand a thief an' I can stand a murderer, but what I
can't stand is a derned ol' fool that stinks worse'n a barnful o' tomcats
in season. For somebody that's so jeezledy anxious to hang on to his
hide, you might think he'd bother to wash it once in a blue moon."

Bain was so glad to get away from Badger that he didn't pause to
take umbrage. He scuttled through the forge and on into the garage.
There Fred Olson had a telephone, which he used to put in his call to
the county jail.

"They said it'd take a while to get here with the wagon, but they'll
send it along as soon as they can," he reported. "They're tickled pink
about Badger. 'Tisn't often we hook a big one like him. Cripes, I'm
gettin' sleepy. By the way, you don't think Sam's likely to nod off
back there?"

"About as likely as a leopard stalking a gazelle, I'd say," Madoc
replied. "Sam's having the time of his life."

Those no-color eyes would stay fixed on Badger for as long as Badger stayed in the cage; and Madoc wouldn't be at all surprised if Sam

managed to wheedle a ride down to the jail out of the police who brought the wagon. He himself would have to be available when they came, of course, but there was no reason why Fred had to stand here falling off his feet.

"Marshal, why don't you go into the house and take a nap till they get here? You've earned some rest, along with a few other things."

Fred yawned again. "Such as what, for instance?"

"A wad of official commendations, I expect, from the police in— let's see, I wrote some of them down here somewhere."

Madoc handed over the list from his notebook. Fred whistled. "Cripes a'mighty, who'd o' thought Badger was so popular? Think I might get my pitcher in the paper? Millie's be tickled at that."

"I don't see why it shouldn't be in a good many papers. This was your collar, Marshal, with a large assist from your deputy, Sam Neddick."

"You wasn't exactly standin' by with your hands folded, Inspector."

"I don't count. I've merely been offering such assistance as any local police are entitled according to RCMP regulations. In fact, however, you haven't filed any formal request, so I'm only here as an interested friend and neighbor. Let's leave it at that, shall we?"

"Why? You got somethin' else up your sleeve?"

"I don't think the case is quite over yet. Mr. Bain is about to cast some further light on the matter, I believe. Would you care to speak your piece now, Mr. Bain, or would you rather go back and keep Mr. Badger company while you get your thoughts together?"

"I dunno what you're talkin' about." Bain tried to talk tough, but his voice was shaking. "I ain't goin' back there."

"Then talk, and talk fast. The marshal's getting impatient."

"Damn right I am." Fred yawned all the way back to his epiglottis. "Come on then, Jase. Why do you think Badger's out for your blood? Was it him or you that blew up your place?"

"Either him or some of 'is men."

"What men?"

"He never said."

"Then how do you know he's got any?"

"They been comin' an' goin'."

"Whereabouts?"

"His house."

"How do you know?"

"I seen 'em."

"When?"

"Now an' again."

"Let's speed this up a little," Madoc intervened. "Were you in company with these men, or were you spying on them from outside?"

"I got a right to know what's goin' on around my own land, ain't I?"

"Did Badger catch you sneaking around his yard? Is that how he roped you in on whatever he's been up to? Or did he find out the sort of reputation you have around town, and approach you directly?"

"I guess he seen me an' asked around," Bain admitted. "Anyways, he come up to the house one day an' wanted to know if I'd be willin' to do a few odd jobs for 'im. I says what sort o' jobs? He says just storin' some stuff o' his in my yard an' maybe doin' a little light truckin' now an' then. I seen no harm in that so I says what about the moncy? He gimme a pretty good figger."

"How good?" Madoc prompted.

"I don't have to tell you my private business."

"Yes you do."

"Hundred a week for the storin'," Bain muttered, "an' fifty extra for each trip."

"Good Lord! What were you storing?"

"He says I better not ask."

"But you took the job on anyway."

"The money was good. Paid reg'lar, too."

"How long has this been going on?"

"Since the fifteenth of October."

"And how many trips have you made?"

"Last night was my twenty-first."

"So you've made six hundred on the storage so far, and a thousand on the haulage."

"Thousand an' fifty."

"Thank you for correcting my arithmetic. And in return for this, you've now lost everything you owned except for that old truck, which might fetch you five or ten dollars if anybody was fool enough to make an offer. It seems to me a man of your vaunted business acumen might have figured out what sort of characters you were working for. Didn't you even snoop into the materials he was parking in your junkyard?"

"I couldn't. It was hid in them seventeen portable privies. Mr. Badger put new padlocks on 'em an' kept the keys hisself. Leastways I s'pose he did, I never got to see 'em. Never tried to force the locks, either, if that's what you're wonderin'. He says if he ever seen any sign I'd been messin' around with 'em, the deal was off."

"How did the stuff get into the privies?"

"I dunno. I think it mostly happened while I was off haulin'."

"And what about this trucking you did? You wouldn't be able to load and unload the cargo yourself, surely?"

"They'd come in the night an' load up."

"Who would?"

"Don't ask me. I'd be asleep."

"All twenty-one times?"

"I sleep pretty sound when I'm paid to." The old sly grin sneaked across his unlovely face, then vanished. "Say, Inspector, you think I stand any chance o' gettin' damages out o' Mr. Badger?"

"I think you could be in more trouble if you try that than you're already in. Mr. Bain, hasn't it yet occurred to you that for the past six months you've been an active accomplice in whatever illegal operation Mr. Badger's been running in and out of your junkyard?"

"I don't know it was illegal, do I? I never seen what he was runnin'."

"Do you really think any jury could ever be persuaded into believing that kind of nonsense? Where did you take your loads?"

"Place over toward Oromocto."

"Whereabouts in Oromocto?"

"I never said 'twas in Oromocto. I said it was around there someplace. Just an old house out on a back road all by itself 'cept for a barn down below it a ways. My orders was to leave the truck by the barn an' walk up an' go inside the house an' stay there."

"For how long?"

"For as long as it took. Sometimes fifteen, twenty minutes, sometimes as much as a couple of hours. Somebody'd come along an' unload my truck, then they'd honk their horn a few times an' drive off. I'd stay in the house till I heard 'em honkin', then I'd walk back an' get in my truck an' drive back home. Them was the arrangements. I didn't make 'em. I just carried 'em out, prompt an' faithful."

"Who lived in the house?"

"Nobody, from the look of it, nor hadn't for some time. Warn't much in it but a rusty ol' parlor stove an' a busted-down chesterfield an' chair. An' a bottle o' booze in the kitchen."

"Was it always the same bottle?"

"Not hardly. I figgered the men must o' kept puttin' one there for when they come by."

"That would mean they used the house for other purposes than keeping you out of the way."

"Oh yeah. I seen fresh footprints, an' sometimes there'd be a fire in the stove that'd been burnin' a good while."

"Did you ever drink from the bottle?"

Bain shrugged. "I ain't much for drinkin'. 'Course the bottle was just settin' there an' I'd be cold from all that drivin'. Badger never told me not to."

"Did you ever ask him?"

"Hell no. Why should I?"

"Was it good liquor?"

"It was free."

"These men who unloaded the truck, they never came in and had a drink with you?"

"Nope. Never laid eyes on 'em. Might o' been women, for all I know. They was always too far away to get a look at. I couldn't see into the barn 'cause the house was up on top of a rise an' set 'way back from the road. The barn was down underneath the hill a ways an' opened right up to the road. They never showed up till I was inside the house, an' like I said, I wasn't s'posed to set foot outside the door till they'd druv off."

"Weren't you curious as to who they were?"

"Not for that kind o' money I wasn't."

"You're a beauty, Mr. Bain," said Madoc. "Now what about this last trip you made on Saturday night? Did it go off just like the others?"

"Nope."

"Why not?"

"The house wasn't there."

"What happened to it?"

"Burnt right down to the ground. An' the barn was all busted in. I didn't know what to do. Drivin' all that way—"

"So what did you do?" Madoc prompted.

"Set an' cussed, if you want to know. Then a van come up."

"What kind of van?"

"How the hell do I know? It was pitch dark. So anyways, the van stopped a little ways in front o' me, an' somebody come out with a flashlight an' opened up the back. Then he waved the light like he was motionin' me inside, so I went."

"Did you get a look at this man?"

"Nope. He had one o' them knitted masks over 'is face, like they wear snowmobilin'. Anyways, he shined the light right in my eyes so I was dazzled, like. Then he slammed the door on me."

"Were you frightened?"

"Hell no. I was tired. I laid myself down on the floor an' went to sleep. After a while, they opened the door an' honked the horn, so I got up an' walked back to my truck. By the time I got there, the van was gone. So I come home an' found I didn't have no home to come to, an' then you come along an' arrested me. An' just as I was gettin' myself halfway comfortable back there, you come threatenin' me an' roustin' me out. Though I s'pose once they've carted Badger off, I might's well move back in an' take my punishment. At least till after breakfast."

"Nothin' doin'," said Fred Olson. "If you think I'm turnin' my lockup into a goddamn hotel, you can think again. You want this ol' coot any longer, eh, Inspector?"

"You're in charge here, Marshal, not I," Madoc reminded him. "We know from his own statement that Mr. Bain is guilty of having aided and abetted a known criminal. We deduce that since the drop Badger had been using was destroyed by fire, he'd decided to work out a different method of moving his goods. That meant he didn't want Bain in the picture any more, so he sent him on one last trip to get rid of whatever cargo was left in the privies. Then he blew up the house and yard to destroy any evidence of what had been going on, and to give Bain a broad hint as to what would happen if he talked. Naturally Badger wasn't expecting to be caught. Even as it was, we saw how mortally afraid Bain was to be put in a position where Badger could get at him. You'd hardly have been so forthcoming just now if there hadn't been all those good, strong iron bars between you and Badger, would you, Mr. Bain?"

The old man growled something they couldn't make out, which was probably just as well.

"However," Madoc went on, "the fact remains that Mr. Bain has made a full confession, most of which is probably true, and that he's already had a pretty severe punishment dealt to him. He'll have to testify against Badger sooner or later, I suppose, but in the meantime I don't see why you and your wife should be put to the bother of looking after him, Marshal."

"Me neither," said Fred. "All right, Jase, git."

"At this hour?" yowled Bain. "Where'm I s'posed to go?"

"That's no skin off my nose."

"But you can't just shove an old man out in the cold an' dark. That's police brutality. I'll complain to the authorities."

"What authorities, for instance? I tell you what, Jase, why don't you hike yourself on over to Maw Fewter's? She's got a spare room I daresay she'd be willin' to put you up in now that Dot's gone."

"Goddamn hogpen. Besides, she'd want me to pay board."

"Look here, Jase Bain," Fred exploded, "if you're hangin' around here tryin' to get pinched again for loiterin', you better forget it. Next time I arrest you, you'll go straight into that cell with Badger an' if you're still alive when the wagon gets here, you'll be sent along to the county jail as an accomplice. Now you make up your mind which you're goin' to do, an' you make it up fast."

Bain said something quite spectacularly obscene, picked up the filthy old bearskin coat he'd brought with him from the lockup, and vanished into what was left of the night. A few seconds later one of Fred's sons, a beefy lad of nineteen or so, charged into the garage with a down jacket tossed over flannel pajamas and his feet thrust into unlaced hiking boots.

"Hey Dad, what's going on? I just met Old Man Bain stomping out of here, cussing his head off. What'd you release him at this hour for?"

"We brought in another customer an' Jase begun makin' a pest of himself. Inspector, you know my son George?"

Madoc shook hands with the good-looking youngster. "I believe we met at the Wadmans' party last month. My sister-in-law tells me you're in line for a hockey scholarship."

"An' I tell him he can play if he wants to, but his studyin' comes first," said Fred. "None o' this not bein' able to read the diploma when he graduates."

"Aw, Pop, I can already read three-letter words if the print's big enough." George grinned and put an affectionate armlock on his father. "No kidding, did you really bag somebody?"

"Yep. That man Badger who bought the old Fewter place."

"Badger the hockey stick salesman? What for?"

"Just about everything, accordin' to the inspector."

Madoc nodded. "He's on a number of most-wanted lists. The latest is for a jail break in Alberta, where he was serving life for arson and murder."

"Him? That's unreal. The kids call him Doughface. How'd you ever get on to Badger, Inspector?"

"Actually, it was your father who put us on the trail. It was also your father who put the collar on him, you'll be proud to know."

"Aw hell, Inspector," Fred protested. "All I done was knock the bugger down an' sit on him till Sam found the rope to hobble his feet."

"You sat on a murderer?" Fred's son groped for words, and finally came up with "Awesome! My old man's a hero."

"Hero be damned," Fred snorted. "I'm too tired to be a hero."

"Then why don't you go grab some sleep? Hey, Inspector, I'll be glad to stay with you and guard the prisoner."

"Sam Neddick has that situation under control, thank you. Come to think of it, though, you might be able to help. I don't know that I've had a chance to tell you, Marshal, but Janet's fingered Jellicoe Grouse as one of the men she heard talking before they set fire to the house Bain had been using as his waiting room. Sam thinks he'll keep till after the funeral, but I'm not so sure. Once the news of Badger's arrest gets around, as it's bound to do once Mrs. Fewter finds Bain on her doorstep, Grouse may be over the hills and far away. Besides, if we take him now, it will save the wagon an extra trip. George, could you ride out to Bigears with me and point out where Grouse is most apt to be staying? Or wouldn't you know?"

"Sure I know. He's shacking up with Nella McLumber."

"What kind o' talk is that?" his father rebuked. "Couldn't you of said he's her roomer?"

"Okay, Pop. He rents the room Nella sleeps in. That make you feel any better? Would you mind waiting a second till I get my pants on, Inspector? Come on, Pop, I'll carry you upstairs."

CHAPTER 21

"How well did you know Buddy McLumber, George?"

Madoc and the marshal's son were riding in Fred's tow truck to create the illusion they were on an errand of mercy in case Mrs. Fewter happened to be peeking from behind her curtains. George was at the wheel. Madoc was slouched in the seat beside him, trying to look like Fred and possibly succeeding, as dawn had not yet broken.

"Buddy?" George shrugged. "Oh, you know how it is, eh. In a place like Pitcherville, everybody knows everybody more or less. He was about seven years older than I, you know. We never hung out together or anything, but he'd offer me a lift if he saw me walking home from hockey practice, stuff like that. Bud was always out driving around."

"In his own car?"

"In whatever came handy. That was the one big thing about Bud. I doubt if he knew one end of a crankshaft from the other, but he could drive anything that had a motor in it better than anybody I ever saw. That's what he used to do, mostly. He'd drive a snowplow in the winter, tractors in the summer, delivery trucks, bulldozers, you name it. They were always temporary jobs, though. Bud couldn't stick to any one thing for long, and I guess people would get sick of having him around. He wasn't a bad guy, but he was one of those know-it-alls, and he'd never shut up long enough to let you get a word in edgewise. But he'd always get hired because they knew he was good."

"And I suppose when he was off driving, they didn't have to listen," said Madoc. "Buddy wasn't the type to have accidents, then?"

"No, never. Sometimes there'd be a breakdown, but that wasn't his fault."

"What would he do then?"

"Panic, mostly. Bud could change a flat and pump his own gas if he had to, but if it was anything more complicated than that, he'd hitch a ride to the nearest phone and yell for my father to come and bail him out."

"What if he couldn't hitch a ride?"

"Then he'd walk, I suppose, but no farther than he could help. Bud without a car was like a goldfish without a bowl. Vehicles were his natural habitat, you might say."

"Then if he couldn't get one any other way, might he have been tempted to steal a car?"

George was silent a moment, then nodded. "He used to when he was a kid. Before he was old enough to get a license, he'd swipe his uncles' cars and go joyriding. I know that for a fact because he was hanging around my sister Margie for a while, and he bragged to her about it. They used to get sore, but they wouldn't do anything except maybe give him a clout on the ear because he always got their cars back without a scratch. Why did you ask that, Inspector? Do you think Bud might have stolen Badger's car or something?"

"Not Badger's. You wouldn't happen to know whether Buddy was working at the store this past Thursday afternoon?"

"I couldn't say offhand. Bud was in and out of the place a lot because he drove the delivery truck for his uncle. He'd been doing that for quite a while. He only started clerking when Henry, the regular helper, got killed."

"Oh? What happened to Henry?"

"He shot himself. He was cleaning his rifle and it went—say, that's pretty strange when you come to think of it."

"Was he alone when it happened?"

"Far as anybody knew. His wife was off to her sister's or somewhere. She came home and found him dead in the kitchen. He'd been out shooting rabbits. There were a couple of them lying on the kitchen table, each with one clean shot through the head. Henry was a fantastic sharpshooter. He had a lot of medals for marksmanship."

"Yet he killed himself cleaning his own gun. Didn't anybody find that a bit strange?"

"Well, sure. But Henry'd been kind of moody lately, according to his wife. He'd done some queer things, too, like staying out all night and flying off the handle when she asked him where the heck he'd been, and picking a big fight with Mr. McLumber the day before."

"What about?"

"Nothing in particular. Mr. McLumber said they were down cellar shifting some stock around and he just got sore and started raving. A customer came in and heard Henry yelling, but couldn't tell what he was saying. So then Henry grabbed his coat and stormed out and went shooting rabbits, and then he came home and shot himself. I guess he figured he was going to get fired."

"How long had he been with McLumber?"

"All his life, pretty much. He'd gone to work there Saturdays while he was still in school and started full-time as soon as he got out. Mr. McLumber says he wouldn't have fired him, no matter what. He thought the world of Henry. He even paid for the funeral. So the relatives kind of leaned on Dad to never mind asking embarrassing questions but just let them get it over with. Dad didn't like that much, but Henry was an Owl and his father's a Past Grand Supreme Regent, and nobody's too keen on the idea of a suicide in the family. You can understand that, Inspector."

Yes, Madoc could understand. He'd run into the same kind of thing himself often enough. The family wouldn't have gone much for the idea of murder, either. Probably it had never crossed their minds, and why should it have? People didn't go around shooting hardware clerks in their own kitchens.

"It looks to me," he said, "as if Mr. McLumber may have some trouble finding himself another hardware clerk."

George chuckled a bit. "I hadn't thought of that. I don't suppose he will, though. There aren't that many jobs going begging around here, and I guess Mr. McLumber pays fairly well."

"Does he, now? I shouldn't think a store like his would do that much business."

"It's not just the store. They do some warehousing, too. That's where Bud would be mostly, making deliveries to other stores."

"What would he be delivering?"

"I suppose the sort of thing you'd find in a general store. Tools such as hammers and screwdrivers and ax heads. Flashlight batteries, weather stripping, stuff like that. The big distributors aren't much interested in filling small orders, so that's where Mr. McLumber came in."

"But is there any real money in that?" Madoc asked.

"Why should he bother if there wasn't? I'd say Mr. McLumber does darn well for himself. He drives a big Lincoln, goes on trips, bought his wife a mink coat for Christmas. My mother told her it was beautiful, though she wouldn't want one for herself because mink makes a woman look so much fatter than she already is."

Madoc laughed, as George clearly expected him to. "George, if you'd like to try some detective work, you might find out—discreetly, of course—where Buddy was on Thursday. On Wednesday, too," he added, recalling Eyeball Grouse and the masked driver of the van at Point C who'd intercepted the army truck on its way from Point A to Point B.

"Sure. I'll ask some of the guys. Discreetly, of course. Say, Inspector, what sort of courses would a guy on a hockey scholarship have to take to get into the RCMP?"

"Why don't you come up to Fredericton sometime soon and discuss the matter with our personnel officer? My wife would be glad to offer you a bed."

George could sleep in the guest room beside his father's washstand wearing its coat of the Loyalist Blue paint Buddy McLumber had been so voluble about. At least Madoc knew where Buddy had been on Saturday.

It was as well George was doing the driving this time. Madoc dropped off to sleep and managed a refreshing nap before they got to Bigears. He snapped wide awake, though, the moment George stopped the truck.

"Is this the place?"

"Not quite. I thought I'd better make sure what we're supposed to do. Were you planning to surround the house or anything?"

"What I had in mind was walking up and ringing the doorbell, if there is one."

"Then what?"

"That depends on which of them answers. If it's Mrs. McLumber, you might greet her politely and apologize for getting her out of bed. You might then say we'd like to talk with Mr. Grouse. Or Jelly, if that's how you normally refer to him. Then I say don't bother calling him, I'll go on up. You stay down here and engage her in light conversation so she doesn't interfere. If Grouse himself comes to the door, you step aside and let me handle him. I mean that, George. Don't do a thing unless he breaks away and tries to make a run for it. Then, if you can do it conveniently and safely, tackle him from behind. If he's armed, stay clear and let him go. He won't get far."

"How do you know?"

"Trust me."

Madoc couldn't think offhand why George should place any reliance on such an unsupportable assurance, except that Grouse probably wouldn't be wearing anything to speak of and charging off half-naked in the predawn chill might dampen his enthusiasm for escape rather quickly. Furthermore, if he'd been enjoying his landlady's charms as George hypothesized, he might be too tired to run anyway. They walked up to the house and rang the bell.

Nothing happened. Madoc rang it again. Then it occurred to him the bell probably hadn't worked in years and the door probably wasn't locked. He eased it open and murmured to George, "Stick your head in and holler for Grouse."

George was good at hollering. "Jelly? Hey, Jelly Grouse. You here?"

Grouse's answering bellow was thick and indistinct. "Huh? Wha' the hell you want?"

"Come down here quick. I need you."

There was some growling and thrashing, a woman's voice raised in sleepy complaint, then scuffing footsteps on the stairway. "What's the matter? That you, Cyril?"

"No, it's me," George replied.

"Me who? Why the hell don't you turn on the light?"

From the sound, Grouse had just fallen down the last few stairs and landed on an umbrella stand filled with pokers and tongs. Madoc turned on the flashlight he'd brought with him. Jelly was a big man, running to fat. He lay sprawled amid a welter of lacrosse sticks and baseball bats, wearing nothing but an unfastened bathrobe. Madoc had a fleeting urge to arrest him for indecent exposure, then decided he'd better stick to the book. He pulled a string to switch on a bulb that shone directly down into the fallen man's eyes. Dazzled, Grouse squinted up at him.

"Who the hell are you?"

"RCMP," Madoc told him. "Detective Inspector Rhys. And you're Jellicoe Grouse, commonly known as Jelly, right? You're under arrest, Mr. Grouse. It is my duty to remind you that anything you say will be taken down and may be used in evidence against you."

"For what?"

"At the moment, you're charged with arson and conspiracy to commit a felony. I expect we'll be tacking on a number of other things once we get you sorted out. There's really no sense in making those obscene noises, Mr. Grouse. We have a positive identification of you from the woman whom Buddy McLumber failed to murder before he stole her car Thursday afternoon. This was after Perce Bergeron's bull box tipped over and burned, as you doubtless surmise, and immediately before you and your confederate dragged the furniture out into the road and set fire to it and the house."

"You're crazy. The woman wasn't there. I mean—"

Jellicoe Grouse realized too late that he'd meant what he said. He tried to get up, caught his foot in a lacrosse stick, and fell again. He must still be half-drunk, Madoc decided, from whatever rite of passage had followed the session at Ben Potts's.

"George, would you mind helping him up? I'll just slip these handcuffs on him first, for form's sake. Perhaps Mrs. McLumber will be kind enough to bring down his boots and trousers."

By now, Buddy's mother was at the top of the stairs, clutching a patchwork quilt around her. "What are you doing to him? He never did anything. He's been right here in the house all the time."

She sounded a trifle smashed, too, Madoc thought, and who could blame her? "Sorry to disturb you, Mrs. McLumber," he apologized. "The crime for which Mr. Grouse is being arrested took place this past Thursday in the early evening. That was the same night your son had the breakdown and came home late from Harvey Station, remember?"

"It wasn't Harvey Station. He'd been out to Bull Moose Portage for one of those meetings Pierre Dubois had been running. I told Pierre what I thought of him for keeping my boy out so late."

"And what did Pierre say?" asked Madoc, keeping his mitten firmly clamped over Jelly's mouth so he couldn't shut her up.

"Oh, he put me off as you might expect. He said he guessed some of the brothers must have got together for a little informal discussion. Cecile claims Pierre took her over to the movies that night, but of course Cecile would say anything Pierre wanted her to."

And of course Pierre had assumed Buddy'd been somewhere he didn't want his mother to know about, which was undoubtedly the truth, and been too noble and high-minded to rat on a brother. He'd check with Dubois as a matter of form, but Madoc had washed out the nature writer as an effective conspirator ever since that inspirational session at the lean-to.

Nella McLumber could be dropped off the list, too, he was sure.

This woman was a natural-born dupe, the kind who could always be fooled because she always knew she was right.

Madoc decided he'd better take his mitten away and let Jellicoe Grouse come up for air. The prisoner at once began to bluster.

"You can't do this to me. I've got influential friends."

"If you're talking about Mr. Badger, you might as well save your breath," Madoc told him. "He's down at the lockup under armed guard, waiting for transport to the county jail. Jason Bain has been arrested and confessed his part in that game you've been playing, in order to save his own skin. You'll be well advised to do the same."

Jellicoe Grouse retorted with a suggestion about what Inspector Rhys could do. As this involved an anatomical impossibility, Madoc took little heed.

"George, why don't you go get the truck? Drive right up to the door. Mrs. McLumber may be saved some embarrassment if we remove Mr. Grouse before the sun comes up and her neighbors begin to wonder."

"They'll wonder anyway," said Mrs. McLumber bitterly.

"Then tell them you went out for a ride because you couldn't sleep, and your car broke down so you called my father and we towed you home," George suggested. "I'll back you up, Mrs. McLumber. Bud used to give me rides when I was a kid."

That started the poor woman sobbing. She made no further comment while Madoc and George bundled Jellicoe Grouse into enough clothes to keep him decent and unfrozen, and stuffed him into the tow truck's seat between them. Here was another tight squeeze for three abreast. Next time he came to Pitcherville, Madoc vowed silently, he was going to bring more adequate transport.

CHAPTER 22

Fred Olson had slept, but not long enough. His eyes were puffy and he was still having to yawn every two minutes. But as soon as the tow truck hove into the yard, he was right there to unload Jellicoe Grouse and hustle him into the lockup with Jelly's influential friend. Sam Neddick was still on guard; Madoc could swear he hadn't moved a muscle since they'd last seen him.

"Prisoner give you any trouble, Sam?" Madoc asked.

"Nope." Sam nodded at a fresh star in the concrete wall behind the bars. "Tried to, once. I had to demonstrate what happens when a rifle goes off accidental in a closed room an' the bullet ricochets. Messed up your wall some, Fred. Lately he's been offerin' me money. Got it up to fifty thousand so far."

"He hasn't happened to mention how he made the money?"

"Nope. Don't s'pose he done it sellin' hockey pucks."

"Would you care to tell us now, Mr. Badger?" Madoc inquired politely.

Mr. Badger, it appeared, would not.

"How about you, Mr. Grouse?"

Jelly, who was shying away from his former boss only a little less cravenly than Bain had done, didn't appear inclined to speak, either.

"Then I suppose we'll have to go and find out. They may think it a bit strange down at the county courthouse if we send in a batch of prisoners and can't tell them why. Fred, how does one go about getting a search warrant in Pitcherville?"

"The marshal fills out a form an' the notary stamps it."

"Who's the notary?"

"My wife Millie. What you want searched?"

"McLumber's hardware store. Would you care to oblige?"

"No trouble at all. I guess George must o' told you about Henry, eh?"

"He did."

"I kept the bullet."

"Good man. Hard luck on Mr. Badger, of course."

Fred stepped into the house and was back in a couple of minutes, waving a sheet of paper. "Signed, sealed, an' delivered. Want me to come along with you, Inspector? I phoned down to see what was keepin' the wagon an' it turns out they've been roundin' up a bunch o' drunk an' disorderlies that was takin' a schoolhouse apart."

Badger sneered. "At least that's one rap you can't pin on me."

"I shouldn't be too sure about that, Mr. Bandicoot," said Madoc. "Marshal Olson is a surprisingly versatile man. Like yourself. George, since you were so helpful about bringing in Jellicoe Grouse, perhaps you'd better stay with Sam and make sure we keep him."

Sam was not going to need any help, but Madoc wasn't sure what kind of reception he and Fred might run into at the store. News of Jelly Grouse's arrest must already have percolated all over Bigears and perhaps beyond. He took the pool car this time, and didn't loiter on the road. Before long, Fred was remarking, "Cripes, if I was outside this buggy instead of in it, I'd arrest us both for speedin'."

"And I'd have no squawk coming if you did," said Madoc. "It's just that I'd like to get to the store before—ah, there he comes now. We'll beat him by a whisker."

They could see a black Lincoln about the size of a battleship coming at them out of the Bigears Road, toward the junction where McLumber's hardware store stood. Its driver wasn't wasting any time, either. Madoc let the Lincoln get to the parking lot first, and pulled in just as McLumber was stepping out with the door keys in his hand.

"Show him your warrant, Marshal. We've got to find out what it is he's been wholesaling before he has a chance to get rid of the evidence."

"This is kind of embarrassin'," Fred muttered. "Ed's an Owl."

"Would you rather I served the warrant?"

"Nope. It's my job. I might as well give the town its money's worth even if I do get hove out o' the lodge for doin' it. Mornin', Ed. Gettin' to work kind of early, ain't you?"

"Have to," Ed grunted. "I've lost my helper, in case you hadn't heard."

"Oh, I heard. The inspector here an' I thought we better drop over an' give you a hand. You goin' to let us in peaceable, or do I have to haul out the warrant?"

McLumber had been a big man when he'd stepped out of his Lincoln. Now he seemed to shrivel. He stared at Fred Olson for a moment, then hung his head. "Oh, what's the use? I told that maniac we'd never get away with it."

"The maniac being the man who calls himself Badger?" asked Madoc. "When did you tell him this, Mr. McLumber? Before or after he shot Henry?"

McLumber jerked his head up and tried to bluster. "What do you mean he shot Henry? Henry shot himself."

"I got the bullet, Ed," said Olson. "What you an' Badger been runnin'? Come on, you might as well show us an' get it over with."

"All right, Fred, I know when I'm licked. Christ! Two of them gone and their blood's on my head." He unlocked the door and led them through the store, down to the basement. It was clean, dry, spacious, and stacked with pasteboard cartons. "There it is. Help yourselves."

"What do you think it is, Inspector?" asked Fred.

"I think it's the reason why Armand Dubois is able to sell his drinks so cheap." Madoc tore open the topmost carton, marked FLOOR WAX. There were a dozen one-liter bottles, each bearing the label of a well-known whiskey. He twisted the cap off one and sniffed.

"Good God! What's in it?"

McLumber shrugged. "I wouldn't know. I was only the distributor."

"How did you get involved with Badger?"

"I suppose it would be nearer the truth to say he was the one who got involved with me. If you must know, Inspector, we've always done a little bootlegging out of the store. My grandfather started it back during the first war when Prohibition came in, and it got to be a family tradition, as you might say. Nothing big, you know, just a jar here and there to a good customer and no questions asked. We ran a little still of our own out back a ways. If anybody ever discovered it, they never let on. But then this Badger blew into town."

The hardware dealer sighed. "He tempted me and I fell. That's the long and the short of it, Fred. He waved this wad of bills big enough to choke a horse in front of my nose, and told me there was plenty more where that came from. Business had been kind of off, and I can't say I rose up in my wrath and told him to take his filthy money elsewhere because I'd be lying if I did. I hemmed and hawed, I suppose, waiting to see what he'd say next. Badger's quite a talker, you know."

"Not to us he hasn't been," said Olson.

"Well, he sure as hell was to me. First thing I knew, he was dropping a few gentle hints that if I didn't run a more efficient operation —meaning if I didn't do it his way—I'd pretty damn soon be in trouble with the excise men, not to mention the customs, considering we happened to have a few customers across the border we'd been supplying. He never threatened, mind you. If he had, I hope I'd have been man enough to tell him what to do with his money, bust up the old still, and walk thenceforth in the paths of righteousness hoping nobody would throw it up to me about having maybe been a little too diligent about following in the footsteps of my forefathers. But Badger was too subtle for that. He kept waving those greenbacks around and harping on modern efficiency till it began to make sense to me."

McLumber sighed again. "I don't know if you can understand, Fred, being a sworn upholder of the law yourself, eh, but Badger made it all sound like what you might call a thrilling adventure. And adventure is something I've never had much of in my life, as you well know. I worked right here in the store ever since I was old enough to see over the counter. When I got through school, it stood to reason I'd go in with Father, Grandfather being pretty bad with the rheumatism by then and me not being able to get into the army anyway on account of flat feet from all that standing behind the counter. So here I was and here I stayed, and when Father went, I carried on by myself. Hardware was in my blood, as you might say. And I'd married Lilybelle and joined the Owls and I can't say it's been a bad life. But as time went on, I couldn't help asking myself, 'Is this all?' So I took Lilybelle on a cruise up the St. Lawrence, but somehow it wasn't enough. Two years later we went all the way to Disneyland on one of those charter tours, but it still wasn't enough."

"You kept on running booze, though."

"Yes, but that was just part of the business. We'd been doing it so long there was no kick to it. I might as well have been selling bug spray."

Fred Olson took another whiff of the stuff in the bottle, then a very cautious sip. "Christ A'mighty, Ed, you sure this isn't bug spray?"

"I already told you I don't know what it is, and that's the God's honest truth. What we used to make in the old still, Fred, that was just what anybody's grandmother might have brewed in her own wash boiler, which most of them did back in those days and don't let anybody try to tell you they didn't. You'd just boil up your wormy fruit, spoiled grain, pig potatoes, whatever you had lying around handy that wasn't going to cost you anything, you'd condense the steam to get the alcohol, add a little caramel syrup to enhance the bouquet and give a better color, and there you'd be. All homegrown and homemade. Nowadays they'd be peddling it in those health food stores as organic whiskey. This stuff here, to tell you the truth, I don't care much for it myself. Badger's been getting it from someplace."

"As you may have gathered, Mr. McLumber," said Madoc, "Badger won't be getting any more. Are you sure you have no idea who his suppliers were?"

"None whatsoever. He said it was safer for me not to know. I didn't catch on to what he meant till the day Henry caught me sticking labels on the bottles."

"How did that enlighten you?"

"Well, see, we never put any labels on in the old days. In fact, we didn't use bottles, not to speak of. It was mostly old pickle jars or whatever came handy. Later on we got more sophisticated and bought up used bottles for a cent apiece. But Badger said we needed more modern marketing methods if we wanted to get into the big time, so he had it put up in nice new bottles, and got a printer he knew to make us up some different labels, just like the real thing."

"Thus adding forgery to your list of adventures," Madoc noted. "What you're saying, then, is that Henry had not till then been aware you'd gone into business with Badger?"

"That's right, he hadn't. You see, Henry was what the Immortal Robbie called unco' guid or rigidly righteous. He'd always known we were doing a bit of business on the side, of course, but he respected our adherence to family tradition and wasn't above taking home a jar himself now and again, so long as it was out of the old home still. But getting it from somebody else, well, that put a different face on the entire matter. So Badger and I talked it over and decided we'd better not let on to him that we'd changed our source of supply. I'd get Badger to stamp the cases turpentine or denatured alcohol, things like that."

"Any one of which might not have been far off the mark," said Madoc. "And that was enough to fool Henry?"

"Well, you see, Henry never had much to do with the stockroom. His job was mostly to wait on the customers. His back was none too good and I tried to spare him any heavy lifting. My nephew Bud would come in and help out when I needed him. Bud was so flighty, speaking no ill of the dead, that I wasn't too worried about his catching on. And Mr. Badger himself, I guess, would bring in the stock and take it out again, all but the local deliveries that Bud handled."

"Why do you say 'I guess'? Don't you know what was happening in your own store?"

"Not about the deliveries, no. The boxes would be here, and then they'd be gone. It all happened in the dead of night. I was supposed to keep clear so I wouldn't be involved in case they got caught."

"Why do you say 'they,' when you've just told me you assumed Mr. Badger brought in the stock himself?"

"Well, I figured he must have had some help. That's a lot of lugging for a man like him."

"If you're tryin' to keep from squealin' on Jelly Grouse an' Jase Bain, you needn't strain yourself, Ed," the marshal broke in. "We already got them pegged. Go on about Henry."

"Oh. Well, it just happened one day I was down here sticking labels on a batch Mr. Badger had told me we had to get ready for shipment and somebody came in needing a light of glass cut. So Henry came downstairs to get it ready for her, and here's me with a Cutty Sark label in one hand and a green bottle in the other. You know yourself, Fred, there were no flies on Henry. I guess he'd been getting suspicious when my ill-gotten gains went to my head and I started throwing money around on that Lincoln and the mink coat for Lilybelle. When he saw what I was up to, he knew."

"Took it hard, did he?"

"Hard? You'd have thought he'd caught me robbing the Royal Bank of Canada. He just grabbed his coat and stomped out of the store as if it had been Sodom and Gomorrah rolled into one."

"You didn't try to go after 'im?"

"How could I? There was a customer to wait on. Mrs. Fiske, it was. Her kids had been having a snowball fight with some other kids. Somebody hove one with a rock in the middle and it went straight through the parlor window. She had cardboard stuck over the hole, but she needed the glass so her husband could set it as soon as he got home. You know Joe Fiske, Fred. He took Elmer Bain's place as foreman down at the lumber mill. Anyway, I figured it was better to let Henry cool down before I tried to reason with him. Damn it, we'd worked together for thirty-seven years."

McLumber was close to breaking down. Fred would have let up on him, but Madoc knew they mustn't. "Mr. McLumber, did you realize Badger had murdered Henry?"

"No, I didn't! Not—not right away."

The hardware dealer couldn't look at them. "I suppose what I really mean is that I did know but I couldn't let myself admit it. You see, I couldn't picture Henry having that kind of accident. He was a crack shot, he knew guns inside and out, and he was precise in his ways. Suppose for instance the customer had wanted that glass to measure fourteen and a sixteenth by twenty-three and five thirty-seconds of an inch or whatever the hell that comes out to in centimeters. That's how Henry would have cut it, not a hair under, not a hair over. Whatever he did, he did just so, and if he couldn't do it right, he wouldn't touch it."

"You're sure about this, I see."

"No question. I ought to know better than anybody else. I worked with him long enough. I can see Henry going out and shooting rabbits to work off steam. Not out of meanness, Henry wouldn't do that, but his wife makes a mighty good rabbit pot pie, so they'd serve a purpose and save a little on the grocery bill. But as to cleaning the gun afterward, if Henry was still upset, he'd have laid it aside till he could do it properly. And all that whispering about suicide some of 'em were doing, that was plain foolishness. He couldn't have, not Henry. What he'd have done, he'd either have given me the cold shoulder for the rest of his life, or else he'd have come back next day and preached at me about sin and greed and the evils of putting the cup to my brother's lips till I broke down and repented and told Mr. Badger I wouldn't work with him any more. Then I suppose he'd have shot us both, and I wish to God he had. What's to become of me now?"

Madoc looked at Fred. "It's your bailiwick, Marshal."

"All right, then. If it's up to me, I'd say let's do what we done with Jase Bain. You're free till they need you down at the county courthouse, Ed, then the judge will have to decide. In the meantime, I'm puttin' you on your word of honor as an Owl not to leave town. This booze better stay where it is for the time bein'. I s'pose we might get Jase Bain over here to take a look at the boxes an' confirm they're what he used to pick up an' take out there to that place on the way to Oromocto."

"Was that what Jase did? I never knew."

"I'm not sure Bain himself knew exactly what he was doing," said Madoc. "He told us Badger kept supplies at his place, but I expect they were only empty bottles."

"Looks to me like Badger was the only one who really knew what was goin' on," Fred remarked.

"Yes, that would be his way of keeping control," Madoc replied. "Badger's an efficient organizer, though his record doesn't show he's ever been mixed up in bootlegging before. Being on the run from prison and probably without capital, I expect he just looked around for a chance to muscle in on some quiet little game where he could turn a dishonest dollar. Your old family business offered the right sort of opening, Mr. McLumber, and he took it."

"But he said we couldn't go on using our still because it wasn't big enough."

"Prob'ly meant he had a better one all lined up," said Fred Olson. "I wish I knew where it was."

"I don't know where it was, but I have a hunch I could tell you where it went," said Madoc. "You haven't happened to notice a sudden stoppage of supplies during the past week, Mr. McLumber?"

"Why yes, as a matter of fact, I have. Mr. Badger got hold of me only this past Thursday night, which he seldom ever did, to tell me not to let Bud make the usual local deliveries on Friday. He said there'd been some trouble with the still and we'd have to slow down and stretch out our stock to keep the big customers on the hook till he could get things straightened out. That's how come you see so much stock on hand right now. Normally this would all have been cleared out and a fresh load coming in tonight. Say, you haven't been bugging my telephone or anything, have you? How did you catch on to Mr. Badger and me?"

"It's a long story, some of which I'm not at liberty yet to tell you. You must realize that when Jason Bain's place was bombed, Badger was the most likely suspect simply because he was the only one who lived nearby. However, that would have been a most unusual thing for a sporting goods salesman to do, so I began wondering whether Badger wasn't what he appeared to be."

"Ain't sportin' goods kind o' thieves' slang for stolen property?" Fred remarked.

"That's true," said Madoc. "I hadn't thought of that. What got to me first, I think, was that little house. It was such a strange sort of place for a salesman to buy. Travelers are gregarious souls as a rule, and here was this chap sticking himself out in the middle of nowhere with a well-known curmudgeon for his only neighbor, and not mixing with the townsfolk. The place hadn't been fixed up at all, but Badger was keeping it tidy, like a man who'd learned neat habits either in the service or in jail."

"He did have a lot o' sportin' stuff around, though," said Fred.

"Yes, but it was oddly arranged: a deep-sea fishing rod with a trout fly tied to the line, for instance, and downhill ski boots next to a pair of cross-country skis. I began to wonder whether in fact Badger knew anything about the goods he was supposed to be peddling. They made me think of Armand Bergeron's dance band, just a job lot of second-hand instruments he'd picked up cheap at an auction. We managed to pick up some of his fingerprints, sent them for analysis, and got back a great deal of information that scared me half silly just to hear. The gist of it is, Mr. McLumber, that once Badger got his hooks into you, you were in a no-win situation. He's left a string of victims everywhere he's been, some of them dead like Henry and Bud, some of them alive and wishing they weren't, like yourself. He's been caught before and escaped before. This time there'll be no question of his escaping. Now if you'll excuse us, Mr. McLumber, I think we ought to be getting back. The marshal's expecting company."

"Are you sure you don't want to take me in, Fred?" said McLumber. "I wouldn't hold it against you, you know."

"No, but the rest o' your tribe would. Specially Nella. She's already had another sad bereavement, in case you hadn't heard."

"Oh, Jelly Grouse. Yes, I'd heard. But Jelly's been getting pinched for one thing or another ever since he was out of diapers. Me, I'm supposed to be a pillar of the community."

"Well, stay propped up till we get Buddy planted. Then we'll just have to wait and see what happens."

CHAPTER 23

Ed McLumber insisted on following the pool car back to Pitcherville in his ill-gotten Lincoln, on the reasonable grounds that he didn't want to be a whited sepulcher. The least he could do, he felt, was confront Jelly Grouse and urge him to repent his evil ways even if it wouldn't keep him out of jail. That was fine with Madoc and Fred. So well did McLumber succeed, in fact, that Jelly broke down in tears and ratted on the man who'd not only helped him distribute the bootleg whiskey but also stolen the tow truck to clean up the debris from the burned-out truck.

Madoc recognized the name. Wolfman Wombatte, a part-time mechanic and full-time rogue, was an old acquaintance. Fred Olson, too, had entertained Wombatte in this very cooler on a disorderly conduct charge. Sam also knew Wombatte, though he didn't explain in what context. The three of them were still holding an agreeable old-home week with Jelly when the wagon appeared to cart the prisoners away.

During this period, George had listened in admiration, Badger in disdainful silence. Ed McLumber, his conscience temporarily at rest, had gone home to put on his good suit for the funeral and, perhaps, try to recruit a new hardware clerk from among the mourners. Then the formalities were gone through, Sam reluctantly uncocked Badger's rifle and handed it over for evidence, and the night's work was over.

Millie, wakened by the to-do, appeared with a coat thrown over her bathrobe to offer breakfast as soon as she could get her clothes on, but Madoc said he and Sam had better get back or Annabelle's feelings would be hurt. Knowing Annabelle, Millie had to agree that they'd better. The party broke up with many hand wringings and backslappings, and Madoc drove Sam back to the farm.

As they drove in, they met Bert crossing the yard. "Where do you two rounders think you've been, eh?"

"To a roundup," said Madoc. "Bain's neighbor Mr. Badger and

Nella McLumber's friend Jelly Grouse are off to the county jail. Sam's earned a damned good breakfast and so, with all immodesty, have I. Do you have time to come in and watch us eat?"

"Watch, hell. I haven't had my own yet. What time do you think it is?"

"Come to think of it, I have no idea. Nor do I much care. I want food and a hot bath and about seventeen hours' sleep. Then I want to get back to Fredericton and tie this case in a double bow knot around a certain inscrutable somebody's neck. Talk about a quiet weekend in the country."

Madoc got his breakfast, his bath, and a sleep of adequate duration, though not seventeen hours' worth and not until he'd phoned Fredericton and asked somebody to nip over to Wolfman Wombatte's house and run him in. That took care of Badger's staff. As to the bootleggers themselves, they'd be Eyeball Grouse's pigeons and were doubtless in the coop already. Then he got up and went snowshoeing with the boys, then he ate supper, then he helped Bert straighten out his goddamn taxes, then he went to bed with Janet and the springs didn't squeak.

Early the following morning, he packed his wife and her washstand into the car, notwithstanding Annabelle's protests that they'd miss the funeral, and drove back to Fredericton. Then he reported to RCMP headquarters and suggested to the deputy commissioner that they perform whatever arcane rites might be necessary to get hold of Mr. X.

"Got things all sewed up, have you, Inspector?"

"I believe so."

"That ought to make him happy."

"I doubt that, sir. I think I've jugged his brother."

"His brother?"

"Or his cousin, or possibly his great-uncle. Family relationships are somewhat confusing in this case."

"Aren't most family relationships? How is Mrs. Rhys?"

"She claims to be quite recovered."

"Good. Please give her my regards. Well, I'd better get on the hot line to Mr. X. Er—would you have happened to—"

"Major Charles Grouse, known to his former schoolmates as Eyeball. He comes from a settlement called Bigears, out back of Pitcherville, where my wife grew up. She spotted the accent as soon as he opened his mouth."

"That odd little way of stressing his word endings? I wondered where he'd picked it up."

"They all do it out there; nobody knows why. My wife thought it tactless to mention the fact in front of him, since it reminded her that one of the men she'd heard talking the night of her adventure was from Bigears, too. She was subsequently able to identify this man as Jellicoe Grouse. He's confessed and is at present lodged in the Adelaide County jail, which appears to have been his home away from home most of his life."

"Oh dear. Jellicoe resting comfortably, is he?"

"I think we can reassure Major Grouse on that point. How soon do you think he can get here?"

"Need you ask?"

"Not really. Then I'll be in my office until I'm wanted."

Madoc was plugging his way through accumulated paperwork and finding it a restful change when the intercom buzzed. Nevertheless, it was with no reluctance that he pushed the work aside, combed his hair, straightened his tie, and entered the presence. Mr. X was there, looking apprehensive.

"Well, Inspector. Mean to say you've caught the rogues already?"

"My wife comes from Pitcherville, Mr. X."

"Oh Christ!"

"That about sums it up, Mr. X. As you'd no doubt suspected, it was Buddy McLumber who drove your stolen object away in Elzire Bergeron's old bull box. Jellicoe Grouse and an old acquaintance of ours called Wolfman Wombatte were the strong-arm boys. The man running the show is an army deserter who calls himself Badger and was posing as a sporting goods salesman. Badger is an escape artist of no mean ability, having served less than his appointed terms in three different maximum security prisons, only one of which was in Canada, I'm relieved to say. He's also used the names Beaver, Bearhound, and Bandicoot at various times. Any one of them sound familiar to you?"

Major Grouse, as he might as well now be called, said they didn't, but anybody who called himself Bandicoot must be a weirdo and he'd be damned if he'd have had a Bandicoot in any division of his. "But what about the bull box? Great Caesar, you don't mean—"

"I'm afraid so, Mr. X. My wife made a positive identification from some photographs supplied by Perce Bergeron. Since she'd met the truck head-on and tried to climb up over the radiator grill to get at the driver, whom she supposed to require rescuing from the cab, she'd had ample opportunity to fix the pattern in her memory. Then there was the fact that she spent considerable time standing there watching it burn after Buddy McLumber had gone off with her car."

"What makes you so sure it was Bud who stole the car?" Eyeball Grouse had abandoned all effort at concealment, but was evidently still determined to defend the family honor insofar as possible.

"Jelly Grouse says Buddy was driving the truck, and there was nobody else around at the time. Buddy's mother admitted he'd been out late that night. I'm afraid the real clincher, however, is that Buddy was known for his inability to keep from blabbing everything he knew, and Buddy was shot through the head, allegedly by Badger, as he was leaving Bull Moose Portage after the dance Saturday night on his snowmobile. The funeral is being held today, as a matter of fact. I'm surprised you weren't notified."

"Can't expect me to drop everything and run down there, can they? How was I supposed Bud's death was connected with—damn it, Rhys, you might have let me know."

"You forget, Mr. X, that I don't officially know who you are."

"Oh well, hell. What was I supposed to do? Damn it, I told you Friday morning I never wanted the blasted thing dumped on me in the first place."

"Stop me if I'm wrong, sir, but would this thing you had dumped on you have been by any chance a still that had been found being illicitly operated by members of the armed forces?"

"On which side of the border?"

"Whichever side you prefer, sir. It would obviously have been a base other than the one at which you yourself are in command."

"Umph. Go on."

"Would the operators have been apprehended and the still shut down only this past week? And was the still removed from its former site for the perfectly sound reason that there hadn't yet been time to conduct a thorough investigation into how many of the personnel at that base not yet under arrest might also have been involved, and it was feared that the evidence might be destroyed either by the con-spirators or by their sympathizers?"

"C.O. was right, wasn't he?"

"Undoubtedly. The willingness of the officers' mess personnel to permit the drivers' thermos to be spiked with ipecac bears out that assumption."

"I never said it was ipecac."

"No sir."

"All right, blast your eyes, it was ipecac. Any tea going?"

"At the door," said Madoc, whose keen ear had picked up the small noises attendant upon balancing a trayful of mugs and fiddling with a knob at the same time. As the door opened and the orderly appeared, Eyeball Grouse stared at Madoc with mingled awe and suspicion. Still keeping a wary eye out, he reached for milk and sugar. After a few steadying sips, he spoke again.

"I suppose you know about the still?"

"Only that it must have been a remarkably efficient one, easily traceable to the place whence it was stolen and sure to get Badger and his crew into the hottest of water if they'd got caught with it in their possession. Or else there was no still at all, merely a load of rocket fuel the bootleggers had been bottling and selling as whiskey," Madoc added, recalling the stuff they'd turned up in McLumber's basement.

"Tasted it, did you?"

"Marshal Olson did. He's a braver man than I am."

"Fred's all right. We went to school together. I suppose he told you they used to call me Eyeball."

Major Grouse selected a pastry from the plate on the tea tray, ate it, and wiped his mustache. "Funny thing, everybody had a nickname, but we never called Fred anything but Fred. So Jelly's in another jam."

From the look on his face he didn't mean that to be funny, as in fact it wasn't. "He's only a kind of second or third cousin of mine, you know."

"There's one in every family," Madoc apologized. "About this still, Major Grouse. Was it something you'd be willing to explain?"

"Oh hell, why not? Can't expect me to go into technical details, naturally. You wouldn't know what I was talking about. Neither would I."

Major Grouse took another pastry. "Gist of it is," he went on with his mouth full, "some of the higher-ups—I'm not saying of what country, mind you—got hold of a bright idea about a new kind of ground-to-air missile. Dull afternoon at the officers' mess, I suppose. So they spent a few million dollars getting it designed and having an experimental model made up. Then of course they had to test it out."

He took another swig of tea to wash down the pastry. "For undisclosed reasons, they decided to shoot it out over the ocean, so they brought it to a place that shall have to remain nameless, stuffed it into a silo, and pushed the button. Damn thing didn't work, naturally. So they got a team of expert technicians and a bunch of mechanics to monkey around with it. Well, the technicians got bored with it pretty quickly and went off to think up another idea. That left it to the mechanics, who found out that by shoving the guts around and throwing out all the electronic garbage, they could convert it, as you deduced, into a remarkably efficient still."

"More tea, Major?" said the deputy commissioner.

"Thanks. Where was I? Oh yes, out in the woods under the silo. Anyway, there it sat and the technical staff were going hot and heavy on the next idea and nobody wanted the confounded thing back, so the mechanics were ordered to chop it up and scrap it, which needless to say they didn't. Lugged it off into a different part of the woods and set up in business, as any damn fool might have known they would. In fact, I gather it was fairly well common knowledge around the base, which was why nobody stopped 'em. Long as enough joy juice got passed out to the right people, it was regarded as sort of a company joke, like—" he glanced over at Madoc.

"Like Ed McLumber's family tradition," Madoc filled in smartly.

"Right. Just testing. But what the company didn't know was how really efficient that still was. They were draining off the booze about a gallon a minute when they could find anything to distill, which was most of the time, I gather, since they were none too fussy about what they bunged into the hopper. And the beauty of it was, they were running the still on—well, if not rocket fuel, something that might, loosely speaking, fall into that general category. This was a special propellant that had been developed specially for the missile that didn't work. A sufficient amount had been shipped to fuel all the experiments that had been intended for the apparatus. Considering the confounded thing fizzled on the first try, that gave 'em enough left over to run the still from here to hell and gone."

"Bit of luck for the bootleggers," remarked the deputy commissioner.

"It was that and then some. Way they had it rigged, they didn't need to use more than a dribble at a time. In fact, they'd have blown the damned thing apart if they'd used more. That meant no smoke, no smell to give them away. They had a perfect setup until somebody who'd also better be nameless twigged on to the fact that they were shipping the bulk of their squeezings away from camp."

"When was this?"

"The day they got shut down, of course. Must have been going on for months. Those mechanics were found on investigation to have a damned sight more money stashed away than they'd had any chance of collecting legitimately unless they played incredibly good poker, which they didn't and never had, according to reliable testimony from their bunkies. What beats me is where they got hold of the bottles to ship it in."

"Those were supplied to them by Badger, who hid them until they were needed inside seventeen used portable privies in Elmer Bain's junkyard."

The deputy commissioner, who had never before been known to evince any strong emotion, murmured a faint, "My God!"

"Or how they managed the distribution," Major Grouse went on. Knowing Jason Bain of old, he had accepted the seventeen privies with equanimity.

"I think the liquor must have been got out of the base by army personnel, who probably were supplied with civilian transport by Badger. You'd know that better than I, no doubt. Anyway, disguised as hardware supplies, it was brought to Ed McLumber's hardware store and put in the basement. Local distribution was handled by Buddy McLumber in his uncle's truck. The larger and more distant customers were served by a rather complicated system. Jason Bain's truck would be loaded with cartons marked floor wax, turpentine, and whatnot—this was all done in the dead of night, needless to say—and Bain would drive the truck over to that abandoned barn where my wife was caught by the explosion."

Madoc took a sip of his own now cold tea to steady his voice. "Bain would leave the truck and walk up into the house, until Jellicoe Grouse and Wolfman Wombatte had come along with another vehicle which he claims he never did see, and transfer the cargo. They'd then honk to let him know the job was done, and drive off. Bain would walk back to his empty truck and go back home. As you know,

Major, people are so used to old Bain pottering around at all hours in that wreck of his loaded with anything under the sun that nobody would ever think twice about seeing him. If Jellicoe Grouse, on the other hand, had ever been spotted driving away from the store in a loaded truck—"

"They'd naturally have assumed he was robbing his uncle blind," Major Grouse finished for him. "At least I would. Though I'm not sure Ed is Jelly's uncle, come to think of it. Seems to me his father was half-brother to Jelly's mother's cousin. I'd have to sit down and work it out."

"Do," said the deputy commissioner. "Genealogies are always interesting. Could you explain to us, please, Inspector, why the man known as Badger happened to shoot that chap you call Buddy McLumber Saturday night in a snowmobile at Bull Moose Portage?"

"Because he hadn't found a chance to shoot him sooner, I suppose," Madoc answered. "Perhaps we might, for the moment, try to see the situation through Badger's eyes. Here's a convicted murderer on the run. He's learned, possibly through a chance meeting with Jelly Grouse, that a respected hardware dealer is supplying a selected clientele with bootleg liquor from a small family-owned still. He also learns, being a man with an inquisitive turn of mind and a desperate need to reestablish himself, that a successful distilling operation is being conducted at a point close enough on one side or the other of the border to make a liaison feasible and a middleman necessary."

"Tea, Rhys?" said the deputy commissioner.

"Thank you. So Badger makes contact with the distillers, who have plenty of merchandise but no distribution facilities, and McLumber, who has excellent distribution facilities but only limited means of production. Keeping tight control by his roundabout system of never letting the various sectors of his operation interconnect, Badger works up a surprisingly lucrative business in a short time. He pays his people well to keep them content with the arrangement and it's all going like clockwork until suddenly the still is seized and ordered shipped away to a place where he can't get at it."

"Possibly in a friendly foreign country," Major Grouse interposed.

"Thank you. Badger then conceives a plan to hijack the still, no doubt with the intention of operating it himself. That will in fact suit him better, because he won't have to go on paying his military confederates and they won't dare complain at being cut off for fear of exposure and court-martial."

"Damn right," snapped Eyeball Grouse.

"Naturally he doesn't let the military personnel know they're being dealt out of the game. Instead, he enlists their help to deactivate the army drivers. He gets his other set of henchmen to steal an unmarked van and Perce Bergeron's bull box. I assume it was Buddy who took the box. Apparently he'd had a youthful habit of joyriding in his relatives' cars. If he was caught, he could pass it off as a mere prank."

"Took mine once," growled Eyeball Grouse. "I was going to warm his bottom for him, but his mother wouldn't let me."

"Too bad," said Madoc. "Anyway, we all know how the hijacking was effected. Jellicoe Grouse has confessed it was he and Wombatte who manhandled the two retching soldiers into the van and left them there. They drove off in Wombatte's car while Buddy drove the truck to where they'd left the bull box. They then shifted the still, not without considerable difficulty because it was a heavy weight for three men to handle. They'd been warned not to tip the still for fear of disturbing the delicate and sophisticated mechanisms inside."

"Is that what they called them, Rhys?" asked the deputy commissioner.

"Grouse referred to them simply as 'the guts.' Anyway, they propped the still up inside the bull box as best they could, and set the barrels of fuel around it. Badger's instructions had been for them to take it to the abandoned house and set it up in the barn next to the road until a better place could be found."

"Thus knocking this Bain fellow off the payroll, too, I assume?"

"Badger might have run into a problem there. Bain's a great one for demanding his rights. Perhaps the bombing of the junkyard was originally planned to discourage him from any such demand. But getting back to the bull box, it's obvious that the hijackers' efforts at securing the still in an upright position weren't good enough. Despite Buddy's expert driving, the still fell over and toppled the truck on that last rise. Out there alone, frightened of being caught with the still and no doubt none too happy about all that fuel sloshing around the box, Buddy panicked."

"He would," snorted Major Grouse.

"Yes, that would have been a normal reaction for him, according to my sources. He hid in the cab until my wife left her car and went into the barn, then stole her car and took off, leaving her stranded. Whether he knew who she was, or whether he deliberately ignited the fuel before he left, I couldn't say."

"Wouldn't have to," said Major Grouse. "Stuff was highly volatile. Had to be shipped in special drums. Must have smashed a few when the still fell over. Soon as a concentration of fumes built up inside the bull box—my God! What would Elzire Bergeron have thought? A part of my own heritage gone. Hell, I can remember when our old cow Geraldine—" in some embarrassment, Eyeball Grouse stuffed another pastry into his mouth. In respectful silence, Madoc sat and watched him chew.

When he'd got his emotions under control and his mouth back in working order, the major stood up. "Well, I'd say that wraps it up. Good staff work, Commissioner. You—er—needn't bother submitting a written report."

"We shall be happy to refrain from doing so," said the deputy commissioner. "Might I offer you a bite of lunch, Major?"

"Got to get back, thanks. Make sure nobody's parked another still on my base, eh. Sorry about your wife's washstand, Inspector."

"No regrets, sir. Fred Olson had one that was just the ticket."

"Hunh. I might have known. Give her my regards. Hell, give 'em all my regards. No, don't bother, I'd better go do it myself. Need a bit of straightening out, eh."

"There's a new chap named Pierre Dubois who could use some advice on paramilitary tactics," Madoc suggested. "He's semiengaged to Cecile Bergeron and planning to blow up Detroit."

"That so? Well, Detroit shouldn't be much of a problem. Might have trouble with Cecile. See you."

The deputy commissioner walked his visitor to the door, came back and considered the last pastry on the plate, but decided against it. "It sounds as if you've had a most interesting weekend, Rhys. Why don't you go home and get some sleep?"

Madoc weighed the prospect of an afternoon with Janet against the prospect of an afternoon at his desk, and went. Janet was delighted to see him.

"I'm so glad you're home. Muriel was just here telling me about this absolutely marvelous Victorian hall rack with a boot box and a mirror and millions of brass curlicue hooks with porcelain knobs she's seen—"

"Jenny!"

"She's seen in that antique shop on Regent Street. What's the matter with you, Madoc? You're getting awfully jumpy lately."

"Lack of sufficient tender loving care, I expect. Come on, love. Give the old man a kiss. Then we'll take a nice, slow, gentle walk down to Regent Street hand in hand, and buy our hall a curlicue."

About the Author

Alisa Craig was born in Canada and now lives in Maine. She is the author of five previous novels for the Crime Club, including *The Grub-and-Stakers Quilt a Bee, The Terrible Tide, Murder Goes Mumming, The Grub-and-Stakers Move a Mountain,* and *A Pint of Murder.*